When Michael Decastro gets an email from Tuki — his long-gone client, the lady of ten thousand mysteries — he doesn't hesistate a moment. He heads to Bangkok to find ... what? He doesn't know. To face what dangers? He hasn't imagined. All he knows is that she's beckoned, and he can't resist her call.

And now, face-to-face with Tuki and a ruby so beautiful it has its own name, Michael must make a choice: move forward, protect Tuki, get to the bottom of her entanglement with the nak lin (cruel Thai gangsters) and see that she's safe, or run back to his father's fishing boat, hiding from the ills of the world beneath a watchcap and a raincoat.

Foolhardy, compassionate Michael hardly has to think ...

The follow-up to the Lambda-award nominated *Provincetown Follies, Bangkok Blues, Bangkok Dragons, Cape Cod Tears* pulses with the heart-beat of the South Seas, and celebrates the vicious mysteries found in the belly of a dragon.

BANGKOK DRAGONS,
CAPE COD TEARS

BANGKOK DRAGONS,
CAPE COD TEARS

A CAPE ISLANDS MYSTERY

RANDALL PEFFER

BLEAK
HOUSE
BOOKS

Published by
BLEAK HOUSE BOOKS
a division of Big Earth Publishing
923 Williamson St.
Madison, WI 53703
www.bleakhousebooks.com

Copyright © 2009 by Randall Peffer

Printed in the United States of America
12 11 10 09   1 2 3 4 5 6 7 8 9 10

978-1-60648-037-3 (hardback)
978-1-60648-038-0 (paperback)
978-1-60648-039-7 (evidence collection)

For Alison, Ben—

Derby Girl & Slugger,

Rock stars, la

Prologue

THE *tuk-tuk* driver slams on the brakes. His motorized rickshaw skids to the curb. Streaks of red, gold, violet light settle into the shapes of saloons, sex parlors.

"This the place. Two hundred *baht*, you pay now."

The American looks up at the sign over the bar. A rose-colored neon image of Madonna's face blows the night a kiss. Beneath, red letters flash bright. Then dark.

SILK UNDERGROUND
Hollywood Girls, Girls, Girls!!!

After a twenty-hour flight from Boston, after a thousand urges to turn back, this is what he gets. The sidewalks of Bangkok's Patpong already crowded with hookers, trannies, pushers, touts. Johns, come to feed their habits, bathe in the blue light of sunset, five hundred neon signs. It is seven in the evening. Still hotter than the engine room on his father's fishing trawler *Rosa Lee*.

He stands before the open door, sets down his yellow seabag, listens to the mating call of Madonna's "Like A Virgin" drifting out from the shadows within. Wonders if Tuki really is waiting for him in there, whether he has the balls to go in. Or whether he should just keep on walking. Before the dragon lady gets her claws into him again.

He closes his eyes, pictures her in flashes. A nest of dark hair, a sexy kid from Saigon, a fisherman's fantasy in a red dress.

Ok. She's a drag queen, a tranny. Well, intersexual actually. Hermaphrodite. A girl with something extra. A diva. So what? She's a client. A long, lost client. She needs him. And it's a little late in the game to get all bent out of shape over her plumbing. We've been down that road before. Like just keep it professional, pal.

So he pushes back the beaded curtain at the door and steps into the dark bar, inhales the fog of cigarettes, perfume, skin.

He really hopes the beer is cold.

• • • • •

The queen behind the bar is *luk sod*, multiracial, like Tuki. Probably in her fifties but looking early forties. She has creamy skin, blue eyes, shoulder-length chestnut hair. She could almost be white, except for the small nose, the arch of the brows, the creases at the corners of her eyes, the high cheekbones. Sort of Kate Jackson meets Lucy Liu, two generations of Charlie's Angels in one. He's heard Tuki talk about her. She's one of the two Vietnamese queens who brought Tuki to Thailand as a toddler. After Saigon fell in '75.

"Brandy?"

"Hennessy or me, la?"

"You."

Brandy puts her elbows on the bar in front of him, slides her chin into her hands, gives him a penetrating look that ends with a squint. "I know you?"

"I got an email from Tuki." He pulls the printout from the inside pocket of his blue blazer, pushes it across the bar to her.

"What it say, la?"

She doesn't read English. He recites the message he knows by heart.

Michael—

I am kind of in trouble. A terrible mix-up. Please come! Silk Underground Bar, Patpong, Bangkok. Don't worry about the cost. I have lots of $ now. But hurry, world's greatest lawyer ... my knight in shining armor!!!!!!!!

Always,

Tuki

A smile spreads over Brandy's face. She steps back away from the bar as if to get a look at him from a new perspective. "So ... you funky white boy she talk about. Lone Ranger gone ride again."

"Can I have a cold beer, please?"

"First you give me kiss, Michael Decastro." She leans over the bar wraps his shoulders in her arms and kisses him on both cheeks. He can feel the ruby lipstick smudging, smell the whiskey and Coke on her breath.

A short, fat Thai down the bar lifts his head, puts on thick glasses, stares at him. Tosses back half a glass of scotch and water.

"We finally meet, attorney!"

"Excuse me. Do I ...?"

The Thai waves for him to come closer.

Michael grasps the freezing bottle of Singha that Brandy sets in front of him, holds it by the neck. Wonders whether he will be using it to defend himself.

"Who are—"

"Varat Samset. Royal Thai Police. You remember? From the telephone? A year, maybe two, ago?" The Thai gets up off his stool, shuffles toward him. There are curry stains on his white shirt, gray pants.

For the first time since he came into this long narrow cave, Michael looks around. Notices Thai versions of Madonna and Brittany Spears wearing G-strings, nothing else, standing on the far end of the bar. They are working a pole dance together, "Material Girl" pulsing from the sound system. Kissing on each other. Not just mouths.

"Get your tongue back in your head, attorney. They're boys, you know?"

"Where's Tuki?"

"You tell me."

"I don't understand."

"Already gone. Flown the coop, as you Americans say … Or hiding. I can't get anything out of this one." He nods at Brandy, leans his back against the bar.

"You're looking for her?"

"And you. You think I come to zoos like this for fun?" He signals for another drink.

"Me?"

"You flew into Bangkok this morning. Thai Airways 921 from Frankfurt." He taps the side of his head. "Varat Samset knows everything."

"Excuse me, but what's going on here?"

The detective casts his eyes at Brandy. "They say these *luk sods* give the best blow jobs in Bangkok."

Brandy sets down the fresh scotch and water, says something in Thai to him. Maybe cursing. Maybe telling him to fuck off.

Samset shrugs. "See what I get? Disrespect. And lies."

"What—"

"Your shemale friend really screwed the pooch this time, counselor. Maybe your Johnny Cochran tricks can get her off for killing in America. But this is Bangkok now. She kills here, she dies here."

Brandy shoots the detective an evil eye. "You bad man! Go now. You no welcome in Silk Underground. Tuki kill nobody!"

Samset shakes his head. "Let me ask you something, Mr. Decastro. You've spent a lot of time with freaks like this. Are they just habitual liars … or do you think those hormone injections they take really distort their sense of reality?"

"You go!"

"Ok. Ok, auntie. But you tell her when you see her, I know she killed Thaksin Kittikachorn. And I will bring her to justice."

"Go!"

The detective gulps the rest of his scotch, slams the empty glass on the bar. Shrugs as he walks out through the beaded curtain to the street. Michael recognizes the gesture. It's the Columbo thing. *Jesus, does everyone in this country think they're in the movies?*

Brandy reaches across the bar and takes his hand, whispers. "You go water taxi stop at Oriental Hotel. Take *rua duan* up river at eight thirty. Tuki find you."

"*Rua duan?*"

"Boat bus."

"What about Varat Samset?"

"Not to worry. He taking long nap soon."

1

HE STANDS in the stern of the boat. The *rua duan* is packed with a crowd of peasants heading home from downtown jobs. Many wear the typical black pajamas, the conical straw hats of farm workers, market vendors, *klong* prowlers.

The ticket man shouts something in Thai, blows a sharp whistle. The engine growls. The boat surges forward, plowing into the current, the black water. The lights of the Oriental Hotel, central Bangkok, slip astern. He feels the damp air off the Chao Prya River start to flow over his skin. Thinks of how the wind starts to cool when the *Rosa Lee* is steaming out through the hurricane dike in New Bedford. Going fishing. The heat of the city and the labyrinth of the law just ugly memories.

He is looking west, watching the spot-lit, pyramid *prang* of one of Bangkok's massive Buddhist *wats* come into view above the river bend ahead, when he feels someone in the crowd around him take his hand.

"Don't look at me, la." It's her. That sultry voice. The voice of Vietnam and Whitney Houston and a midnight train to Georgia all in one. "Don't say anything."

He feels a body mold a little against his back. Her heat.

"You came for me."

He wants to tell her, *Of course I came*. Wants to tell her how hard it has been for him since she just plain vanished from Cape Cod, from America. Before he tied up the lose ends in the Provincetown Follies murder case. Before she was fully cleared for the death of Al Costelano and her Thai lover. Wants to tell her that he has resigned as a public defender, given up the law. Tell her that Filipa dumped him. Broke off their engagement. And … and there was this other girl for awhile, an Indian from Cape Cod. Awasha. His last client. Shot. Dead. Because of his stupid mistakes. So … he's gone back to fishing out of New Bedford, Nu Bej, with his father and Tio Tommy on the *Rosa Lee*. Fluke and summer flounder.

But when he opens his mouth to speak, he feels her finger cross his lips. Her breath on his right ear.

"We get off at the next stop, la. Temple of the Dawn, Wat Arun. Go into the temple grounds. Turn right, walk until you see a small temple with two giants guarding the door. One white, one green. Wait. I will be there."

· · · · ·

The temple door is open. It is dark inside except for a bar of amber light filtering in from the glow of spotlights on the *prangs* outside.

"Just hold me, la." Her strong arms grab him from the shadows, circle his back. Hands slide up over his shoulder blades, lock together behind his neck. Her breasts full against his ribs.

He pulls his head back, half to get a look at her after all this time, half to thwart the kiss he fears is coming. *Cristo Salvador!* After all the worries that she could be dead, after missing her for nearly two years. She's back in his life … against all odds …

He just wants to see her. Keep her from harm if he can. Still, he can't imagine what he was thinking when he boarded the plane back in Boston, came here. Maybe that she does not deserve more misery. Maybe that the world sparkles a little more as long as Tuki Aparecio is in it.

But he hears the voice of his father, the *pescador*, the bad-ass Vietnam vet, in his head: *Jesus, Mo, we're talking about a drag queen here. An illusion. A cheep gook trick. Just walk away.* So ... there will be no kiss. He can't go for that.

"You're trembling, Michael."

"Maybe this is all a mistake. Maybe I shouldn't be here."

She gazes up at him, still holding his neck. Her black eyes glisten with doubt. And a new sadness.

She's like a different person. More flesh and blood, less fantasy. No longer the *diva* of Provincetown Follies, no Whitney Houston or Janet Jackson clone. Not the drag queen superstar he helped beat two murder raps back in the U.S.

Her hair is not the fountain of sun-streaked, funky curls he remembers. It falls black and straight, a simple pageboy cut, like so many women he has seen in this city. Her body seems a touch fuller beneath the black pajamas, not so nearly anorexic. Hands softer, skin smoother. She's more like his mother now. Well, if his mother Maria were half-Asian, not Portagee. And alive.

Only the grin, that huge, amazing smile, coming out of the blue night the way it does, is the same. It starts with her full lips and straight white teeth, spreads to her chin. Two dimples bloom on her cheeks. But now the effect is somehow less catlike, more something else, than he remembers. Something more vulnerable.

"Jesus, Tuki!"

"You don't like me."

"No. You look really ..."

"I've changed, la."

"It's just that ... I don't know. Everything is so different here. Not like on the Cape. This is YOUR home. I feel all turned upside down. And that detective, Samset, told me—"

"I mean, I've REALLY changed." Her lips part. She has more to tell. Something stops her. She puts her head on his chest.

"What happened? Samset is ape shit."

"I saw a murder. Saw *nak-lin* kill Prem's father." Her voice, little more than a whisper, echoes in the limestone temple.

Prem. The sick bastard who touched off the whole catastrophe for her in the U.S. Her ex-lover. The ghost who stalked her from Bangkok to Provincetown.

He reaches up, unclasps her hands from his neck, steps back. Stares into the eyes of this smooth face in the shadows. He can no longer see her African-American father at all in those wet pools. Only her Vietnamese mother.

"*Nak-lin?*"

"You don't want to know."

"Some kind of gang?"

"They work for the *jao pho.*"

"The who?"

"Godfathers."

He asks her: Is she saying that Thai mafia killed Thaksin Kittikatchorn, Prem's father? Tried to make her look like the killer?

She closes her eyes, blotting something out. "Tried to kill me too. Not like on Cape Cod. Not with guns. Asian style. Now everybody is after me."

He feels like he has walked into the wrong movie, at least half of him wishes he were back home fishing on the *Rosa Lee.* Jesus, what has he gotten himself into now?

2

SHE stares up into his unshaven, beautiful face in the half-light of the temple. Wants to clasp her hands behind his neck again. Wants to tell him how this current nightmare started. Tries.

Buddha. It began as a Buddhist act of contrition. An extreme attempt to shed her bad karma. To start a new life for herself. She came back to Thailand, to Brandy and Delta, to the exact place where her great love and great misery had begun. Came back to the River House, on a smoggy, moonless night. Came to return what her dead Prem had stolen from his father. What his father had stolen, too.

• • • • •

Thanks to the services of a long-tail boat, she's face-to-face with Prem's prick of a father, the billionaire producer of sleeping pills, the collector of stolen artifacts, the crusher of an only son. Here on the waterside deck of the River House, bathed in the tangy scent of fresh-cut teak.

The house is bigger, more ornate, than the old one. The one she burned to the water in a storm of anger seven years ago. The house where she loved her sad, sweet Prem. The poor rich boy. The pung chao *addict, heroin junkie. Here. River House. On the* klong *in Thonburi, near the royal barge sheds. She will complete this cycle of her life and his. Make her peace, in the dark, where it all began more than ten years ago when she was the reigning princess of the Patpong. And not much more than a teenager.*

"Khwan pha sak, Miss Aparecio. I have been waiting a long time for this moment. My wife thinks I am a fool to see you here alone at night without my bodyguards. When you are as well-known as me, when people covet your wealth and power, Bangkok is a very dangerous place."

She knows he bites his tongue, wants to call her Prem's sin, call her his son's luk sod *Patpong whore. Shame her one more time, the way he did seven years ago when he made Prem give her up.*

So … She glares at Thaksin Kittikachorn. Late fifties. Very much the ex-navy gunboat captain, the champion handballer, the way he carries himself. Predator in a golden shirt. Self-assured. But his eyes dart between her and the river. The klong. *The dark. Worried about something. Maybe looking for someone else.*

"Do you have the Heart of Warriors?"

Until now, she did not know the stone had a name. But, of course, it must. A thing so beautiful. She feels in her handbag with her fingers, touches a cool, oval gem. Remembers one night seven years ago after all the trouble started between her and Prem. After his addiction and his family began to steal him away from her. Back when they both were trying to hang on to love, to each other for a little longer. Despite the heroin, despite the pressure from his family to end it …

One night when Bangkok looked like a fairy world from the river taxi. Just a night or two before Prem's family swept him away for drug rehab at the Hill Station in Malaysia. There in the river taxi he slipped the eighteen-carat ruby into her coat pocket. He said it was a stone that had vanished during the madness of the Vietnam War. A gem from the crypt of Wat Ratchaburana at Ayutthaya. The ancient royal capital of Siam. Circa 1400. He guessed that his father paid thieves or grave robbers to steal it for him. The gem had been on display in a glass case in the living room of the family mansion for as long as Prem remembered. His father's prized possession. Sitting right next to the collection of Buddha's heads stolen from wats in

Cambodia. *His father has a fascination for the rare, the ancient, the mystical, the forbidden. Covets them. Possessing things like the Heart of Warriors makes Thaksin Kittikachorn feel his balls.*

That's why Prem took it. He wanted to strip his father of that awful power the man held over him. He wanted Tuki to have the ruby, the power. Gave her the wine-red miracle as a symbol of his eternal love. She told him she would guard it with her life. That seemed to make him breathe easier.

"But if I die …," he said, "if you stop loving me, you must promise to return it to Ayutthaya. You must free yourself of any bad karma that comes with keeping a stolen thing without the justification of love. You must free me too. You must make our peace with Buddha."

A month later, when he emerged from rehab at the hill station, she learned that he had caved in to his family's pressure. He left her for the daughter of a silk merchant, left her for a loveless marriage. Left her with a heart in ashes. But in love … for years. Guarding the stolen ruby with her life for five years of hell in New York, then on Cape Cod. The last eighteen months traveling in Southeast Asia. As if the thing has magical properties. As if it could someday make her life better.

But now … Now Prem has been dead for nearly two years. And her soul has changed. The love she felt for him is just a sad memory. She has to let him go. Has to let go of the Heart of Warriors. Get on with her new life.

"If I give the ruby to you, you have to promise to take it back to Wat Ratchaburana at Ayutthaya."

"Yes. Of course. It is a national treasure. But quickly. How much money do you want for the …?"

"I'm not here to SELL it," she says.

She wishes she could just take the ruby back to Ayutthaya herself. But it is not that simple. She has talked this over with many monks, many times, since she has gotten back to Southeast Asia after her five years in America. They always speak in parables. But what she thinks they are saying is that she will lessen none of her karmic load, none of Prem's cosmic burden either, if the original thief remains alive and does not make amends for his theft. Like no pain, no gain, la. Her problem is that she really doesn't trust this man, feels she needs to test him.

"This is not the time to …" Kittikschorn's eyes dart out to the dark river again. The klong. Out and back once more.

She sees a life-size, bronze statue of the Buddha seated in the lotus position on the corner of the deck over the klong.

"Promise before the Buddha and the eternal spirit of your son that you will take the stone back to Wat Ratchaburana."

"Please. You don't understand. We should not be here like this …"

"Promise … Say, I promise before Buddha to return the Heart of Warriors."

The father twitches. "Yes, I promise before Buddha and my son and all the angels of Bangkok. But surely you must see how dangerous it is for us to be here like this. Alone without the protection of my body … The jao pho are—"

"Ok."

She feels in her bag among the clutter. Finds the oval gem she wants to give him, cups it in her right hand. Is stretching out her arm to offer it to this tiger of a man. The lights of Bangkok and Thonburi are twinkling in its facets when she feels something buzz past her ear, hit the teak wall with a thwack.

Thaksin Kittikachorn's face blooms blood. He topples backwards. Hits the wooden deck. Life surging away from a wound in his neck, soaking him in gore. His carotid artery severed as if by an invisible knife of epic sharpness.

She wheels, looking for an assailant, a weapon. Sees two silhouettes— or maybe it's just a single guy, she can't be sure—slipping back into the shadows where the house meets the porch rail at the far end of the deck. Sees the flash of a green satin jacket as a figure vanishes.

Standing at the top of the steps to the boat landing, ten meters away, are two masked men in black. One seems to be holding a cell phone, taking a picture. The other has a pistol.

This girl of the Patpong needs no second warning. She knows that the nak-lin have come for the ruby. Will kill them both for the Heart. So she drops the stone. It clinks on the teak deck … Just before she imagines the voice of her lawyer saying, "Get evidence." Just before she makes a flying leap into the klong.

She comes up to get air, check her bearings, once … before she slips out of her black skirt, red silk blouse, and swims toward the royal barge sheds. Hides in the shadow of the queen's dragon boat. Knows already that this is just the start of a terrible journey to see the Heart of Warriors safely back to Ayutthaya. A terrible fight to leave Southeast Asia behind. If such a thing is even possible.

3

"TUKI says some men killed Kittikatchorn."

"You saw her, counselor?" Varat Samset's at his desk in Bangkok's central police station. Concrete walls the color of puke. The desk fan blowing only on the detective. The rest of the room a sauna.

Michael stands there sweating.

"I went to a temple. She was there. Told me she saw Thaksin Kittikachorn murdered by the *nak-lin* on the deck of the house near the royal barge sheds. Then she disappeared."

"Somebody knocked me out last night."

"I wouldn't know about that."

"Of course not, counselor. You don't know about anything."

"Pardon?"

"You have any idea how dumb you sound when you say *nak-lin?*"

"What? Why?"

"*Nak-lin* just means gangsters. You have any idea how many gangs we have in Bangkok."

He shrugs. "Can I sit down?"

"Chinese, Burmese, Malay, Indian, Laotioan, Hmong, Vietnamese, Thai, Russian."

"What?"

"We got *nak-lin* in all shapes and sizes. Someone's store gets firebombed, somebody disappears, a corpse is floating in the river. Always the same explanation. *Nak-lin.* BULLSHIT! I have witnesses: the wife and servants of Thaksin Kittikachorn, his bodyguards. They all say he was going to the River House to meet your shemale client. He said he thought she was going to blackmail him for something."

Michael feels the back of his polo shirt soaking with his sweat. "She was trying to give him a gem, a ruby."

"A ruby?"

"Something called the Heart of Warriors."

"Really?"

"She said Prem gave it to her."

"Before she killed him."

"He shot himself."

"You say."

"Ok, have it your own way ... She was giving it back. The stone. She says it was stolen."

"Oh yes."

"Prem took it from his father. His father took it from some temple."

"The Heart of Warriors vanished from a temple in the ancient city of Ayutthaya, valued at something like eleven million. Where is the ruby now?"

"Tuki said she dropped it at the River House and ran. After the *nak-lin* killed Kittikachorn."

"You believe that? Oh, yes, maybe I guess you would. You probably believe in what Americans call the tooth fairy too."

His whole body is dripping. Underwear sticky and knotted in his crotch. *Fuck this place!* What made him think he had any business coming here? He should know by now that justice does not dwell in cop stations. Maybe nowhere.

"Go ahead, counselor. You want to tell me to piss off? Tell me to take my little Asian country and stick it up my ass? You ready to quit on that shemale yet?"

He feels steel rods shooting up his neck, piercing the back of his skull.

"Please … be my guest. Go back where you belong."

Something deep between his ears cracks. "Back off, Detective! Give me a break here. Give Tuki a break!"

"Oh look, watch the white boy do anger. So Clint Eastwood. So not Thai."

"Listen, you bastard! She gave me this. Said it was how they killed Kittikachorn, tried to kill her. She said you would understand." He fishes in his leather backpack, takes out a wrinkled, red, silk blouse and unfolds it, exposing a steel star about four inches in diameter. Stained brown with dried blood.

Samset gets up from his desk chair, pulls rubber gloves from his desk drawer. Puts them on, picks up the star. "You know what this is, attorney?"

"Someone threw it at Thaksin Kittikachorn. It stuck in a wall."

"A *tonki*. Some people call it a *shaken*, a Chinese throwing star. This one has an unusual design. Its three blades fold up to look like a cyclone for safekeeping."

"Crazy."

"Very unusual. Not what we normally see here in Bangkok. Very dangerous."

"I told you she didn't kill Kittikachorn. She said one of the ambush guys was wearing a green silk warm-up jacket."

"You think that's going to help me find these boys?" He laughs.

"Tuki's your eye-witness."

"Oh, yeah. Just perfect. You know what that means?"

"What?"

"The guy in that green jacket finds her before we do, you can kiss her sweet little ass goodbye."

4

IT'S A BARRY WHITE kind of night. The dance version of "You're My Everything" is pounding. She can already feel the bass jiving her heart. And she has just passed beyond the doormen at a night-club called CM2 in the basement of the Novotel at Siam Square.

I'll meet you at the wine bar, she told him two nights ago when they met in the *wat.* When she gave him the *tonki* wrapped in her silk blouse. *Eleven o'clock, la. Friday night. We will see where we stand.* Now she's unsure of what she really meant. Yes, she meant "stand" with the police, the *nak-lin* and some gangster in a green satin jacket. But her heart tells her she meant more. *Like where do we stand with each other after nearly two years apart, la?*

Typical Tuki. Her words confusing even to herself, always laced with layers of meaning. Her intentions habitually obscure.

Moving into the Boom-Boom Room, she sees faces, bodies, flashing in and out of the darkness. Snapshots of ecstasy, of bump, of grind. In red, blue, gold, flaring phosphorescence. Thai women in cocktail dresses, Thai men in silk shirts. Lots of upscale *farangs.* Expats, white and Japanese businessmen. Their eyes glazed. Brains blowing circuits.

And Barry White so loud the music pumps through her lungs, thick as the stage smoke. The room so crowded every step toward the bar means another grazing of hips, the rub of her breasts against someone's upper arm, chest. The relentless scent of citrus perfumes. Shampoos. The brilliance of black hair. Sometimes a man's hand on her forearm. Just to steer him past her body. Or an invitation. Even the Dentyne in her mouth feels electric by the time she catches sight of the wine bar. By the time she sees him waiting for her at the end of the bar with a glass of pale wine in his hand.

He looks nervous, the way he holds his glass so close to his chin. But it can't mask those bedroom eyes, the fine, tan symmetry of his face. The slight shadow of a beard she loves. Something about his close-cropped hair—or maybe the way he stands with all of his weight on his right leg in those khaki chinos and white polo shirt—reminds her of a Brazilian football player she saw on TV.

"Hey." She stretches out her arms, beckons to him from ten meters away. Feels every inch of her body calling to him from beneath this little, golden dress. It is nothing more than the thinnest veil. A film, really. She can't help herself. Here. Now. She's offering to take him away from the killing, from that ferret Varat Samset. From the *nak-lin*, the *jao pho*. Away from his failure as a public defender, failure with the law. To someplace he has never been. To drown in the amber rivers of Southeast Asia for a while.

But she doesn't want to scare him away. She wants to draw in his mind, his ceaseless curiosity. And that huge Portuguese heart. She wants to share her deepest secrets with him. She pushes through the crowd to him at the bar.

"Michael," she says, taking his glass of wine, sipping. "Listen, la. I still have it."

"Yeah." He's looking into her eyes. "You sure do."

"I mean the stone."

"The ruby?"

"Well, sort of."

Her hand, a mind of its own, slides into the pocket of his chinos. Just halfway.

"Dance with me …" Her words are bursts of air in his right ear. "Like that night in Provincetown. Please."

He hesitates. Al Green is singing "Let's Stay Together" over the sound system.

"Don't be ashamed. No one knows us here … And I told you, I've really changed."

He squints, doesn't understand.

She can't help busting a huge smile, stretching out her hand a little in his pocket. "My plumbing, Michael. I've changed … you know?"

"What?"

"I'm a real girl. Female." If he only knew what she has gone through to be able to say these words, how good they sound sliding off her tongue. "Nothing extra, la. In Hanoi, last year. I had the operation."

"A girl?"

She can see him trying to take in the substance of her words. Trying to understand how this changes the way he thinks about her.

"You're a girl?"

"One hundred percent girl … who really wants to dance."

• • • • •

A slow dance. His parents' music, her parents' music. A crush song from American bars during the Vietnam War. And Saigon bars. Barbara Lewis, "Hello Stranger." *Seems like a mighty long time.*

It's not like that dance they shared two years ago at the Carnival ball in Provincetown, when she was the brightest star of Provincetown Follies' premier drag show. That dance had been a cha cha. This is the other thing all together. A slow burn. He's thinking he's more lost than ever. He's never seen a light show like this, not on Cape Cod, not in New Bedford or Providence, not even in the clubs in Boston where Filipa used to take him back in their courting days. He feels vacant-headed, *despistado*, hears a voice in the back of his head telling him he needs to stop with the chivalry and get the hell out of Dodge.

"Hold me tighter, la."

That voice again. Her. The orphan from Vietnam. The love child of the black marine from California and the bar girl from Saigon's Dong Du Street. No longer the girl in the black pajamas and short hair from the temple. She's changed again. Glossy red hair, falling almost to her waist. A diamond choker. Cleopatra eyes. Body by Bowflex. *Cristo!* A girl. He feels something rip in his groin, feels the pain as he imagines her surgery. Feels his old fear of being too close to that body of hers. Damn, it's already lifting him away from the humiliation Filipa heaped on him when she canceled their wedding. Already lifting him beyond his last case, the tragedy of Awasha Patterson's death last year.

He feels awkward, confused. Keeps wondering if he's crossing some kind of straight-guy line here. He should just stop dancing … But the music's weaving itself into his thoughts, into his muscles. His skin, too. Heat rising from every relevant inch of her body. And his.

You could die here, he thinks. *Save yourself while you can, fool. Girl or not, let be!*

She presses into him, wraps both her arms around his neck. Whispers. *Here's the truth.* The ruby she took to the River House, the one she dropped on the deck before leaping into the *klong*, was a fake. Glass. Why? Two reasons, la. One, she had worried there was a chance that the *nak-lin* might try to ambush her at the River House so she was not going to expose the real ruby to theft again. Two, she didn't trust Thaksin Kittikachorn. She wanted to test him. If he actually took the fake ruby back to Ayutthaya then she would know he had honorable intentions, know that he had what Buddha calls the karma cleansing of *right purpose* and *right action*. She had planned to check with the monks in Ayutthaya. If they received the fake ruby, she would replace it with the real stone. Meanwhile, she had tucked the real Heart of Warriors away under a bush. It's probably there where she hid it in the courtyard of a small monastery in Bangkok's Banglamphu district.

But she has not gone back for it. She's afraid the *nak-lin* are even now following her. She needs him. *Please help me, Michael.* She has to get the stone back, return it to Ayutthaya. Cast off the bad karma. Find closure with her lost love. And get out of Thailand before the police send her to the Bridge Over the River Kwai Death Camp ... or someone kills her.

But first this. The dance. She's singing in his ear. *Hello Stranger.* Her voice changed from her diva days, changed since the man who killed Al Costelano squeezed her throat in the vice of his hands, put her in the hospital for weeks back in Massachusetts. It has gotten lower, raspy. Sultry in a sort of Tina Turner way. But she can still sing. Her vocal chords sear him.

And damn. She really is a girl now. He can feel her. Every curve, every hollow. Smell some secret signal in the musk of her hair. Even though it is a red wig. *Hello Stranger.*

"I just want to know ..."

He doesn't answer.

"I just want to know, la, if ... if I could ever be more to you than a client, a challenge, a victim to rescue."

He stares up into the flashing disco lights. Feels her thighs slide against his thighs. He smells the musk, hears the beckoning words of the song, sees the reflection of the strobe lights on his cheeks. Her cheeks. The arc of her shoulders. The smooth plane of her neck. Her lips.

He is raising her face to kiss when she jerks away.

"Come on, la!"

"Huh?"

"I've got to go."

"What?"

"*Nak-lin.*"

"Here?"

"At the bar."

"Are you sure?"

"Go to the Wat Chai Chana Songkhram, in Banglamphu, tomorrow, six in the morning, when the monks gather for their prayers. I will come. I promise."

5

A GONG SOUNDS. The monks, with their shaved heads, their saffron robes, have finished their prayers. They file from the temple, fanning out across the courtyard to the streets of Banglamphu, to beg alms. By his watch it is already 8:37. The morning mist off the river has given way to a gray, hot day. The air drips with humidity, the scent of spent gasoline, garbage. A pair of Brahma steers munch grass in the shade of the whitewashed *wat*.

She has not come. And now he wonders if he has been a fool. Whether the red hair, the musk, the hand in his pocket last night were all about setting him up as a decoy. Someone to distract the bad guys while she makes her escape.

He would not know a *nak-lin* if one spit in his face ... unless maybe the guy is wearing a green satin jacket. But maybe they have followed him here, are watching him right now. Waiting for some sign of her or the ruby. Thais with their foam cups of coffee, their morning papers, crisscross the temple courtyard on their way to work. Any number of them could be gangsters or plain clothes cops.

For the first hour he sat in the lotus position, faced off with a statue of Buddha and made like he was meditating, but then his legs cramped and he had to get up. Now he has bought a small sack of rice, is trying to look inconspicuous as he casts handfuls to the pigeons. *Fat fucking chance!*

So what should he do? Give up on this place? Tardiness has never been one of her flaws. If she is this late, she must not be coming. Either standing him up was always part of her plan … or she saw that he was being watched here and decided to bug out. Either way, feeding these pigeons is a waste of time.

Maybe he should get on a bus or a *rua duan* and try to lose whoever is tailing him. Check into a new hotel. Maybe hide among the other *farangs* loafing in the cafés, bars on Kao San Road where all the international backpackers hang out. Maybe … *Shit!* He has no clue. This is not his universe.

· · · · ·

With his street map in hand, and his mariner's love of navigational challenges, Michael has decided he should try to find his way to the water taxi landing in Samphya and see if someone follows. He's just a block from the river when an old monk walks up to him. The man is about five feet tall and thin as a goat. He wears wire-rim spectacles and has his hands pressed palm-to-palm beneath his chin in prayer.

"*Sawat dii khrap.*"

These are just about the only words in Thai Michael knows. A greeting. And he knows he should make his hands like the monk's and bow his head in return. Tuki taught him this.

The monk steps closer. "Michael?"

"I am Michael."

The monk opens his hands as if begging for alms. Raises his hands right beneath Michael's eyes. Cupped in one hand is a small ball of red silk wrapped with a rubber band. It is like the blouse Tuki had wrapped around the throwing star. Maybe a torn-off pocket.

"You take. Go now *rot fai!*"

The monk takes the sack of rice from Michael's hands and subtly drops the tiny package in its place.

"*Rot fai?*"

"Train. *Pai!* Go Hualapong station!"

· · · · ·

Not until he is alone in a men's room stall at the station in central Bangkok does he open the little silk package. Inside is a brilliant oval ruby the size of a playing marble. And a second-class, one-way, railway ticket to Penang, Malaysia.

His chest tightens. Locks.

He pictures her smile. And for the first time he suspects he knows what calls to him from the sparkle in her eyes. From that grin that starts with her full lips and straight white teeth, spreads to her chin. To the two dimples on her cheeks. Trust. It could be trust. And maybe something more. Freely given. No conditions. Rarer than a stolen gem. Most rare in the life of an attorney, a fisherman, an American.

So he smiles back. And lets the steamy air of Siam fill his lungs.

He knows better than to go back to his hotel for his seabag. Samset or the *nak-lin* might be waiting. Ready or not, he is skipping the country. On the midday train. Heading south. With a heart full of questions about justice, trust, smiles. An eleven million dollar stone tucked beneath his tongue.

Looking for Cinderella.

6

ROLLING SOUTH from Bangkok. A second-class sleeper. Fans in the coach humming their nocturne.

He's not in the mood for alcohol, doesn't want to let his guard down. But he takes the bottle, anyway. Sips. The Mae Khong whiskey is a sizzling current in his throat, sweeping away the pain in the back of his neck, filling the emptiness in his chest.

The caution lights are starting to pop on in his head—like *needy boy beware*—every time she gives him a cockeyed look and speaks. Her name's Wen-Ling. A Chinese Thai.

She's the one plying him with this rice whiskey. The woman sitting next to him tonight on the train. A middle-age siren. Cougar in an expensive white suit, the hem of her skirt riding up so high on her thighs that her legs seem impossibly long. She reeks of cigarettes, pungent perfume, the strange whiskey. Jasmine, maybe. A witch in a French-style straw hat. Broad brim, pink ribbon for a band, trailing off down her back with her ponytail.

"Don't these trains always make you feel like a spy?"

That's it. After logging fifteen thousand miles to get here. After all those night moves back in Bangkok the last few days, after stashing a ruby in his mouth and fleeing the City of Angels, he finds a fellow traveler who has the words for the feeling he has been getting for the last six hours on this train. Maybe everywhere he's been since landing in Indochina.

"See what I mean?" She points out the window with the whiskey bottle.

It's sunset. The train has begun to brake. It threads along a network of *klongs*. A warren of stilt houses cover the bank. Charcoal braziers burn in the doorways. Figures paddle narrow boats through the shadows.

He wonders if the Kittikachorn's River House where Tuki unleashed the demons so many times looks just so. Whether Cholon, where American GIs like his father kept their love nests thirty-five years ago, their hooch girls on the fringe of Saigon, had this darkness. This smokey look.

An old man stands up to his knees and naked in the *klong*, soaping his thighs in slow strokes. A girl leaps from porch to porch above the water, pursued by a band of boys waving a snake. For a second, Michael thinks he hears them laughing like crows.

She offers him the whiskey again.

He takes the bottle, drinks deeper this time. Giving in to the whiskey's release. The glass bottle warm and wet from her lips. The whiskey burns him right down to his toes. His eyes—big, wet—search his reflection in the window, the night beyond. He sees the desperate sag to his cheeks, his jaw, etched over the blur of a twisting *klong*, stilt houses, flaring fires, silhouettes of women, children. Here. Gone. And the caution lights popping on at the back of his brain.

"What's the matter? What you looking for? What you lost, honey?"

· · · · ·

He's having a memory.

A beach house in Nantucket, the master bedroom. A king-size bed. The comforter, the sheets, the pillows tangled together. Clothes. A man and a woman's. Tuki's black bra. Her thong. Trailing across the rug to a Jacuzzi on an outdoor deck beyond the open slider.

Blood. Swirls of it. Coiling, ebbing, flowing through the water in the hot tub.

A body. Nude on a bench seat in the spa. Head buried in a forearm on the edge of the tub. A hole in the side of the head where the bullet came out. It's Tuki's ex-lover. The poor little rich boy Prem from Bangkok. A thread of blood leaks from the corner of his mouth. Next to his hand is a .357 magnum.

Michael staggers out of the house to the beach. He had hoped that Prem Kittikatchorn would just disappear from Tuki's life, stop hounding her. But not like this. And she was here too. In that house. In that room. With her clothes off. But now she's gone. The beach is bare. The ocean is empty.

• • • • •

He can't remember exactly what he was thinking that day on the beach in Nantucket, what he was picturing. But now here on this train hissing through the hot Thai night, he sees dead women just beyond the windowpane. Women he has loved. Awasha Patterson, gun shot, lying on the floor in a pool of blood … last year. Three EMTs pressing enormous gauze pads to her right cheek, chest. His mother Maria in her hospital bed just a few months before Awasha died. Strangled by her cancer until she was the shadow of a Holocaust victim. Then just a whisper. A word. *Love.* Then nothing at all.

He feels something tightening in his chest. All the air going out. His legs shiver.

The train wheels are rumbling through his mind—a terrible pulsing—when he sees Tuki again in flashes, flickers. Out there. In the night. Rising above the other ghosts.

She's onstage, belting out "This Old Heart of Mine." The crowd clapping to the music as she works the runway, singing, strutting. A love child, an old soul, a holy child of Buddha. Head high, chest out, hips swinging. Smiling when he loses her.

7

"YOU WANT to talk about it?" She takes a slow swallow from the bottle. Eyes him over the rim.

He looks away. Stares into the night outside from behind the glass, from this train. Knows he should stop drinking, thinking, talking. Wishes the porter would come to make up the berths and save him from going into the rabbit hole with this stranger.

"You see bits of secret worlds on a train," says Wen-Ling, "and you want to see more, ride forever, know those secrets. It is like what Thai people call *pung chao*. White powder, heroin. A craving deep … here, honey." She presses her hands, the whiskey bottle, to the hollow beneath her breasts.

Jesus. That about sums things up, he thinks. Tuki is like this to him. *Pung chao.* And now he can't find her. Again. All he has is this hard, red little souvenir of her beneath his tongue. And a net of tangled memories. *Pass the bottle.*

• • • • •

The Provincetown ball, the summer Carnival. Almost two years ago when Michael was fresh on the Follies murder case, when he was Tuki's public defender. A club called the Boat Slip. He got roped into coming to this gay dance. It's payback for information he needed from a crazy old drag queen named Chivas.

A slow set comes on. The DJ spinning a tune from Pretty Woman, *a sexy number called "Fallen."*

He's leaning against a wall, sucking on a beer, listening to the song, watching all the drag queens and kings dancing when he feels someone grab his elbow. His client. The murder suspect. Tuki.

"Can I have this dance?"

He wants to beg off, lie. He cannot dance with a tranny.

But her hand holds on. Until they are dancing. She feels as light as a phantom in his arms. His feet remembering eight years of dancing school in Nu Bej.

She's so smooth, so easy on her feet, so straight, so strong, so subtle. They spin together, his thigh grazing the backside of her left leg. The blade of his hip slides against hers.

He wants to swear. This just cannot be happening to him. He cannot really be dancing like this. Not here, not now, not with this person. Not even if this is what a defender has to do to make his case ...

• • • • •

"They call this the railway of many souls." Her eyes are closed, face turned to the dark ceiling. The lights so dim in the railway coach that indoors and outdoors blur together.

He has the odd sense of hurtling through a thunderstorm. Hot, wet air making his breath quick, shallow. The rumble of the wheels, sky. Vague flashes of lightning. The scent of ozone. A heaviness in the back of his brain, his chest. *Fucking rice whiskey.* It must be almost midnight, the bottle's more than half-empty. And the porters have still not come to make up their berths. *Jesus!*

She talks. Drinks. Talks more. Tells him this railway cost more lives to build than Egypts' pyramids. Since the British stretched the first tracks north from Singapore in 1903, perhaps as many as a hundred and fifty thousand Malay, Chinese and Tamil coolies lost their lives pushing the rails through equatorial jungle and swamp. Sixteen thousand British, Dutch and Australian POWs died extending the death railway to Burma during World War II. Cemeteries at the bridge over the river Kwai serve as unforgettable reminders.

The Bridge Over the River Kwai Death Camp. The place Tuki always seems most to fear. Has she already gone there? Is that where this train is really taking him? Is Penang nothing more than a waystation on this night train to oblivion?

The whiskey has made a soft, lazy song of her words. Almost Tuki's voice. But the accent is a bit different. She says she was a bar girl once. Bangkok, Singapore, other places here in Indochina. *Long time ago, honey.* She found love and moved to Australia with her man. But she lost him. *Very sad. Nothing is forever. Know what I mean?* So she is coming home. Taking her own sweet time. Riding the rails from Bangkok to Singapore. The night train, the sleeper. A sentimental journey. A refugee of love.

"Very hard, American. Sooo hard, honey ... Maybe I break up this trip. You know Surat Thani?"

He shakes his head no. Takes the bottle from her, tips it to his lips. Part of him just wants to pass out from the whiskey, end this night as soon as possible.

"I know a little hotel. A place to forget everything." Is she offering him this? Offering him pleasure? Is that what she wants with her whiskey and her questions? With her eyes ... and the ring of laughter in the dark, swaying car? *What's the matter, honey? What you looking for? What you lost?*

He can picture it. She gets off. He gets off. There is a railway hotel like some place he's seen in the movie *The Killing Fields.* A town throbbing to the beat of a night market. The party goes until the moon sets, the stars fade away. Almost like Provincetown back home on the Cape.

Her warm hand moves across his thigh. His mouth salivates, tongue surges. The ruby rolls against his gums. He has to work it back into the pit of his jaw before he can speak.

"I have a long way to go. Someone I need to ..."

She stares away out the window. The moon on the paddies. Shadows of oxcarts, water buffalo.

"Where? Where is she, American?"

If only I had the faintest clue, he thinks. Listens to the fans in the coach humming off-key. Strange, there are no porters to make up the berths, to put an end to this whiskeyed intimacy. And her head is settling onto his shoulder. A fine head. Long soft hair with the scent of some … something sweet …

For a second he wonders what the *nak-lin* think if they are watching him now. If he's been followed … Or … maybe there is even something weirder going on here. But he can't think. His mind now a muddy river flowing from a place he can't even imagine toward a sea he's never seen.

He wants to jump to his feet, shout for the porters, or run.

But his eyes close, his body heavy as bilge lead, words unraveling in his head. *If I had the faintest clue …*

8

WHEN THE TRAIN shuffles to a stop at the Malaysian border crossing, she stirs against his chest.

He opens his eyes to a bright morning sun. A golden haze of a day.

"If you have any drugs or contraband," she says, "now would be the time to flush them down the toilet. Possession means death in Malaysia."

He feels muzzy, parboiled in the heat. Still drunk. Can think of nothing to say except, "Shit." Just shit.

The ruby digs into the root of his tongue as the train crew and border guards herd him off the train to an outdoor queue at the immigration/customs station. The sun witheringly hot.

· · · · ·

"Passport!" The Malay agent grunts from inside a wire cage. "Show now!"

From behind him in the queue, she prods his lower back with a finger to get him out of his fog, this wicked hangover. He pushes his passport forward into the cage.

"How long you coming to Malaysia, American?"

She pokes him again—*speak.*

"I'm on holiday. Two months." He mumbles. But his words sound like shouting in his head. He squints with the pain. Thinks maybe the Mae Khong has permanently seared the inside of his skull, melted the chambers of his brain. Wonders if his eyes are hollow, black.

"You no have return ticket. You rich boy?"

"No." His voice breaks. The ruby is a hot coal in his mouth, nearly closing his throat. He wants water. Needs water. About ten gallons.

"You must have return ticket or lots of money to come my country. Bums stay Thailand. No bums here. You bum, you go jail … or we send back now."

He tries to say that he has money, but the words come out a jumble of Portuguese and English. *Freaking whiskey! Damned ruby!*

"You drunk?"

"No, I …" He fumbles in his pants pockets for the pack of traveler's cheques to show he is not indigent.

"You no speak right. You got something in mouth?"

The ruby slams back against his wisdom teeth. "No, I …"

The immigration officer's eyes search beyond him, look for one of the armed guards on the railway platform. Catches one's attention, beckons him.

Oh shit!

"What wrong with you?"

The guard is nearly on him, cocking his submachine gun.

He feels like he is going to faint. Or spill the ruby if he tries to say another word.

"Hey, American. Answer me."

The guard is raising his gun toward Michael's chest … when Wen-Ling steps between them.

"He ate some beef *satay* from a vendor when the train stopped at Hat Yai. It made him sick. He threw up all over the train. It was this awful yellow and green. You know, with chunks of meat and …"

The immigration agent looks ready to gag. Sighs. Shakes his head. Wags a finger at Michael. "You listen to what Haji say, American. Malaysia, Moslem nation. You eat no sacred cow!"

He nods. Feels his eyes burning.

The agent slams his stamp down on Michael's passport.

"Go in peace, *ferringhi*. But … no more cow!"

Wen-Ling whispers something in his ear. He's not sure what she says. Not even sure she speaks in English. He just knows her voice sounds plaintive at first. Then resigned. As if she has reached a decision. Or is saying goodbye.

With no luggage, he hopes to breeze through customs. But he gets stuck behind a long line of Malaysian Tamils returning from shopping sprees in Bangkok with mounds of gear. When he finally clears the border, looks around for Wen-Ling on the railway platform, most of the travelers have already climbed aboard the shiny, new Malaysian train. He wants to thank her for saving him from the death squad boys. From what surely would have been a strip search, an interrogation, an arrest. The loss of Tuki's ruby. But she's nowhere in sight. Like Tuki, like his mother dead from cancer, like Awasha shot, wiped off the Earth. Filipa gone, too. Another tangled memory. Another woman vanished from his life. Another female he never understood …

And now he wonders again. What if someone has followed him here, watching for him to lead the way to Tuki and the ruby?

• • • • •

It's not until he locates his coach, locks himself in its bathroom, that he actually heaves. The Mae Khong gushing out of him in torrents into the toilet. But the ruby's safe. First, caught in his cupped hands. Then stashed in the toe of his sneaker.

So now he's walking with a slight limp as he looks for his seat … But he feels a bit of alright. He just wishes he knew why. Whether something in him is healing now that he is alone again. Or whether this is what it feels like to be doomed. To have bad karma. Stuck on an endless mission, scripted by inscrutable forces. With the demons closing in.

At this point, all he can do is take the ride, hope he can find Cinderella. *The problem is that's not enough, is it?* She's not safe, he's not safe, until he can figure out who really killed Thaksin Kittikachorn and deliver the killer or killers to Varat Samset and the law. Not until he can find some guy in a green jacket.

How the hell you going to do that, counselor?

9

THE CONDUCTOR shakes him awake as the train slows for Butterworth.

"You get off here. Follow signs to Penang ferry."

When he steps off the train, he thinks he sees Wen-Ling, the straw hat, at the far end of the platform. But then he's jostled by the crowd pushing past him toward the ferry terminal. And when he looks back down the platform the hat is gone.

And no one is at his back. But just to make sure he's not being followed, he goes into a stall in the bathroom, stays for half an hour. When he comes out, the ferry is long gone and the terminal deserted. He drifts out onto the non-descript streets of Butterworth in search of bottled water. He stops at a vendor's stall, drinks three bottles. Nearly buys some beef satay, but then remembers the customs agent's counsel—no more cow.

It's almost sunset when he hits the bathroom again, changes out of the white oxford shirt that might have made him stand out in a crowd. Now in a gray polo that he just bought, he blends with the rush-hour crush of Brits and Aussies heading home to Georgetown on Penang island from work on the mainland.

The ferry's bench seats are full. He claims a space among a group of white men, leaning on the bow rail of the big, yellow ferry with its blue and red stripes. For a few seconds he has the feeling he's aboard one of the lumbering ships of the Massachusetts Steamship Authority, heading for Martha's Vineyard. Or on the *Rosa Lee* with his father and Tio Tommy steaming offshore for summer flounder or cod.

He takes a long breath, looks out to sea. Rainsqualls are towering above leaden waves. The clouds violet pillars. He can smell the pungent scent of fish. Doesn't know why he loves the smell so much. Birds wheel and dive after the silver shadows of fins. Mostly the birds come up wet and floundering and empty handed. But they struggle into the sky. Spin and dive again. Ever hopeful … or maybe just dumb creatures. He hears his father's voice. *We're fishers, Mo. Stop with the self-pity, the* saudade. *Get your net in the water.*

His mind staggers. Part of him wishes he never got on the plane that brought him to Bangkok. Part of him sees nothing but pain and darkness ahead, wishes he could catch the next flight off this continent. But another part feels the need to be of help, to stand by Tuki. He feels this strange obligation to her that he felt during the Provincetown Follies case. Maybe it has something to do with his father's service in the Vietnam war, the hooch girl his father left behind. But his father's ghosts are not the only pull on him. There's affection. He always liked Tuki. Now that she's a fully fledged woman … Cristo, *who the hell knows? Feelings are complicated.*

So are thoughts. There are a multitude of questions buzzing through his brain that won't let him rest. Questions about where he will find Tuki, whether she is safe. Who killed Thaksin Kittikachorn? What about the shadowy *jao pho?* Or Varat Samset?

What's that ferret clawing into now? And how … how can you know for sure whether Kittikachorn's murder and the nak-lin's *pursuit of Tuki are truly about the stolen ruby? All you have is her word on this … and she has not always been the most reliable source. A chronic liar by omission.*

So, no surprise, he's wondering again if someone could be following him. Wondering how long it will take the bad guys to find the ruby he has now tucked in his jeans pocket …

He closes his eyes to clear his head, to get a grip on his next move. What if he left the ruby with monks somewhere, hoped they'd take it back to wherever it came from? Then maybe he can forget about the former princess of the Patpong once and for all. Catch the first flight home to Massachusetts. Go fishing again. Who knows, maybe he can patch things up with Filipa. That would make his father and a lot of other folks back in Nu Bej happy.

But when he opens his eyes again, all he can see is Tuki. Sort of. Almost alive. Everywhere he looks. In the clouds clotting on the dark green slopes of Penang Hill ahead. In the violet haze of sunset hanging over Penang's main city, Georgetown. In the smoke of incense, coconut fires, roasting chili peppers, frying fish rising from the houses on the edges of the North Channel. In the mist settling over the *sampans*, the waterfront restaurants, the plumes drifting off the barbeque pit at the Eastern & Oriental Hotel.

Her. The orphan from Vietnam. Love child from Dong Du Street and the Patpong. Out there on the island. Sometimes the girl in the black pajamas and a pageboy. Sometimes the woman with glossy red hair, falling almost to her waist. Cleopatra eyes.

His client. And who knows what else.

The sultry voice. The voice of Vietnam and Whitney Houston and a midnight train to Georgia. The girl it seems everyone is chasing, wants to kill.

Michael—
I am kind of in trouble ... Please come ... Hurry ...

Cristo, he thinks. *Spies or no spies.* Nak-lin *or no* nak-lin. *Killers or no killers. Net in the water. And no more cows, buddy boy!*

· · · · ·

"You want good, cheap hotel?" The tricycle rickshaw driver in front of the ferry terminal to Georgetown, Penang, has the sweat-stained skin of a man who hasn't bathed in days.

I need to buy more clothes than what I scored in Butterworth, he thinks. But what he says is, "Why not?"

He climbs in the rickshaw, his head staggering under the aftershocks of the Mae Khong. His mind already getting lost in the maze of Georgetown, the mountain forest rising behind it. Much of this city of nearly five hundred thousand looks like it did during the British Colonial days. A set worthy of Indiana Jones.

Dense neighborhoods of Chinese and Indians claim the heart of the city. Malay fishing *kampongs* dot the coast. Night markets, cafés, food stalls, rickshaws fill the evening streets. In one block he sees a crowd dodging the charge of a Chinese paper tiger. On the next street his rickshaw stalls behind the sway of a Hindu procession—drums, flutes, genii, goddesses. Further up the street, music in five languages pulses from the speakers of vendors selling pirated CDs. At tables in the streets, people linger over coffee, fresh fruit juices, Dutch beer and shrimp *satay* on long bamboo skewers.

Fleets of motorcycles buzz off to far corners of the island.

"Jesus, where do I begin?" he asks, mostly to himself.

"No matter," says the driver, huffing over the pedals in front of him. "First we get you good massage. Then blow job."

10

HE'S LOOKING over his shoulder, wonders if the yellow rickshaw a half block behind is following him when his driver makes a sharp turn onto a narrow street. Small Chinese hotels press together in a row. Something about their look reminds him of the Patpong. Maybe the neon signs, maybe the pimps in their black, lycra shirts leaning against the walls, green bottles of beer in hands. Then he sees the street sign: Love Lane. Penang island, it seems, is a place that tells it like it is.

"How about you take me to a bar?"

"Ok, Joe. Girly-Girly bar?"

"Someplace I can speak English." *Someplace I can ask people if they've seen a girl who looks like a miracle. A girl with the voice of a diva. A heart bold as Harlem, warm as a Bangkok night. Vulnerable as a kitten.*

"No problem. Girly show, massage, blow job, beer. All same place."

• • • • •

He remembers the house lights going dim:

Saturday night and Provincetown Follies in meltdown. A blue spotlight picks her up. His new client. The drag queen, the accused killer. She's the figure in a red, sheer evening dress, standing at the top of the stairs leading down to the stage. A diamond choker glitters at her throat. She's Whitney Houston tonight. Her hands in prayer, fingers beginning a slow rhythmic snap. Her hips picking up the beat. The mic rising to her lips. She begins Whitney's torch of torches from the final scene of The Bodyguard. *A song about bittersweet memories, about forever love.*

The sound system weeps with violins. Her blurry eyes find him. Find each heart in the room. Her lost lovers. Her parents. Her children.

• • • • •

"Haiphong Bar next block, Ok, Joe?"

The driver pumps the rickshaw uphill, rises off his seat with the effort. The long sleeves of his shirt creep up his arms as he struggles with the weight. Michael sees red needle tracks running from wrists to elbows. *Pung chao.* It made a ghost of Prem Kittika-chorn ... Then the dominoes started falling. One by one. Continue to fall.

Who's next? He looks back down the street. The yellow rickshaw still there, coming. Gaining. Flickering in and out of the neon lights. And traffic stalling in front of him.

"I can walk from here." He jumps from the rickshaw while it is moving. Tosses the driver twenty dollars U.S. He's overpaying, but screw all. *Time and tide wait for no man.* He can already smell the *tempestade* starting to swirl around him. The shit storm. And he's not even through the swinging doors of the Haiphong yet.

11

"I KNOW that bitch." The Tamil bar girl slurs her words, leans an elbow on the bar. Fingers the bottle of Amstel he just bought her. "But I no remember where I see her last."

The Haiphong is filling up. German merchant seamen, Aussies from the airbase in Butterworth, Indian whore mongers, teenage Chinese hookers. A crew of college lesbian backpackers from UCLA, tossing darts. Two Malay boys dancing in a corner, groping each other's butts. Percy Sledge, "When a man Loves a Woman," churning from the juke box.

The B-girl tilts her head, rolls her eyes at him. Looks with amusement at the Durian shake he's drinking, probably imagines his hangover. Something about her look, maybe the orange feather helmet or the green lipstick, remind him of a long-dead jazz singer. Billy Holiday maybe. Or Josephine Baker. But taller. Tall as him. With the hint of a mustache.

"You want buy some magic pills? I got all kind pills, cute boy. Pills make you stand up straight and tall. Sharkfin pills."

"If I buy the pills, you think you could try to remember where you saw this girl last?" He taps the postcard laying on the bar. It's a picture of Tuki. The one the touts in P-town used to pass out to promote her show at the Follies.

"She no look like that anymore."

He's not sure what she means.

"You girlfriend tranny, heh?"

"Not exactly."

· · · · ·

More than two years ago … One of those mornings a guy tries to block out of his mind and never can. A raid on Shangri-La, Big Al Costelano's compound in rural Truro on Cape Cod. Michael caught smack in the middle of the bust … while visiting his client.

Gestapo in full battle gear—walkie-talkies, blue windbreakers with ICE in gold letters on the back. State cops, too. Not only do they suspect that Tuki and the other queens who live here as guests of the newly murdered Costelano are illegals, but they claim the queens are keeping a disorderly house for immoral purposes. Michael's some of the evidence. The feds trying to say he's a John.

The Gestapo are bending their captives over the dining room table for body cavity searches when Michael hears an agent shouting.

"This one has a pussy … under his lil' pecker!"

"This one" is Tuki.

Her lawyer feels something twist in his guts. Just when he thought he had Tuki figured out, she turns out not to be a tranny. She's a hermaphrodite. An intersexual. One, according to her examiner, with an IUD inside her. So … she ovulates. Cristo!

· · · · ·

"Maybe I remember …" says the B-girl. "One pill fifty ringgits."

He lays some bills on the bar. "All I have is a few dollars." He doesn't mention his eighteen hundred in traveler's cheques.

The girl picks up a twenty dollar bill, pauses, takes another.

"What?"

"I remember something. Restaurant, beach place, out of town. End of the north shore road. In Teluk Bahang. Called Silver Moon. They got band. Good-time place. Maybe find you tranny there."

"Really?"

She slides two small yellow caplets into his hand. "You better buy more pills. I got love potion, too. Fifty dollars."

"I think I'm ok."

"Maybe not, cute boy. You go need serious magic."

"How's that?"

"You know big, black fellow? Look like you American actor Lawrence Fishburn?"

12

IT'S ALMOST MIDNIGHT when the taxi drops him. As soon as he gets out of the cab, he looks around to see if he has been followed. The road is peppered with people on motor scooters, their headlights coming, going, milling around the Silver Moon. *Cristo,* any of these people could be watching him. Maybe even the man in a green satin jacket that Tuki saw at the River House murder.

The place is living up to its name. A nearly full moon cuts a path across the Straits of Melaka, right to the spot where the parking lot meets the coral shore. Besides the scooter traffic, the restaurant, lit with about ten thousand tiny, twinkling lights, is the solitary sign of life in this fishing *kampong*, a collection of small shops, homes, guest houses. Built on low stilts out over the water, the Silver Moon is a horseshoe-shaped pavilion opening like a man-made cove to the sea. Dinner and cocktail tables on the left side, bar/dance floor to the right. Live band perched on a low stage in the middle, a river of moonshine at their backs.

Even from the parking lot, he can see hundreds of people juking to a six-horn combo rocking the Sam & Dave funk classic, "Soul Man."

Jesus, he's sick of bars, booze, crowds. Wonders why he can't have a client who works on a farm, a mountaintop. Or a boat.

But then he pictures that smile of hers when she sees him, the ruby he has tucked in his jeans pocket, a cyclone-shaped throwing star. And he remembers the B-girl's cryptic words. *You go need serious magic ... You know big, black fellow?*

He swallows the two caplets of ground sharkfin. Then it's into the madness. Past the pool filled with giant, golden carp. Through the open doors, straight to the bar.

• • • • •

He's got his back to a seaside railing, eyes glued on the stage, clutching a five-dollar glass of lemonade when the horns in the band finish their bridge. He half expects Tuki to rise out of the crowd and bust out the next verse of the song. But the singer turns out to be a Malay dude, about three hundred pounds. Huge fro, a blue sequin jumpsuit.

All around, a sea of babes. In jeans and tank tops, shorts and halters, little silk dresses. Yellows and wine-red the preferred colors. Their mouths opening, lips moving, singing, laughing ... But he can only hear the horns. While he inhales the scents of these night flowers in bloom, searches their faces. So many beauties. So many not the former diva of Provincetown Follies.

Until his eyes land on a girl carrying a tray with what looks to be a bottle of Heineken and a glass of champagne to one of the tables on the restaurant side of the pavilion. She's tall, blond hair, pink highlights. A pixie cut. Teased out, punky. Odd, pale skin. Bright green eyes—nearly Western—sparkling with the twinkling lights. Sort of butch-looking in tight jeans and a man's white dress shirt. Unbuttoned down to the black bra, shirttail hanging loose.

The walk gives her away. There's only one girl he knows with that voguey runway bounce. One foot in front of the other. Hips swaying, a fisherman's dream ... And she walks right up to a little cocktail table. Right up to a black man with his hands pressed palm-to-palm in front of his lips. He's fit, bearded, bald, wearing the white frock and pants of a cook or chef.

She bends, kisses him on the forehead, serves him the Heineken. He smiles up at her, says something that makes her face curl into a laugh. She sits, lifts the champagne. They toast.

Something twists in his chest.

Shit. Now what? Suddenly he understands what the girl was trying to tell him back at the Haiphong. About Tuki's looks ... And this black man. With a face he's seen somewhere before.

Has she just been using him as a mule to get the ruby safely out from under the prying eyes of the cops and the *nak-lin* back in Thailand? The slow dancing, the hugs, even the train ticket, just bribes to get him to do her dirty work? Does she have a thing going on with this black guy that she's been trying to hide from him? His heart doesn't want to believe it, but that kiss, smile, laughter looked like real affection.

His first thought is to just grab the ruby from his pocket and throw it into the ocean. Then go back to the bar and line up the shots of Mae Khong. But instead he walks over to her table, eases the Heart of Warriors into his hand. Wipes the fingerprints off with his shirt, sets the stone in the middle of the table.

"You probably want this."

She looks up. Her white-girl makeup crinkling, cracking around those fake green irises of her contact lenses as she soaks up his sudden appearance, his distress. Her panic blooms. Lips parting, cheeks sagging.

"Oh, la!" She jumps to her feet, tries to throw her arms around him.

But he steps back, avoids the embrace. "I've got to go."

She grabs his wrists with both hands. "What's wrong, Michael?"

He looks down at the black guy at the table, that face so familiar. But from where? "It's none of my business. I don't know why I ever ..."

"What?"

He tries to pull free.

But she squeezes his wrists, suddenly seems to connect his hurt with the man at the table. "It's not what you think ... Michael, listen to me!"

"You don't have to explain."

"But I do. I ... He ..." Her body's trembling, eyes welling up. Suddenly the black man is on his feet.

"My name's Marcus Aparecio, Michael. I'm Tuki's father, her *bpaa*," he says ... Then he wraps both of his long arms around Tuki, drags her to his side as if sheltering her.

Now Michael remembers. This is the guy in the picture she sent him eighteen months ago from Vietnam. The Polaroid snapshot. Tuki and this man. They were dressed in khaki shorts, white polo shirts, standing in front of a large stone pagoda. He's tall, slender, black. Looking like Lou Gossett, Jr.

Not Lawrence Fishburn at all. This long-lost father, this ex-marine. This Vietnam vet.

"Everything's going to be alright." The voice is a resonant baritone. He continues to hug Tuki.

"I don't know."

"What do you mean?" She reaches towards Michael with wet eyes.

"I think someone's been trying to follow me."

Marcus Aparecio grabs a wooden cane hanging from the back of his chair. Raps the floor with it. "Goddamn Sunny!"

13

"WHO'S SUNNY?"

She doesn't answer him, turns her eyes away. The white-girl wig and makeup are gone the green contacts left behind in the little apartment she shares with her father. It's over the kitchen at the Silver Moon, and Michael gathers from the amount of gear they have collected, the number of disguises, that the place has been a hideaway, an oasis, for Tuki and her dad. He gets the idea that this Sunny guy is somehow connected to the *nak-lin*, and that Tuki and her father have been dodging these bad guys for quite a while. Months, or maybe even since she skipped bail and split Provincetown nearly two years ago. They've been hiding out here on Penang, submerged in these new identities. Marcus cooking at the restaurant. Tuki hostessing, waiting tables.

The whole situation makes him nervous, makes him wonder where all this is leading. What's Tuki's end game? Is she just trying to find the most difficult way in the world to return a stolen ruby? Or is there more to this mess than he knows? He came to Bangkok thinking he was coming to render legal support, not get dragged

into a deadly game of hide-and-seek with Thai gangsters. *Cristo!*
Is he getting sucked so far down the rabbit hole he may never see
daylight? What would his father tell him to do now? He needs
to think.

But right now he can't concentrate. Right now he's too tired,
too hung over, too hot and sweaty to think about much more than
water—lakes and oceans of water. Too tired to do anything but
just stare at Tuki. Who doesn't seem to feel any of the panic he
sensed from her back in Bangkok. Maybe the girl's just pretending.
Needs to pretend for a while that she's safe here, they're all safe.
Hidden away from cops, Sunny Whoever and the *nak-lin.* Hidden
in a parallel universe called Penang. He can't get a clear read on this
whole situation …

But, Jesus, Tuki's easy on his eyes just now. She's looking very
mermaid in her silver string bikini, reclining on a large, smooth
rock in a mountain creek that spills into the pale ocean near the
lighthouse at Maku Head. This morning she's golden. Her hair,
even shorter that it was back in Bangkok, is black, wavy. Tucked
behind her ears, slick like her skin from swimming.

He's breast-stroking against the current rushing around the
rock, playing peek-a-boo with a pair of curious sea otters. Trying to
work out the kinks in his back after sleeping on the floor of her
apartment last night.

"Hey," he says. "I asked you a question."

"Better you don't know, la!" She has a small, plastic bag of tiny
green fish for the otters. Throws two to the pair, closes her eyes
against the glare of the morning sun.

He stops swimming, scrambles up the side of her rock. The
green surfer jams, borrowed from Marcus, dripping water. "Look,
I've pretty much turned my life upside-down to get here. Because
you asked for my help. But now that I'm here, you sandbag me."

"I don't understand this sandbag, la."

"You shut me out. Just like you used to do back on the Cape …
when your secrets almost got us both killed. And now the reptiles
are …"

She takes his hands, draws him toward her.

"We hiked all the way out here through the jungle so that we could finally be alone. Look at me. I'm a girl, Michael. Just a simple girl. No more ... you know? Don't you finally want to kiss me?"

He feels her warm cheek slide against his, smells the coconut on her skin. Thinks, *Christ yes. Right here, right now, in this paradise. I could kiss you until our flesh melts and the oceans sweep us away. But at this very moment there could be a whole nest of serpents like this mysterious Sunny her father mentioned ready to ...*

She presses her lips to his. He tastes hot, smooth plums. Then her tongue finds him. And his mind curls into a tiny ball around his words, his fears.

He feasts.

They feast. Eating, drinking each other with their eyes wide open. His hands locked in hers as she pulls him prone on the rock. His nose to her nose. His arms to her arms. Chest to her chest, hips to her hips, bare thighs to her bare thighs. Knees gently plowing. Her toes, his arches.

He's sure that the otters, the rushing stream, the ocean waves, the wind in the palms, the monkeys in the trees, even the seabirds, the butterflies in flight, must be pausing. Stopping. To witness this kiss. This girl, this intimacy, this affection, so long in the birthing ... growing wings.

• • • • •

The sun is hot on her cheeks when she hears something coming from the jungle. From the trail back to the village at Teluk Bahang. A noise like fish heads tossed into a barrel in the kitchen at the Silver Moon.

"Someone's coming, Michael." She disengages from his arms, sits up. Looks around, wondering if any of this is real. The sun, the sea, the rock, the man. The kiss. Or whether the cops or the *nak-lin* have already found them and this is her death dream.

"Get in the water."

She obeys. Rolls on her belly, feels the moss against her skin as she slides noiselessly down the face of the rock, eases into the stream. Watches him follow. The muscles in the backs of his arms, shoulders, legs, taut chords she wants to knead with her hands, her fingers. Inhale with her lips.

"Come on."

His shoulders, then head, sink under water. She follows, barely swimming. Drifting downstream with the current. The water in the stream so soft, so fresh, so clear. She can see the grass waving on the sandy bottom five feet below. The two otters circling them. Dark little rockets.

And the flinty taste of him soaking into her heart.

It is not until they surface behind a clump of reeds that she remembers her paper bag of fish. She left it behind. On the rock, la. For anyone to see. Mistake #854! She hears people speaking in Thai. Maybe *nak-lin*. They are talking about the bag of fish, the shadows wet bodies have left on the rock.

Michael is still up to his nose in the water, trying to peep through the reeds toward the rock, toward the place where the path meets this little river upstream.

She tries to look too, tries to see if it is Sunny, but Michael squeezes her hand. Holds her back. It's no use, anyway. The reeds are too thick to see through in that direction.

There's a splash. Maybe twenty feet upstream. Another. A third.

Through the curtain of the reeds to her right, she can just make out pods of dead fish drifting downstream. More sailing through the air, landing like bombs. Coming closer to where they're hiding.

"You want to stop with the games, Decastro, and come out of those bushes." A man's voice in English, Thai accent. But not Sunny's coastal drawl. It's more city, more Bangkok.

"We know you're in there." This time a woman's voice, speaking English. But not with a Thai accent, exactly. Something else, Asian though. "Come on. Come out. I promise no one will get hurt, Michael … honey."

His hand, her heart, freeze at the sound of his name, the endearment. She can almost feel him grit his teeth as he squeezes his eyes closed with pain. *Somebody out there knows him. A woman. Calling him* honey.

"I've been such a fool." His voice is an angry whisper. "I should have known."

She wraps her arms around him from behind. His whole body is knotted, trembling.

"Make this easy on us, counselor."

"Is that you, Samset?"

The detective?

"Just be glad I found you first."

"Go away, Samset," says Michael. "This is not your country."

"We want to talk to Tuki. She has something ..."

She thinks about the ruby she hid beneath her father's pillow for safekeeping earlier this morning as he slept. Know's he'll keep it safe for her—just like always—when he wakes up.

He squirms in her arms. Tries to push her away. "Go. Swim. Get out of here!"

"Not without you."

She takes a deep breath and dives for the bottom ... scissor kicking into the current. Her fingers hooked beneath his watchband. Coaxing him. Pulling him. Her knight in shining armor ... While her mind curses in Vietnamese. The bastard cop Samset on shore. And the woman. The one who sounds like she's Samset's sidekick. Another police. The bitch behind that strange accent, who has just been speaking to Michael like a sweetheart. *Who the hell is she, la?*

14

"MAYBE we should just stop all this running, and give the Thais their ruby back." This is something he has wanted to say since that night in Bangkok at the club in the Novotel. Now he just flat-out lets it fly. Her Buddhist idea about making the original thief Kittikachorn return the gem seems null and void now that the man is dead. Why are they risking their lives to hang on to the Heart of Warriors? What's he missing here?

He aches from the swim down the stream, then in the ocean, all the way around a steep rocky point … He's a little out of breath from the twenty-minute jog in bare feet along a jungle path. The frantic effort to wake up Tuki's dad back at the apartment in Teluk Bahang, grab the ruby, some clothes. Wigs.

Now he's collapsing in the back of a beat-up, red Mercedes sedan. Dust swirling in the open windows. Tuki's beside him, her skin and hair dry, but that little silver *tanga* of hers is still damp, warm against his thighs. Both of them are trying to keep their heads down, out of sight … as Marcus rockets the car over a dirt track through the jungles, the hills of central Penang.

"Really. Why don't we just give back the stone?"

"You mean turn it over to the cops?" Marcus' voice sounds heavy. He's not wide awake. Still the gruff, mercurial fellow who slunk off to bed last night with no more than a few words for Michael.

"Yeah, Varat Samset."

"It's not that simple, Michael."

"Why not?"

"Tuki!" Marcus Aparecio's voice is a warning. *Let be!*

She shoots her father a sideways look. "Complicated, la."

"Come on, Tuki. You asked me to come here to help you. I'm here. What the hell's going on?"

"I think this is one of those times. You know, man …? Like no good deed goes unpunished." Marcus lets out a strained sigh.

Michael looks at Tuki. "You don't really believe that?"

Another funny glance between Tuki and her *bpaa*.

"*Nak-lin* never forget."

"Are we talking about someone named Sunny?"

She looks away.

"Does he wear a green jacket? Does this have something to do with the murder?"

"I don't know."

"Who is he?"

"*Ya fun foi ha takhep.*"

"What?"

"Don't turn over the rubbish to look for the centipede."

"Can you be straight with me?"

Marcus looks over his shoulder at his daughter. "I guess you better tell him."

• • • • •

December. About six years ago. Twelve months after Prem dumped her, caved in to family pressure to marry the daughter of a silk merchant.

Ten months after she torched the Kittikachorn's first River House for revenge. Like burn, baby, burn. Just take it all away, la. Take the hammock where she first made love, the bath where Prem used to wash her, worship her. Take the cowardly lion who stole her heart. Please! Please take the pung chao *that has eaten away his will, her soul …*

Nine months since she fled Bangkok's police. Nine months since she fled Thaksin Kittikachorn's vengeance. The man no doubt guesses she's the one who burned the River House, she's the one who has the ruby his son stole from him.

Nine months since Brandy and Delta raided their savings account to buy her a ticket to escape to NYC on China Airlines. Nine months since she arrived for safekeeping at an upscale Vietnamese bistro north of Canal Street run by an old friend of her mother's from the war, the amazing René Parish. Nine months since he gave her this hostess job at the Saigon Princess.

Nine months and she has almost stopped looking over her shoulder for Thai police or Thaksin Kittikachorn's muscle boys.

Parish is a former Saigon bar keeper from the war years. African-American, sixty to sixty-five. A large, portly James Earl Jones type. A teddy bear. Tonight he's closing out the register, counting the receipts at a table in the rear of the restaurant. She's resetting all the tables out front, when someone knocks on the locked glass door of the Princess.

There's a man outside. He's Asian. Thai … or Vietnamese. With his elegant brown bomber, half-dozen gold chains around his neck, five hundred dollar shoes. She's guessing he's in his late twenties, early thirties. Prem's age. But much fitter, with broad shoulders, a thick neck. And he's shorter. Shorter than her. With a baby face. Smooth, full cheeks. Black, little eyes. Razor-cut hair oiled, neatly combed across his head. Almost like some of the boys who went to Christian missionary school with her in Bangkok. Except for the unconscious smirk on his lips.

Parish hears the knock, looks up from the table where he's counting the cash, sets it down. She sees his right hand reach for the Walther he keeps on his lap when he's counting money.

"He wants us to open the door," she says.

"Tell him we're closed."

Her hands wave back and forth across her chest, like go away, la. Restaurant closed, ok?

The boy-man outside, his breath puffing in the frosty air, pulls one hand out of his jacket pocket, flutters his fingers beckoning her closer. Grins at her. That smirk still on his lips. Leans to within inches of the glass door.

"Tell you boss, Robsulee have message for him. Very important. You open now." His voice comes through the heavy plate glass of the door, muted but sharp.

Robsulee. The name stings her. Something coming out of a dream, something whispered on a hot night in the River House when she was making love to Prem. Something forgotten, buried. Just the shadow of a ghost. It must be just a coincidence. It must be that Robsulee is a common American name.

But something is definitely wrong, la. Right here, right now. The voice, the smirk, the schoolboy look of the man on the other side of the glass. She wonders if this is how what Americans call a stick-up *goes down; if the next thing she knows, this guy will be coming through the door, guns blazing.*

Now he's pounding on the door with both fists.

"René! He says he has a very important message for you."

"What? From who? Jesus!"

More pounding. The boy-man is smiling.

"Robsulee … somebody."

"Robsulee?"

"That person."

"For Lord's sake."

She hears Parish push back out of his chair, walk toward the door. When she looks back at him, she sees he's got the Walther in one hand pointed at the figure outside the door. A baseball bat in the other. He looks like some kind of terminator, except for the slight twitching at the corner of his right eye.

"Open the door."

The boy-man puts his hands over his head. He's still smiling as she swings open the door, seems undaunted by Parish's massive body, the weaponry he's wielding.

"Ok, homey, get your ass in here. And listen up. You try to mess with her or me, I'm going to shoot you in the head and pound it into duck sauce!"

"If I meant fuck with you, you already dead, nigger!"

A silent concussion ripping through her belly.

"I really didn't hear you say the N-word, tell me I was just imagining ..."

The boy-man is smiling. "You lucky, motherfuck. I no like niggerboys. You know that? But Robsulee say no hurt you. What she say rule."

Parish growls. "Get the goddamn hell out of here, you little ..."

The boy-man starts backing up toward the door. "Ok, monkey face. I go. I tell Robsulee you no care pay her what you owe. That good?"

"She knows I always pay. Right on time."

"She say you pay more now."

"Let her tell me that herself. Not send some boy with the message. Who the hell are you, anyway?"

His smile blooms. "You can call me Sunny. I'm the one you talk now. Forget Robsulee. I'm the one collect Robsulee's debts for her. I'm the one tell you, you cute little princess got big price on head. Very rich man Thailand want Tuki Aparecio, former queen Patpong Road. Want her bad."

Another explosion in her stomach.

"What?"

"Now you pay me ten thousand dollars month keep princess secret. You know, safe here in cozy, little restaurant. Or ... somebody cut her balls off. Stuff them down you throat. How you like that?"

15

THE FORTY-FOOT wooden sampan rolls in the waves. *What a poor excuse for a boat ... what a half-assed escape plan*, he thinks as he pulls a mildewed blanket over his head and tries to sleep on a mound of nets, spooned against Tuki's back.

They've been at sea all night, chugging south along the west coast of peninsular Malaysia. Marcus Aparecio dry heaving over the side every quarter of an hour.

Tuki's *bpaa* seems flush with cash. He has paid two hundred dollars to a fisherman from a *kampong* on the south end of Penang to ferry them down the coast to a village where they can catch a local bus for some city he's never heard of. Marcus says the idea is to lose the Thai cops, and everybody else, once and for all. He has Vietnamese friends who run a little hotel in the city. They can crash there until they plot their next move. Until they figure out how to get the ruby back to Ayutthaya, figure out how to appease or neutralize the *nak-lin*.

Neutralize?

The whole scenario sounds like a recipe for catastrophe to Michael. This run-and-hide business is not his style. Not legal. Not even smart. So how the hell's a guy supposed to get any sleep with a thousand questions about tomorrow buzzing through his head? While his arms are wrapped around this golden angel. His dick hard from the touch of her hip, from adrenalin, fear.

"You want to tell me what your father means by *neutralize*, Tuki?"

She stirs, rolls to face him. Her eyelids closed, lips smiling faintly.

"Kiss me."

"I think I'm going to jump out of my skin here."

"You don't want to kiss me?"

"I'm going crazy."

Her hand is under his polo shirt, gliding across one of his pecs. "Please!"

"What?"

"You know you're lovely as hell."

"Yes ... So kiss me, Michael."

Fingers sliding below his belt.

"Tuki."

He looks around. The fisherman is just a shadow in the wheelhouse. Aparecio is a lump of clothes curled on a docking line back aft. Finally empty, finally asleep.

"You want to ... you know?"

"Jesus."

"What?"

He grabs her hand. "Stop. Ok. Just stop. Plaeeeeeeeeeeeeeese!"

She gives a low growl. Part frustration, part challenge. Presses her forehead to his and looks him in the eyes.

"You still afraid of me?"

He sucks in his breath, counts to ten. "Maybe."

"Oh, la!" She presses her cheek to his chest. "Oh ... la."

"It's not what you think."

"Then what?"

"You never answer my questions. And—"

"Will you kiss me?"

"First answer my question."

"About what?"

"What does your father mean by neutralize the *nak-lin?*"

"That?"

"Yeah, that."

"He means ... kill Sunny Janluechai."

"That's what I was afraid of."

"Now kiss me, la."

"Before we all go down in flames at sunrise?"

"You want to die a virgin?"

• • • • •

They haven't been ashore in the little fishing village for more than forty-five minutes when he feels the urge to strangle Marcus Aparecio. But he really doesn't want to pick a fight.

"I see that hairy eyeball you're giving me. We going to have a problem, boy?"

He looks at the tall black man standing in the shade of a palm grove by a narrow beach. The khaki shorts, the orange Hawaiian shirt, NASCAR driving shades. One arm leaning on his cane. Skin glowing again, sparkle back in his eyes. Thick beard, kempt and washed. A miraculous recovery from seasickness thanks to three glasses of rambutan and soy milk whipped in a blender, a bowl of coconut rice mixed with anchovies that the street vendor called *nasi lemak.*

"I'm not a boy."

"Shit. I'm pushing sixty-four. So you're a boy to me."

He feels tiny beads of sweat sprouting all over his back, wishes Tuki were here to intervene, not bathing and changing her clothes beneath one of the fish boat piers.

"Then I have to ask you. Why do you think I'm here?"

"You're in love with her ..."

He doesn't know what to say. The word love has never been spoken between him and Tuki. Never even been spoken to his secret self.

"… and she's in love with you. Why do you think she went through three months of hell with her surgery in Hanoi? You think she really cared about some extra flesh between her legs?"

"I really doubt—"

"Listen to me, Michael. She did it for you. She wants to be the girl you always dreamed of."

"She sent me an email asking for my help."

"I told her not to do that. But she didn't listen."

"Too bad. Maybe if she had listened, it would have saved us all quite a bit of trouble."

"You want to go? Go. Just do it now, before you hurt that girl worse than she already is."

"Somebody could kill her."

"I have everything under control."

"Is that why someone almost cut off her head with a throwing star?"

"How were we supposed to know the *nak-lin* were on her trail?"

"I got the impression that you are something of an expert on this Sunny Janluechai character."

Her father says that for the better part of the last year he and Tuki had a good thing going at the Silver Moon. It seemed like the perfect place for Tuki to recover from her operation. The perfect place to hide from Sunny Janluchai, the *nak-lin*, Thaksin Kittikachorn, Thai police who were after her for burning the River House seven years ago. He and Tuki both loved being back in Southeast Asia. Loved Penang. Until she decided that she had to go back to Thailand. She couldn't be stopped. She kept saying her life would be cursed, Prem's soul cursed, until she got the ruby back to Kittikachorn and made him return it to the place it was stolen.

There's something in the black man's eyes now. Not actually a tear, but some kind of pain. The thing Michael has seen in his father Caesar's eyes when someone mentions his dead mother.

• • • • •

About eighteen months ago. Yellow leaves falling around them. Maria. His mom. She's holding his hand, hugging him to her chest. She's just told him that she has ovarian cancer, that she only has a few of months to live.

"Why ...? I mean, I don't understand how this kind of thing ..." *His voice breaks.*

"Remember when you were a teenager? How I used to tell you to go gently, go slowly with your girlfriends? To stand in awe?"

"You said be patient, a woman's body holds a thousand mysteries."

"Well, this is one of them, meu meninho."

He wants to hold on to her forever. Never leave this place. Just hug his mother, hug this mystery. Shelter her from the dark, winged creature diving down for her, talons spread, sharp. Sing to her a lullaby. Sing to her the songs she raised him on, her favorite songs from Bob Marley. "No Woman, No Cry." *Never, Mamãe. Te prometo. Seguro. Te amo. Te amo. Sempre, Mamãe. No crying.*

• • • • •

"Look, Marcus. We barely know each other. I don't want a beef with you. It's just that you seem hell-bent on us running. That crazy car ride through the hills yesterday, the midnight boat to wherever the hell we are. And now you want to get on a bus for—what's that place again?"

"KL."

"KL?"

"Kuala Lampur. It's the capital of Malaysia, you know?"

"No. I don't know. That's my point. I'm way out of my league here. It's like I've accidentally signed on to an epic journey to Neverland or something. I feel like I'm going to implode unless we slow down and get a grip on things."

"What do you suggest we do then?"

"I don't know." He looks out at the white sand beach, the pale blue lagoon. Pictures schools of tiny painted fish drifting with the current on the reef just offshore. "Maybe we could stop running for a while. This fishing village looks like a pretty good place to hide, catch our breath. Rest."

"Trust me, nobody's more tired of all this than me."

"Then let's stay here for a while. I've got plenty of money, you seem to have plenty of money, and—"

"You don't understand, Michael."

It's Tuki. She's come back from the shadows under the pier, dressed like someone he has never seen before. Like the many Muslim women in the village. She's wearing a green *abaya*, a plain white *hiyab* shrouding her head.

"Why?"

"The fisherman who brought us here is a poor man," she says. "He owed us nothing but a ride. When he gets back to Penang he will sell what he knows about our travels to the highest bidder. Maybe the police, maybe *nak-lin*. Maybe both."

"I think the bus to KL stops up the street by that little mosque." Her father lifts his suitcase, straightens up on his cane. "Are you with us, Michael?"

He looks at Tuki, her golden cheeks. Hidden beneath those swaddling clothes, she could almost be his mother. A picture he found of her in her youth, dressed for some long-ago Portagee *festa* back in Nu Bej.

He reaches out, takes her right hand.

Then he turns to her father, who has set down his suitcase again on the dusty road. The man has opened it, taken out a garment. Is now slipping a long gray robe, a *dishadasha*, over his head. Capping his shaved crown with an embroidered *kufi*.

"Peace, ok, Marcus?" His voice sounds dry, shakey. "But just for the hell of it, somebody want to tell me what the penalty is for possessing a stolen antiquity in Malaysia?"

Aparecio hands him a *dishadasha* and a *kufi* to put on.

"You know, I really liked having my daughter to myself, Michael."

16

ALMOST *ten at night at the Delta baggage claim. Ft. Lauderdale/ Hollywood International Airport. The carousel starting to clatter, the chute spitting out bags.*

She's scanning the crowd for a man. For the bpaa *she has never known.*

And then, suddenly, there he is. Popping up right in front of her. Just like Brandy and Delta said, a long, tall drink of water, la. Looking like Lou Gossett, Jr. in An Officer and a Gentleman. *Actually wearing his Marine Corps dress blues, as he promised—so you can't miss me, sugar. Perhaps looking almost like the young man her mother Misty, Huong-Mei, saw the night he walked into the bar where she was dancing off Dong Khoi in central Saigon.*

Almost that young warrior still ... except for the full beard.

Her hand, a mind of its own, reaches out. Reaches up, touches that beard. The cheek. Fingers brush over his lips.

"Oh, la! Is it you? After all this time? You? My father? My bpaa? *Really? You?"*

"You're a sight for sore eyes!" He sweeps her into a hug.

The tears are running down their cheeks. People looking, smiling to themselves. The slender young Asian woman in the black suit, the handsome

American vet. This image of reunion, reconciliation. Almost the perfect couple.

So she does not shatter the moment.

Does not say this is what my lawyer never knew. I was there on Nantucket when the nak-lin shot my ex-boyfriend Prem. Does not say she jumped naked from the second-floor deck of his bedroom before they could shoot her too ... Does not say she stole a tank top, shorts, flip flops, driver's license from a sleeper's bedroom at another house on Madaket Beach ... Or that she hid in the back of a Roto-Rooter truck when it took the ferry off-island back to Hyannis.

She cannot tell him yet that she left her sweet-but-hopeless lawyer to pick up the pieces of the murder case against her ... that she has a stolen ruby worth more than eleven million tucked up her ass in a condom. That Sunny Janluechai will probably rape and pillage cities to find it.

No.

Now is not the time to do anything but hug this man who has been following the story of her arrest for murder online, who has called her out of the blue while she was in the hospital recovering from her close call with the real killer of Big Al Costlano. Who has begged her to meet him in Florida.

Not the time to say she shoplifted this suit from the Hyannis Mall, that she gave some high school boy with an SUV a blow job to drive her to the airport in Providence. Not the time, la, to admit she would have thrown herself into Nantucket Sound, ended the whole nightmare, if her bpaa hadn't called her. If he hadn't bought her this ticket to Florida online, even as she waited at the airport in Providence. If he hadn't been a dad, right from the get-go ... and given her a reason to live.

Not the time to ask why he hadn't made himself known to her before this.

Not the time for anything but embracing ... At least for a while.

"You want to get out of here?" He releases her from his hug, looks in her eyes.

"Out of America. Far away as possible, la."

"Hey, sugar, you in trouble?"

"Just a little."

"What do say we fly now, talk later?"

"Where we going?"

"How about Vietnam?"

"All I have is a borrowed driver's license."

He hands her an envelope. Inside is a brand new U.S. passport.

"How did you get the picture?"

"You're quite the star on the internet."

"Is this passport real?"

"We better hurry."

· · · · ·

"You want to tell me how you ended up in Florida, la?" She tugs on his shirt sleeve.

It's one in the morning, They are just two hours into the fourteen-hour leg of the Cathay Pacific flight from L.A. to Hong Kong, final destination Ho Chi Minh City. She's already so nervous she's been to the toilet five times.

Her father keeps the palm of his hand over his eyes. "Can we just be glad we found each other again?"

"I have so many questions."

"Some things, I've found, are better left unsaid, sugar."

"You think we'll find her?"

"What ... who?"

"My mother. Misty. Huong-Mei?"

He rolls his shoulders. Pushes the blanket off his chest. Seems anxious. "So long ago ... I kind of doubt ..."

"But you promised me we'd look, la."

"Yes, but ... what are the chances really that we—"

"Are you afraid?"

"To see her? Why?"

"Because you left her."

"You think it was my choice? There was a war. Nineteen seventy-two. Things were crazy."

"Misty was pregnant with me."

"Listen, Tuki. Vietnam was madness. The U.S. couldn't pull troops out of the country fast enough. The NVA was kicking our ass at An Loc. Jane Fonda on Radio Hanoi, for Lord's sake, talking about an immoral war. The Watergate Scandal back home."

"Did you love her?"

"Love wasn't enough. Everything was coming apart in Saigon. People spitting on soldiers. Bombs going off in the GI zone. New rumors every day that the government was going to collapse, that legions of South Vietnamese troops were throwing down their guns and going home ... or crossing over to the Viet Cong."

"But didn't you love her?"

He rubs his eyes with his fingers, strokes his beard.

"Hell! Yeah, who wouldn't?" he says finally. "She looked just like you, sugar. A beauty. One in a million. Tall, thin. But with the curves of a '68 Corvette Stingray. That long, black hair right down to her waist."

"You remember Brandy and Delta?"

"Like it was yesterday."

"They use to tell me, 'When you mama dance that Gladys Knight Midnight Train to Georgia, everybody in Saigon thinking they must go get good lala quicky quicky.' She was some sexy girl, la?"

He closes his eyes, maybe hearing music, watching a film play back inside his head.

"Oh yeah."

"I picture her. All the time since I was a little girl. Dancing in the shadows at the far end of some soldier's bar to ease her heart, to feed the baby growing inside her belly."

"My bar."

"What?"

"That's how we met. She started dancing in my bar. The Black Cat."

"But you were a marine."

"Not when I met her. I was a marine in Nam, 1965-66. After I mustered out of the Corps, I went back to Saigon and opened the Black Cat."

"Brandy and Delta never told me."

"They wouldn't."

"I don't understand, la."

"The Black Cat was not a nice place."

"You ran a whorehouse?"

"I was young and wild."

"Misty was a whore? My mother?" Her voice loud, shrill. Passengers in nearby rows pop their heads up, shoot dirty looks.

"*She was just a kid from up the river. Eighteen years old. Needed a job. My manager hired her when I was away in Sidney on vacation.*"

She stands up, pushes into the aisle. "*I want off this plane, la! Tuki is all done with pimps and whores! This is the biggest mistake of my life!*"

He reaches out and tries to take her hand. She shakes it off.

"*I fell in love with her the moment I saw her. It was a mad love. Crazy insane. I swear I never …*"

"*Then why did you leave us?*"

"*She made me go.*"

"*What? Why?*"

"*Somebody wanted to kill me.*"

She sits back down. "*Because you were American?*"

"*And other things.*"

She waits for him to explain, but he shakes his head. Not going down that road.

"*I cried the whole way home on the plane to San Francisco.*"

"*And then you never looked back.*"

He reaches over, wipes the tears from her cheeks with his fingers. "*It wasn't like that. Really.*"

17

"SHIT!" Marcus Aparecio is scowling.

It's nine in the morning. He's standing in bare feet in a pale blue *dishadasha* at the foot of the stairs. Baking in the sunshine that's blasting the alcove entrance to the Vinh Long Guest House in KL's Chinatown. Squinting at a dozen pairs of shoes left here on the stoop by guests like himself, according to the custom of the country, before they retired last night to their rooms.

"What?" Michael shakes one of his own shoes, a white Nike, before he puts it on, to make sure no nasty little creatures crawled in overnight.

His brain is barely buzzing. Spending ten steamy hours alone in a tiny little cubicle, with nothing but a mattress on the floor and a pole fan hardly made for sound sleeping. Especially when the laughter of the hookers and the groans of their Johns from rooms down the hall kept him up half the night. Especially when he kept wondering what he would do if Tuki came knocking on his door. Her dad in the adjacent cubicle.

Four nights in a row of this torture is way too much.

"Where the hell are my shoes?" Her dad.

"What do you mean?"

"They're gone."

"So are mine," says Tuki, coming down the stairs and searching the shoe collection. Someone lifted our shoes."

"You sure?"

"I think I know my own shoes, Michael."

Marcus Aparecio kicks the line of sandals and sneakers. "God-damn it!" A shiny, black scorpion scampers out of one.

"You're kidding, right, Tuki?"

"I really liked those shoes, la." She's doing her Muslim maiden look again—*abaya, hijab.*

"Wow. They actually took the bait, sugar."

"I don't understand." Michael watches the scorpion scuttle onto the sidewalk, street, down a storm drain. *Crazy.*

"Yesterday when Marcus and I were in the park, we felt like someone was following us, watching."

"Why didn't you tell me?"

"Maybe it was nothing."

"We decided to set a trap." A smug note has settled into Apare-cio's voice.

"A trap?"

"I sat down on a bench, took the ruby out of my bra. Wrapped it in some tissue and stuffed it into the toe of my shoe. Then I put my shoe back on."

Michael almost wants to laugh. He's heard of silliness before, but this … "You actually imagined such a trap would work? You thought the *nak-lin* would believe for a second you would leave that stone in the shoe overnight?"

She shrugs like *Guess what, the shoes are history.* "Desperate peo-ple believe what they need to. If you wanted that ruby, la … if you saw me put it in my shoe, would you not check my shoe the first chance you got? Even if it seemed like an impossibly stupid place to hide a gem?"

"So … someone was definitely watching," says her father.

"Varat Samset would not be stealing shoes."

"No. I fear not."

"Is this the work of your pal Sunny?"

"At least now we know what we're up against." Aparecio clears his throat.

"The *nak-lin*."

"In all their glory."

"So … the ruby was actually still in your shoe?" Michael's squinting as if this will help him focus his brain, get his head around this latest manifestation of the insane world he's fallen into.

She purses her lips for a second. "Sort of."

"I'm lost."

"It was a fake."

"Another one?"

"Yes, la."

"How many fakes do you have?"

"One more," she says. "I didn't think they'd actually take my shoes, too."

"Or mine, goddamn it! But this buys us a little time. They'll drop their guard, until they realize the stone is bogus." Marcus leans against the wall with his eyes closed.

"So now what?" Michael feels a headache coming on.

"You ever been to Singapore?"

He rubs the sleep out of his left eye. "Can I ask where the real ruby is? What Tuki did with it?"

"Women, whoever knows?"

"Yeah."

"They get their hooks into you until you can't see straight. Mess with you day and night. And after they're gone, it's like some kind of wildfire burned you up."

"Yeah."

"You haven't the smokiest notion what they were all about. But you can't forget them. Know what I mean?"

• • • • •

A Harvard Square café. Midwinter. Someone calls his name. He looks up from his coffee, sees a woman. Stiffens. Long black hair in braids trailing over the shoulders of her deerskin coat.

Her name is Awasha. She's a Wampanoag Indian. Daughter of his former landlady on the Cape, Alice of Chatham. The direct descendant of Awashonks, a woman warrior almost three hundred years ago in King Philip's war. And she needs a lawyer, needs a legal advocate.

She's the one. His last client. The one who gets her hooks into him. When he's a mess after the Provincetown Follies case goes to hell. A year after Tuki left him professionally and emotionally shipwrecked.

18

THEY'VE MOVED UPTOWN, from the scorpion nest owned by her father's old friends from Saigon, to a hotel that looks like something he remembers from a vacation on Nassau's Paradise Island ... but Michael's not smiling. He looks out from the window on the ninth floor and bares his teeth at the Petronas Twin Towers, rising like immense salt shakers beyond the tinted glass.

"We've spent all day hiding in this pricy hotel room, running up credit card debt, wringing our hands. And we don't have a plan." Michael's voice has a jagged edge.

Marcus Aparecio takes a long swallow from his fifth bottle of Tiger beer fresh from the mini-bar.

"Don't worry about my credit card. I got that covered."

"What about a plan? We can't go on like this, running from place to place. Living minute to minute."

"Tomorrow morning you two take the train. I will come later on a plane. Go to the Raffles Hotel, Beach Road in Singapore. I'll meet you there."

Tuki is curled up, completely buried under the comforter on the king bed. "The *nak-lin* will be expecting us to dress like Muslims. We have to change our drag, la."

"It's a bad idea to go shopping together." Michael is still looking out the window, watching the setting sun turn the twin towers golden.

"Right, man. You want to do the honors?"

He turns, sees her father flipping through the channels on the TV until he finds one showing *Stars Wars* in Bahasa.

This pecker is trying to get me killed, he thinks. But what he says is, "I'm going to need some help. Tuki?"

Her body stretches out beneath the comforter. Arms and legs spreading. A giant butterfly. He wonders if she can hear the coded message in his voice. *I'm scared. I don't know how much more of your father, or this random flight, I can take. Give me some kind of sign. Tell me where we're headed. What's your endgame, Tuki?*

No one speaks for at least a minute.

Then the comforter explodes off the bed and Tuki's standing close enough to touch. An orchid of a woman in nothing but her Victoria's Secret.

"Meet me in Chinatown on Jalan Petaling an hour after dark. By the guy we saw yesterday telling fortunes from the *I Ching* and making potions from the entrails of a monitor lizard."

· · · · ·

She feels Michael before she sees him. Feels his awkwardness and caution. A dark energy pushing through the throng of shoppers in the night market, a momentary hush, a gust of wind as the locals take him in. As they watch this handsome, scowling Westerner sneak up on her.

It's hard to concentrate on what the old Chinese fortune teller is saying. He's squatting next to the dried carcass of a large monitor lizard. Crushing a piece of the mummified heart to powder in a bowl with a pestle in one hand, holding her one hundred ringgit note in the other. He's muttering about wind and thunder. The fingers of her right hand play idly with two live juvenile monitors in a wicker cage, their forked tongues flicking in and out of her palm as if they've discovered something sweet, raw.

"Hi." Michael puts his hand on her shoulder. The touch damp, metallic.

She turns, rises to face him. "What's the matter, la?"

"I just really needed to see you. Alone."

She smiles, thinks of what the fortune teller has just told her about danger. And what he told her yesterday about love. "You want to sweep me off my feet, la?"

"Your father hit a nerve in me today."

"He's doing his best."

"I don't think he likes me."

"He doesn't think you like him."

"Well maybe he …"

She takes his hands, leans toward him until she can smell the fresh sweat of his skin.

"You jealous, la?"

"It's a possibility."

"Just a possibility?"

"I don't know."

She drops his hands, steps away. Looks back toward the fortune teller with his lizards. His hand holds out a small, red porcelain cup. "You drink now."

The liquid tastes like stale tea.

A smile spreads across her face as she looks at the two juvenile monitors nipping at each other in their cage. Then she scans the crowd on Jalan Petaling. It's closed to traffic for the market. Neon signs glowing. Chinese lanterns twinkling on strings above the street vendors' red-and-green umbrellas. Shrimp and pork stir-fry sizzling.

"Listen."

The Eagles "Hotel California" is playing from a nearby boom box on a card table where a teenage Indian kid is selling CDs and DVDs.

"What?"

"I can take you there, la."

"Where?"

"Hotel California. You know, the other side of a dream?"

"Aren't we going to buy some clothes in the market?"

She sees the way his forehead wrinkles. "You look like some kind of sick cat."

"Gee, thanks."

"You do, la."

"I just don't understand any of this."

"Kuala Lumpur?"

"Everything. The people, the languages, the cultures. Fortune tellers. These caged dragons. Your father. The *nak-lin*."

"Me?"

"A woman's body holds a thousand mysteries."

She sighs.

"I'm sorry."

She wants to feel his hand again. Maybe if she holds it long enough she can melt the hardness under his skin.

"We should go back to Thailand. Maybe I could get Samset to drop the charges against you if we tell him you have the stolen ruby and we offer to give it back. Then we could go to the States and—"

"I used to think this was just about the ruby," she says. "I was so wrong."

"What do you mean?"

"Walk with me. Let me hold your arm." *Before the* nak-lin *find us. While we have time to be a woman and a man. Before some funny-talking woman police jumps out of the dark and starts calling you "honey" or something.*

He twitches as she snakes her arm through his.

"*Nam Khun hai rip tak*, Michael."

"What?"

"Let's make hay while the moon shines, la."

He looks at her. She sees something starting to soften in his eyes, knows maybe she looks beautiful tonight. She has to. The fortune teller told her yesterday, and again tonight. She has to put her fears aside, stop thinking about Sunny, the *nak-lin*, Samset and his female sidekick. Tonight is do or die for this new love she has been hiding in the back of her heart for almost two years.

So now she's betting on a thin, black, linen dress that clings to her curves. The see-through red shawl falling back off her shoulders. The open plain of golden skin, rising above the not-so-subtle cleavage. The diamond studs in her ears. Her short hair swept across her forehead like Audrey Hepburn in *Breakfast at Tiffany's*. Do or die.

She leads him through the crowd.

"Why do you think this is not just about the ruby?"

"I promise I'll tell you later."

She turns a corner with him, leads him down a twisted alley.

"Where are we going?"

Her feet stop walking, her body leans back against a stack of fruit crates in the shadows behind a restaurant. She smells mangosteen, rambutan, hot peppers, coconut milk as she pulls him into her, her arms curling under his, fingers spreading in the curls on his neck. Closing her eyes, lips pressing. Opening to his.

Until his tongue finds hers. His hands trace the outer edges of her breasts and the sparks start shooting in her chest.

"This is crazy! We have to shop."

"Do you love me, Michael?"

His lips glide down her throat. "To the moon and back."

Every tiny hair on her body lights up.

Her hands, wild animals now, undo the belt on his jeans.

She feels the muscles in his belly, thighs. Knotted, quivering. His skin smoldering to her touch.

"Jesus."

Do or die, la.

"Cristo."

"Close your eyes," she says as she slips down on her knees.

"Tuki!"

"Welcome to the Hotel California."

19

HE CAN'T get that Eagles song out of his head. Or the memory of last night in the shadows. The scents of hot peppers, the fruit, coconut milk. They have been swirling around in his brain since before he got on the morning express train to Singapore with her. The two of them dressed like a sikh couple ... complete with appropriate Malaysian passports courtesy of Marcus Aparecio's Vietnamese friends back at the Vin Long Hotel.

Even after seven hours on the train she looks fabulous, glowing, in her last-minute night-market purchases. A maroon *sari*, scarf, costume jewels. Vermillion *tilak* spotting her forehead. His scalp is itching from the turban, but he kind of likes how cool his torso feels in this night-shirt-sort-of-thing she bought for him. He is starting to get used to the beard that is coming in fast since he stopped shaving a couple of days ago.

Now as she steps down from the coach in the Singapore station, he takes her hand. Feels the softness of the skin, the sure grip beneath. For the moment she is all his. No prickly father, no *nak-lin*, no whiskey-pushing female cohort of Samset. No Varat Samset either. No dude in a green jacket with a throwing star.

Just Tuki. In a city so shining and clean it makes him think of weddings.

"I love you," he says. Can't believe the words flow so naturally from his mouth.

But it's true. The emotion, the ease.

She leans into him, kisses his neck. "I love you too."

He tells himself she is no longer the drag queen, the transsexual, the hermaphrodite. No longer that freak of God's and her own invention. The siren and the accused killer whose dark eyes mask ten thousand secrets.

After thirty-one years, she has emerged from the neon jungle, a most amazing woman. She made him buy condoms last night on Jalan Petaling. Confirmation once again that she ovulates, must make smart choices about birth control, sex. Especially now that she's stopped using an IUD.

Jesus. Last night was just an appetizer. Tonight ... Cristo, *tonight we'll stop running, hide from the world. Even her* bpaa. *Get a room of our own somewhere in this crystal city and ...*

She squeezes his hand with a sharp urgency.

"What?"

There's a short, round Thai with thick glasses, walking toward them. Flanked by two cops in berets, blue fatigues tucked into their jackboots. Each has Marcus Aparecio by an arm, his hands cuffed in front of him. His eyes blank with shame.

"I told you, counselor. You can run, but you can't hide!"

· · · · ·

He feels the hot sun, southerly breeze on his cheeks. It's late June. Lighthouse Beach, Chatham, on the Cape. About a year ago. The solstice. Summer people—couples, families, teenage au peres *with toddlers replacing the play of seals here on the broad sand apron.*

The girl has been dead more than a month. Lost. Awasha the brave. He's feeling a riptide in his chest. Saudade. *The compulsion to bark until his voice gone. It was her time, Mo. Like for everything there is a season ... Don't give me that shit, Dad!*

He squeezes his eyes shut, pushes back the waves in his head, watches the blood racing through his lids, brilliant little torpedoes.

When he opens his eyes again, she's here. He sees her. Almost close enough for shouting. Down the beach fifty yards, where the tide pools are filling with the silver sea. Her cheeks sparkling with brine. The wind lifting strands of black hair off her back. She stands in the bright sun balancing between land and sea ... her yellow fleece pullover. Jeans. One hand on her waist, her eyes fixed on him, beckoning.

So this is what the old Wampanoags call a tcipai. *A ghost.*

• • • • •

"Put these on and come with me. Hurry!"

He jerks his head off the table. After five hours of almost constant interrogation by two really persistent Singaporean detectives, and Varat Samset, he knows he's just about ready to admit to anything. Including aiding and abetting a murderer ... and international flight from justice.

"Michael!"

His eyes open. He turns to look over his shoulder for the source of the female voice.

In the bright lights of the detention room, Wen-Ling's face is just plain heart-freezing. So white, so hard, with unnaturally red lips. A geisha's mask from some ancient play or nightmare.

She's standing in the open doorway, tossing him a pair of jeans and a T-shirt.

"What?"

"Don't ask stupid questions, Michael. You want to rot to death in Changi Prison, stay here. You want to see your girlfriend again, come. Now!"

His skin feels suddenly frozen. *How the hell did this siren get here? What new torture does she have planned?*

"Don't be an idiot. Let's go!"

He doesn't know why, but he follows orders, lets her lead him out into a hallway.

"If you say anything, I'll kill you." She shows him a paring knife in her hand.

The next thing he knows she's gripping his wrist and jogging down a long, dark stairwell. At the bottom a metal door opens into a parking garage. There's a car stopped in the middle of the exit lane. A gray eighties Beamer with its engine running. A young Chinese man is behind the wheel. Another Chinese guy riding shotgun, a submachine gun cradled in his arms.

Someone opens a back door from inside the car.

"Get in, Michael!"

"Where am I going?"

"Freedom, la." Tuki's voice. Her, the shadow in the back seat. Sitting next to her father. She stretches her hand out to him.

He takes it, ducks to get into the car. Suddenly stops. Turns back to Wen-Ling.

"Why are you doing this?"

"You could call it sentimental reasons."

"Get in the car, Michael."

"This is bad business!" says Marcus. There's an odd note in his voice … dread, perhaps … as if he knows more than he's saying.

"Where's Varat Samset?"

Tuki tugs on his hand.

"This isn't his party," says Wen-Ling. "Now go. Just go."

"So everything you told me on the train wasn't a lie?"

A sad little grin spreads over Wen-Ling's face. She pushes him into the Beamer, slams the door. "Goodbye, Michael."

The car starts to roll, gains speed, darts out the exit onto a busy city street. It's a thick, hazy night. The asphalt glistens with humidity. Singapore's towers sparkle, doing their crystal palace thing.

Tuki leans her head against his shoulder. "I hope I did right, la."

"You gave her the ruby?"

"The last one in my handbag."

"The fake?" he whispers.

"She doesn't know that."

He can't believe she's pawned off yet another bogus gem. The girl is a wonder. "There's going to be hell to pay when Wen-Ling and Samset find out they've been tricked."

"We've got to find a real smart place to hide." Marcus Aparecio sounds totally exhausted, has his forearm over his eyes. "That woman's a cobra. Trust me."

"Where's the real ruby?"

"Maybe we go get it soon."

20

SHE CAN tell by the roadsigns that they are heading toward Changi International Airport when the Beamer veers off the expressway. Not at on an exit ramp, but down a dirt track twisting through brush and high marsh grass.

A crunch of brakes. The car slams to a stop just feet from a chain-link fence. The driver gets out, breaks a lock with a set of bolt cutters, opens a gate.

When they start moving again, she taps the guy riding shotgun on the shoulder. "Where are you taking us?"

"You leave Singapore."

"This doesn't feel good to me," says Michael.

"They took all my money and ID." Her father's voice sounds sluggish.

"Mine too."

Another tap on the shoulder. "Hey, la. We need our passports and money!"

The gunner says nothing. He just keeps glancing at his watch.

The car hits a pothole, bottoms out with a jolt. The Beamer skids. It doesn't feel like they are driving on dirt anymore.

When she looks ahead through the windshield, she sees a put-ting green, a sand trap. They are driving on the fairway of a golf course. Turning into a stand of trees and bushes.

Suddenly the whole car shakes. A whining roar—so loud her ears hurt—crushes them from above. She grabs Michael's hand. Feels its sweat. Closes her eyes and waits for who knows what. Death maybe.

"Jesus Christ!"

Her father wraps her in his arms.

When she opens her eyes she sees through the side window the lights of a jumbo jet climbing out of view. Smells jet exhaust, knows she's nearly under the departure end of the active runway at Changi.

The driver cuts the headlights, rolls to a stop, cuts the engine.

"You get out now!"

"We should run," says her father. "Before the cobra comes back."

Michael squeezes her hand three times before he gets out of the car. Like he's sending her a signal or something. Or maybe it's just his way of telling her goodbye.

"I don't want to die a virgin, la."

· · · · ·

He's thinking he has been a fool to trust Wen-Ling—especially now that she thinks she has the ruby—when their hike ends on the shore of a small cove.

"Boat now." The gunner waves his weapon at a wooden lugger, painted orange and blue, its bow pushed up on the shore of a little cove. A narrow plank stuck over the side for boarding. The engine making a thumping bass sound.

"You go!"

There's no moon, no stars. Just the light of one small LED flash-light in the hands of the driver. But he can see that this boat is much bigger than the boat they took from Penang. This is as big as the old Portagee fishing boats, the Eastern-rig draggers that tie up at the wharves in Provincetown. As big as his father's first *Rosa Lee*. As big as the family-run freighters he saw carrying rice and cattle to Bangkok on the river. But he can see no family here, no crew.

"Shrimp trawler," he says as he scuttles up the plank after Tuki and looks around at the nets. Even in this light he can tell that the fishing gear is shit, rotten. The boat doesn't smell like it has fished in ages. Not a good sign. This is a smuggler, sure as hell. Its crew probably about as far as you can get from honest fishermen.

"We need our passports, credit cards, money!" Her father is standing on the shore, up in the face of the gunner as if he will not board unless he gets what he wants.

The car's driver appears out of the dark with a blue gym bag. "All in here. Now you go! Police be here any minute!"

Marcus Aparecio grabs the flashlight from the driver, opens the bag and rummages. He seems to be searching through his wallet when she hears the boat's diesel rev.

"Come on, Marcus." Tuki's voice.

"Fuckers stool three thousand dollars."

The engine revs again.

"Marcus!"

"You go now, black boy!" The gunner pokes Aparecio in the ribs with his weapon. Shouts something harsh in Chinese.

The boat starts backing off the mud. The gangplank falling away over the side just as Aparecio and the gunner scramble aboard.

Another jumbo roars overhead.

As soon as the boat is steaming into open water, Michael wraps Tuki in a hug, needs to feel her warmth. Whispers in her ear, "Can you distract the guy with the gun for a minute?"

She gives him a brief kiss on the lips, then pushes him away. Turns to the gunner.

"Hey, where's a girl pee around here, la?"

• • • • •

Now it's the men's turn to piss. They're standing side-by-side at the stern rail.

"We're fish in a barrel. You know that, Michael? That woman back at the prison. She's capable of—"

"Quiet." The gunner at their backs.

"Dude doesn't really sound like he's here on a mission of mercy, does he? I figure this jamoke's going to try to pop us soon as the next airplane flies over to muffle the shots."

"I count three of them aboard. Trigger boy. And captain and a deckhand in the wheelhouse."

"Quiet!"

"Can you run a boat like this?"

"Raised on one."

"Quiet." Gun in the back. "No more talk!"

"Hey, man, chill out! I'm trying to take a piss."

"You finish piss now."

"Ok, bro," says Michael. "Just let me zip my pants."

When he pulls his hand out of his fly, it's holding the cargo hook he snatched from atop the capstan when Tuki made her pee call. He nudges Aparecio with his elbow to show him.

Suddenly the older man spins around, hands on his throat. "Help!"

For an instant, the gunner looks confused … then raises the butt of his weapon. He's stepping forward to thrash Tuki's father when Michael strikes.

There's a sucking sound and a crunch as he feels the wooden handle of the cargo hook shudder. The steel point catches the gunner right under the ridge of his lower jaw, puncturing the skin. Coming up hard against the molars.

It was her time, Mo. Like for everything there is a season … Don't give me that shit, Dad.

The gun drops to the deck.

Then, just like he's landing a skilly, a white marlin, Michael puts the full force of his shoulders into swinging the body flat on its side over the rail. But this fish isn't coming aboard—he's going the other way. Tumbling into the foaming wake without so much as a whimper.

When he pops to the surface, they can see him wrestling with the hook in his jaw before he disappears into the darkness. The runway lights of Changi just now appearing about a half mile off to port.

Aparecio picks up the submachine gun. "I think it's time for the other two jazzbos in the wheelhouse to take a swim too."

Michael's suddenly feeling weak and out of breath. He settles on the deck.

"I never felt like this before."

"Like what?"

"Like I could actually kill somebody."

Aparecio puts a hand on his shoulder. "Your stock's going way up in my book, boy!"

21

"YOU KNOW where we are?" Marcus Aparecio comes into the lugger's wheelhouse to stand his watch. Their second morning at sea.

"I can read the chart. We are about a third of the way up the east coast of Malaysia. Passed an island called Tioman about four hours ago."

"The way I see it we have two problems. First, at some point somebody is going to come looking for this boat. Second, except for the three hundred dollars Tuki had stashed in her bra, we're out of money, and using our credit cards will no doubt bring that cobra bitch, and maybe the *nak-lin*, down on our heads again."

"There's a third problem."

"What?"

"We have about enough fuel to last us another six or seven hours."

"How screwed are we?"

"I don't know. Where's the ruby?"

"Not here. Tuki stashed it somewhere last week. And it's not like we can sell that little darlin' anyway."

"Oh yeah, I forgot. I flew halfway around the world to commit a list of felonies I haven't even tallied up yet—and nearly get killed—just so Tuki can give, GIVE—in proper Buddhist fashion—this gazillion-dollar stone back to its rightful owners, the people of Thailand."

"Are you going to get all righteous and indignant now?"

He takes a swig of brownish water from a pickle jar by the engine controls, spits it out the window.

"I've had about five hours of sleep in the last two days and nothing to eat but some boiled rice and a couple of bowls of something that looked like ping pong balls. So … sorry. I'm not at the top of my game."

"Leechee fruit."

"Ok, leechee fruit. Whatever. I could go for a little *paella* about now."

"Yeah, well remember this. You didn't know about the ruby when you came here. You came for that girl sleeping out there on the deck. You came because of something inside you."

"I must have been crazy. Fucking gangsters, cops. And whatever the hell Wen-Ling is. *Cristo Salvador*! What kind of bad movie is this?"

"Michael, do your love my daughter? Yes or no?"

He looks out the window at the figure just stretching her limbs in the black pajamas. She rises from the deck where she has been sleeping with a sack of rotten rice for a pillow. Her hands brush the hair off her face. She looks back at the vee of the boat's wake, squints hard as if she is watching something for several seconds. Then she looks off to the west, the coast of Malaysia just a green smudge on the horizon. Turning east she takes in the pearly vacancy of the South China Sea. Smiles. Her full lips, straight white teeth. Dimples. That grin he dreams about, spreading to her chin. Her cheeks glowing red in the early morning sun.

"Yes or no?"

"Yeah, ok, Marcus. I love her. But what's that get me?"

"How about a jolt of adrenalin to start your brain again."

"What are you talking about?"

"We're about to be up a damn creek without a paddle ... unless somebody here begins thinking on his feet."

"So far so good, la." Tuki enters the wheelhouse still smiling. "True, we got a lot of sharks following us. But no sign of pirates yet."

"Yet?"

· · · · ·

"Where's the gun?" Michael is demanding, not asking.

"You have a funny look in your eye." Tuki says.

"I think I've got a way to get us some money."

"What?"

"We're going fishing."

"With a machine gun?" Tuki again.

"For sharks."

"You must be kidding." Marcus is shaking his head.

"Those are blacktips following us. In the U.S., blacktip shark is worth three-fifty a pound fresh off the boat. Even if it's only worth a dollar a pound here, there's two thousand dollars swimming behind us."

"How in the hell—"

"All we have to do is slow down and lure them close enough to shoot."

"Lure?"

"We have to put something in the water to attract them."

"Not my black ass. And not my daughter's."

"We're just about out of tricks here. You got a better idea?"

"You ever fired a machine gun, boy?"

"That would be your job, Sergeant."

"And yours is to be the bait? To get in that water with those sharks?"

Michael sighs, looks at her. A hint of pink sunburn across the tops of her cheeks, the bridge of her nose. No makeup. Threads of hair blowing around her face in the wind coming through the open wheelhouse windows.

"If we ever get ashore in one piece, promise me, no more running, ok? We figure out how to give back the real ruby, get the *nak-lin*, Samset and Wen-Ling off our backs. Then disappear to some grass shack on a deserted beach. Forever maybe."

"You must really love me," she says.

. . . . .

He eases over the side in his boxers with a line tied around his waist. "Pull me in when I shout, ok? Fast!"

She's standing at the stern, rope in both hands, front teeth biting her lower lip.

"Really fast, ok?"

She nods. Doesn't look able to speak.

The boat's barely chugging along, no one at the wheel. Marcus is perched on the roof of the wheelhouse, his legs spread to steady his body against the roll of the boat drifting in the light swell. He's looking down on the stern of the lugger, Tuki, Michael. And the sharks thirty yards astern.

In the time it takes him to say two Hail Marys in Portuguese, he has slipped halfway back to the sharks. He's floating on the boat's cargo hatch, kneeling the way he has seen surfers do in movies. Now he takes a fishing knife he found, sterilized over the galley stove, cuts quarter inch gashes in his thumbs. Presses them with his fingers until the blood flows freely.

He stretches out on his belly and paddles the hatch until it is facing the back of the lugger, leaves his hands dangling in the water.

He can see the faint trail of blood spreading from his thumbs out into the water to his sides, behind him.

The sharks, six of them milling around, basking in the noon sun on the surface maybe fifteen yards further off, pay him no attention.

"I don't think this is going to work," he says.

Just then one of the sharks thrashes with its tail, twists on its side, dives.

"Jesus Christ, he's coming!" Her *bpaa* shouts from the roof. "They all are."

She doesn't wait for him to tell her to pull. She bends to the task, is heaving on the rope when the machine gun starts to rattle and the water explodes.

The sky thick with a pale red rain.

• • • • •

"You still got all your parts, boy?"

"That's not funny!" says Tuki.

"Well look at him, girl."

He lies collapsed on the deck, covered with blood, hyperventilating. Face to the sun, eyes closed.

She dips a bucket of sea water, pours it over his chest to rinse some of the gore off his skin. In his mind he's counting all his fingers and his toes.

Slowly, after the third bucket, he opens his eyes and grins at her. "I really want you in a grass shack on the beach."

"Me too, la." There's a thin note in her voice, something uncertain in the way her eyes hit his, dart away. "*Chua chet thi. Di chet non.*"

"What?"

"Every cloud has a silver lining."

You hope.

22

WITH THE HEADS cut away at sea, a buyer from a local resort hotel restaurant never sees the devastation a Browning submachine gun can wreak on flesh. And, in the end, they get almost seven thousand ringgits for the six sharks that Michael has dressed with elegant precision on the docks in the port of Kuantan. Enough to buy a rusty, blue Nissan from a local fisherman, add a lot of financial stuffing to Tuki's bra. And beat it out of town with just a nameless Singaporean lugger left behind as the only evidence that they have passed this way.

"Where to now?" Aparecio is at the wheel.

"How about a shack on a beach … miles from nowhere?" Michael's riding up front, map of Malaysia on his lap.

"First KL," says Tuki from the back seat.

"The city, KL?"

"We need to get the ruby, la … and our time is running out."

Her father stomps the brakes, turns to look over his shoulder. "Where did you put that stone?"

"Somewhere no one will ever find it … for a while."

She sees Michael close his eyes, knows he's really getting tired of all her little mysteries.

"What do you mean *for a while?*"

"How long can a dragon hold its shit, la?"

· · · · ·

She's squatting next to the old Chinese fortune teller for the second day in a row. To one side of her is a dried carcass of a large monitor lizard, on the other, two live juvenile monitors in a wicker cage

Here, finally—just maybe, she hopes she has stumbled upon the place that might have answers to all of her questions. Well, at least the two that kept her awake last night. Where do I go from here? And how can I keep the ruby safe?

So now the fortune teller's consulting the I Ching. She's watching him cast copper coins, three at a time, six times, onto the red batik cloth spread out on the sidewalk. With each toss he counts the heads—two, the tails—three, until he has all the numbers totaled for the hexagram.

"Number thirty-two," he says. "Heng. Wind and thunder. Go forward in the same way and spirit. Perpetual, regular, self-renewing. The moon is nearly full."

"I don't understand."

"You are in danger. There will be many barriers in your path. But you are on the right path now, and you must push ahead with all your soul and heart for an enduring relationship, for commitment. Now is the moment to press on. You know? Do or die."

She thinks maybe she's being hustled, that this is the worst kind of hokus pokus. But then she feels the Heart of Warriors cupped in her bra, pressing her breast. Pictures shadowy arms cocking with throwing stars, Sunny Jan-luechai putting a pistol to the temple of someone she loves. Pictures her father. And Michael. Sweet Michael. His olive skin, shadow of a beard, bedroom eyes, razor-cut hair. Broad chest, shoulders, arms. Muscled thighs built for Thai-bo.

"What must I do? I told you yesterday, I'm in love, and I'm afraid, la."

"I can give you something to make you bold for a hundred ringgits. You want?"

She sees her chance here, it's like a great, golden hole in the air right in front of her face. "Please."

"This could take some time."

She smiles, says almost to herself, "Ya phat wan prakan phrun. *Let's get on with it."*

As the fortune teller snips a piece of flesh off the dried heart of the monitor, she reaches in her bra, retrieves the ruby.

He puts the dried triangle of heart in a bowl and starts to grind it to powder with a pestle.

"I prepare drink for you. Give you courage of a dragon."

"Dai yang sia yang," *she says. "To get something, you must give something."*

He nods, turns back to his grinding.

It's this moment when she slips her hand with the ruby into the wicker cage, offers it to the smaller lizard.

And with the zip of a tongue, the stone's gone ... eleven million dollars down the hatch. Where not even the nak-lin *will think to look.*

The fingers of her right hand play idly with the monitors in the cage, their forked tongues flicking in and out of her palm as if they've discovered something sweet and raw.

• • • • •

It's after dark when they roll into KL, into Chinatown, start up Jalan Petaling on foot. The night market pulsing with people. The CD vendors rocking Boyz II Men, Nirvana, Celine Dion, Kanye West.

"There's our guy," says Michael.

The Chinese fortune teller is right where they left him at his spot just beyond the Nini Cosmetics and Accessories shop.

When she reaches the fortune teller, she feels her spine freeze. The lizard cage is empty. "*Mai klai fang!* Now I am truly a tree on the bank."

"What?"

She searches for the American phrase she heard the queens at Provincetown Follies use to explain impending doom. Her voice little more than bursts of air as she says, "My foot is in the grave, la. The ruby is lost."

"*Heng*," says the fortune teller, recognizing Tuki, remembering her hexagram—even though she's wearing jeans and a tank top, not a filmy black dress tonight. "Number thirty-two. Thunder and wind. Danger. Perseverance."

"What happened to your lizards? The ones in the cage last week?" Her father points to the empty cage.

The fortune teller looks away into the crowd. "Dead."

She wonders if this old man sitting on the carpet holding the *I Ching* in his hand already sees that the color has left her face, her fingers shaking. Already has found the ruby in the belly of the dead monitor … or in its shit.

Michael takes her hand. "It's going to be ok, really."

Suddenly her father's eyes brighten. "But you have the bodies?"

"Very valuable."

Marcus Aparecio reaches into the pocket of his khaki shorts, pulls out a huge wad of ringgits. "I want to buy one."

"Whole dragon?"

"Yes."

"They not dried out yet."

"Can we see?" She feels the first shoot of a lotus in her voice. Hope.

The fortune teller gets to his feet, cocks an arm at them. "You come."

· · · · ·

They stand on the roof of an apartment building above Jalan Petaling, KL spread out around them in a constellation of twinkling lights. The fortune teller lifts what looks like the trunk lid from a compact car. Splayed out on a sheet of corrugated steel beneath are the bodies of the two monitors who licked her fingers last week. She remembers the way the flicking of their forked tongues tickled the palm of her hand. Now they stink like three-day-old chicken livers. Or dead frogs baking in the road after a hard rain when the sun is blazing again … But they are both intact.

"Not ready yet." The fortune teller waves the rank odor of decay away from his nose with his hand.

"Which one, Tuki?" A tense quietness has settled into Michael's voice.

She squeezes his hand, feels his long fingers absorb her stress, then squeezes back. "The smaller one."

"You give me five hundred ringgits. I save for you. Dragon dry, ready, next week."

"You're sure. The smaller one?" Her father gives her a deep look. She nods.

"I'll give you seven hundred ringgits now. It's for my daughter." He gestures to her. "She's sick."

The old Chinese man purses his lips. Frowns. "Number thirty-two," he says, ruminates. "Thunder and wind."

"Too much, la!" She closes her eyes for a second. "Too much thunder and wind."

"Please help us," Michael says. "Help her!"

The fortune teller's eyes soften. "Let me get a bag ..."

"A dragon for the princess," says her father, handing over a fist-full of bills.

Suddenly she is loving her American men very much. Her Michael, her dad. The music drifting up from the street feeling just right for this moment. Abba, "Dancing Queen."

She can't remember how the Thais say this thing she's thinking. Doesn't care. *But here's the story, la. What once was lost, now is found.*

23

"MISTY? Is that you?"

Five thirty in the afternoon. Saigon. Ho Chi Minh City. Rush-hour traffic. Squadrons of motorcycles buzzing behind her, out in the street. The Cathay Pacific flight, a month of traveling, searching in-country. The networking with the Amerasian Foundation, Red Cross, the census keepers of Ho Chi Minh City. Maybe it all ends here ... with her father's mad, mad question ringing in her ears.

Sometimes she can't believe the man's absolute fearlessness when it comes to a thing he wants. She lags behind him, watches him weave his way though the customers into the neat shelves of books. He's homing in on a woman at the back of this second-hand, foreign-language book shop on Nguyen Hue Boulevard near the Kimdo Royal City Hotel.

The woman's shelving American paperback mysteries—Raymond Chandler, Eric Stone, Victoria Houston—from a cardboard box on the floor.

"Misty? Is that you? Huong-Mei?"

She freezes with an armful of books clutched to her chest. Stares. Her eyes widening to take in the tall, slender black man standing in front of her. The beard, the polo shirt, the cargo shorts, the wooden cane.

Oh, la, her? My *me*, my mother, *she thinks. Hears her* bpaa's *voice in her head.* "She looked just like you, sugar … One in a million. Tall, thin. But with the curves of a '68 Corvette."

She is not like Brandy and Delta, not an aging beauty trying to dress like someone on TV. Her face is smooth open, white. Whiter almost than the masks the queens paint on their faces when they try to look like Marilyn Monroe. But without makeup. Pretty. Her hair dark brown, full, shiny. Recently washed and trimmed, parted a bit to her left, hanging to the shoulders. She's pushed it behind her ears, holds it in place with a silver headband. Little jade triangles dangle from her earlobes. A set of reading glasses, the kind with just the lower half of the frame, perch on the edge of her nose.

"Ten toi, la … Huong-Mei," *she says.* "I am she." *Her body's stiff. A simple brown cotton jersey shows the broad shoulders, full breasts, narrow waist of a woman who is a size four. Her black skirt comes to the knees. The calves below are firm, slender, athletic.*

An old conversation replaying in her head again: "Misty was a whore?" *My mother …?* "She was just a kid from up the river, sugar. Eighteen years old."

"I thought you were dead. When you didn't answer my letters, I guessed …"

She drops the books. They hit the floor, a soft rustling.

"Marcus? Is that you, my Boo? My American?"

"Oh mercy, mercy, mercy." *The sobs just tumble from his throat.*

Suddenly they are hugging. Squeezing so hard that sweat shadows blossom on their clothes where they touch.

The customers withdraw to the corners of the shop, seemingly certain that they are witnessing the onset of something no one is ever meant to see.

Tuki feels her ribs buckling in her chest, the tears starting to blind her.

"Where you come from?" *Her mother's voice now almost a wild laugh.* "There's someone I want you to meet."

Oh no, please!

· · · · ·

"It's too late, Marcus." Huong-Mei turns her back on him, on Tuki, too. Puts her face in her hands. "Thirty-five years too late."

Her father looks bewildered, his gaunt cheeks suddenly sagging around the jaw. His hands folding and unfolding into each other.

"You cannot be here. It not safe. For you. For me."

"That's what you said in 1972."

"Please!"

"I'm sorry. I know this must be a shock, but—"

"Misty is dead. I have new life. Three children. All grown up. My book shop. Husband. Very good man. Government lawyer ... Very big in Communist Party. He knows nothing about ..." *She shakes her head wildly, hair swishing across her pale neck.* "I have been a little bit happy ... Now ... you ..."

"But this is your daughter, our daughter. She ..."

Huong-Mei's hands flutter around her face. "That not possible, la ... My little boy, Dung. He ... he died on boat to Thailand."

She wants to say no. No, this is not true. I'm here. I lived, Mother. I've been dreaming you for almost thirty years ... you dancing on that bar, the Midnight Train to Georgia ... and everybody thinking they need to get some good lala ... It's just that I was never Dung, never a boy except for the strange little chaang between my legs. She wants to open her mouth and spew. But she feels her me's silence, her confusion, fear. Maybe even guilt. Her mother's heart and her own just splintering. This is a terrible mistake, coming here without warning. All too much. Just as it was too much when Prem came back for her in Provincetown after five years, with his pung chao addiction and his gun. An impossibility. A nightmare.

"Come on!" *She takes her father's hand.* "We have to go."

He holds his ground. Leans on his cane as if it is a pike pinning him to the floor of the book shop.

A slight young man in a white shirt appears from the back room, seems to size up the situation. He crosses the shop, rushes between the shelves of books, puts his arm around Huong-Mei's shoulders.

"Please, please excuse my mother. Sometimes she gets very emotional when she meets Americans."

Her father thrusts out his hand to shake with the young man. "My name is Marcus Aparecio. Your mother and I were friends ... a very long time—"

"No, Boo, please!" Huong-Mei's face presses to her son's chest.

"So you're the one," says the young man. "The marine in the picture she hides in the back of that book by Hemingway, A Farewell … to something."

Huong-Mei howls. Unearthly pain scorching the room. Everything going up in smoke and flames.

"Let's go." She tugs on her bpaa's free hand again. "I'm begging you, Dad."

She's never called him this before, can't believe she has said it now. Dad.

He yields. Reaches out to Huong-Mei, touches the ends of her hair with his fingers, lingers for a second, then turns away.

When they have reached the street, have started east down the boulevard toward the river, she hears a shout. It's the young man. He's running up to her.

A smile starting to spread across his lips, cheeks, eyes.

She can feel something here. A welcome. A bond, maybe.

"I'm Tran," he says. "So … So I have an American half-sister?"

With a stolen ruby, she thinks … and a chaang I'd like removed. "You know a plastic surgeon, la?"

24

"STOP!" She motions out the passenger's window of their Nissan. "Look!"

The car lurches, grinds to a stop.

He stirs from his sleep in the back seat, kicks the plastic bag at his feet that contains the rotting, fully intact monitor. A gust of foul air rises from the lizard.

They've been driving all night, trying to put as many miles as they can between them and anyone who might have seen them in the streets of KL or on the docks of Kuantan. Now it's mid-morning and they are heading up the east coast of Malaysia in Terengganu state, her father driving as usual.

There's a coconut grove on the right-hand side of the road, trees towering in subtle arcs, a golden beach, a sapphire sea beyond. Surf rolling ashore in long, white plumes, spindrift hanging in the air above the foam in small violet clouds that appear and dissolve before his eyes.

"What about this place?"

He sees now that she is not pointing to just the coconut grove, but to a pair of small cottages on stilts set back under the palms.

Thatched roofs. No glass in the windows. Red checkered curtains blowing in the wind. For Rent sign posted at the entrance to a sandy drive.

No other houses in sight. No other cars on this coastal road. No people. Just some monkeys in the trees.

Her father clicks the car back in gear and rolls closer to the sign, reads:

Long-Term Rates Negotiable
Contact Hadji Bin Mohammed, Marang Village

"I could have a place to myself," says her father.

She turns to Michael. A pink blush spreading over her cheeks. Her eyes sparkling. "What do you think?"

He wants to say, *I think you look like Christmas this morning. I think I'm dying for you*, minha querida. But what he says is, "Let's look around."

Even before he's totally out of the car, she has run up the steps and is on the porch deck, looking in the windows.

"You have to see this, Michael!"

When he's beside her, she pushes back the curtain on a window. Suddenly he's looking in on a small bedroom with a queen-size mattress on a platform suspended from the ceiling by thick ropes. Picturing their bodies intertwined, there on that swinging bed, swaying gently in the wind. The moon rising over the South China Sea, washing over them in their tender fury ... While the monkeys chatter in the trees.

"How about I stay here and clean the dragon, find the ruby? You and your dad go to Marang and deal on the rent?"

"You know why they build the houses on stilts here, Michael?" Her father has a little cockeyed grin on his face.

"Protection against a storm surge? A *tsunami*."

"No. I think it's the tigers. You know? They come prowling at night."

"Sweet."

She leans into him, her arm sliding behind his waist, her head resting on his shoulder. "You remember that night in Nantucket?"

He winces.

"Tonight is your chance to get it right, la."

· · · · ·

Her hand reaches over the table, grabs his as he lifts his wine glass for another swallow. The entrees have not arrived yet, and he has single-handedly downed well over half the bottle of Merlot. They are sitting near the storefront window of a quiet little restaurant called Black-Eyed Susan's. A soft violet light bathes India Street outside. Couples stroll the sidewalk, flickering in and out of the glow of the streetlamps that have just come on.

"Please, Michael. Take your time."

"Sorry."

"You don't have to get drunk."

"How do you know?"

"I need you tonight. What's the matter?"

He puts down the wine and looks her square in the eyes.

"It's not worth talking about."

"Please, la." Her hand on his again. "Do not shut me out. Not tonight. Just talk to me."

"You really want to know what's wrong?"

"I am so afraid." Her eyes stare at the flickering flame of the candle on their table.

"So am I, Tuki. That's what's wrong. I feel all torn up inside. I'm scared as hell. 'Face your fears and they will shrink to the size of bugs,' my father always told me. I have always believed him. But now I … I don't know. This is too crazy."

"What?"

"I think I'm in way over my head."

"You want me to get another lawyer again?"

He hears a hitch in her voice.

"It's too late."

"Buddha says it is never too late."

But it is. This night. At least when it comes to tenderness. Because he passes out in her bed. A sea-view room at the Jared Coffin House Inn. His

clothes still on. His Portagee heterosexuality a little tarnished. His reputa-
tion as a charmer and a Knight of the Round Table shot to hell.

25

MAYBE *the fortune teller was wrong,* she thinks. *Maybe my persever-ance is not enough to overcome all this wind and thunder.*

Because, look, it's too late again. He sleeps, la. Again. This man run ragged.

She's in the swinging bed beside him. Her father settled into his own cottage down the path. It's well after midnight and she has been watching this man sleep since she and her dad got back from Marang so many hours ago. Hoping he would stir from his nap. Hoping for the moon to come and tease him awake. Hoping tonight will be their night.

Now, at last, a tardy moon rises over the sea. A pale orb shin-ing through the open window of the cottage. The lunar light on his face is doing nothing to rouse him. Worse, it seems to wash away his soft breathing with its cold, blue tide. She holds the Heart of Warriors in her fingers, notices how it seems to just suck up the moon and give nothing back. Wonders how this stone can be the cause of so much trouble.

"I love you." Her words are silk as she brushes his hair out of his eyes. Her fingers trace his brows, the line of his jaw, his lips. "You came for me."

She slides close behind him. Curls an arm around his waist, closes her eyes and smells the scent of coconut soap on his shoulders from his shower before he came to bed, feels the warm wind blowing in off the ocean. The night birds are fussing in the trees, the waves combing the beach. From far off in the jungle come sounds she can't identify. Crying maybe. Or a mating call.

"I can wait," she says. "As long as it takes."

• • • • •

He wakes to her at sunrise, feeling her against his back, smells the fruit of her hair before he sees her. Maybe he's still dreaming of tigers hunting, prowling, chasing each other, fishing on the beach, he's not sure, when he turns to her and slides his lips along the rim of her jaw, reaches her mouth.

His lips brush hers. Soft, sweet slices of plum.

Her tongue stirs. He feels it trace the edges of his mouth, the palm of her hand settling behind his left ear, pulling him into her. The fur rising on his chest, his legs. The first rays of sun flirting with those red highlights in her hair.

"Good morning, love."

"You taste like a good time."

"Try me," she says.

He slides his lips to her collar bone, inhales her skin, her breasts. He drinks the wetness from her mouth. Then her belly.

"Remember the Hotel California?"

"Ummmmm."

"Now it's my turn." *And this is just the beginning.*

Her body feels so small and delicate, but immensely strong when she puts her hands beneath his shoulders and pulls him up to her, onto her. Tears at his back with soft claws.

"I've never done this ... you know," she says. "Not like this."

"I love you."

"Ouch."

"What?"

Her hands are in the hair on his neck. His ears prick to her fast breathing. The bed starts to sway on its tethers. Her body melts against him. Absorbs. His mouth, his heart, *meu cristo*, his soul. The rest. Her finest, smoothest, secret skin against his own. Nothing at all separating them.

"Never let me go."

He feels the sun warming his back. Smells hot, wet fur. Tastes brine. Tigers are loose on the beach. Charging. Pouncing. Swaying in and out of the surf. Fishing. The spray soaking their bellies, flanks. Tails flying in the wind. Eyes not seeing the *tsunami* rushing toward them.

Until it's catching them.

Sweeps them through the coconut grove.

Carries them into the jungle.

The black mountains.

Wave upon wave tumbling them.

Crushes them together.

A ball of flesh, fur, desperate

Mouths. Roaring back at this

hot sea ...

Even as they sink. Sucked down through a rending fissure into the planet's blood, their own.

When the bed is still, she kisses him alongside the ear.

"Maybe you could just mail the ruby back to them."

"And stay here forever."

"Twice."

26

DAY SIX in paradise. They are cuddling together in a hammock strung between two coconut palms on the high rim of the beach, letting the sea breeze dry them after a long swim, when her father shouts.

"Hey, Jesus! You better look at this!" He jumps out of his beach chair, the Sunday edition of Singapore's *Straits Times* in hand. Limps over to Michael and Tuki. "Here's trouble."

She reads the headline he's spread in front of her:

Drag Queens Nabbed For Murder Of Thai Mogul

"What?"

"Read on."

> Bangkok. Royal Thai Police have announced that two Vietnamese drag queens have been arrested for the murder of pharmaceutical czar, Thaksin Kittikachorn.
>
> In a raid Friday night at the Silk Underground, a Patpong drag bar, police took into custody the two proprietors, known locally as Brandy and Delta, for the April 10 assassination of Kittikachorn.

> The victim died from an attack by a martial-arts-
> style throwing star at his retreat on Klong ...

"Varat Samset did this," says Michael.

"We have to try to help them."

Her father bites his lower lip. "That's what the cops are counting on, sugar."

· · · · ·

She's calf-deep in the surf, striding toward the wreck of a freighter
washed ashore in a typhoon. Prince Charming at her side. Her
hands are pressed to her head to stop the explosion. Blue sarong
riding up above her knees with each long stride. Her bikini bra suddenly a bundle of taut cords pinching her chest. Her breath comes
hot, fast. Her throat too parched to cry.

"This is really bad, Michael."

"Maybe there is someone in Bangkok who can help them.
Surely they have lots of friends, a lawyer ..."

"You don't understand. The bail is forty million *baht*, more than
a million dollars! And they are not in the Bangkok city jail. They are
in Bangkwang."

"Bangkwang?"

"You never heard? The Bangkok Hilton? Hell House?"

He squints, confused.

"Thai people call it the Big Tiger ... It eats you alive."

"Executions?"

"Like eight hundred people on death row."

"But Brandy and Delta haven't been convicted of anything.
This is just Samset's way of baiting us."

"Doesn't matter. Worse than Bridge Over the River Kwai
Death Camp. *Kathoey* go there, she never come out."

"Kathoey?"

"*Sao praphet song, phet thee song.* Ladyboy, third sex."

"Oh."

She says there are seven thousand prisoners in there. Very
nasty men. Jail is the end for a *kathoey*. You want to die?

• • • • •

The Barnstable county lockup. She remembers the handcuffs on her wrists. Cops at her side, rushing her down the corridor. A dozen men hanging on the bars of their cells hooting, grabbing their crotches, licking their index fingers. It smells like cigarettes, the burning scent of ammonia masking something worse.

She's still in her makeup, her costume from the show. A black spandex dress from Frederick's. The police took her down the second she came off stage.

One of the inmates has his face to the bars eyeing her breasts, his tongue flicking in and out of cracked, bloody lips.

She feels like she's being strip-searched. Brandy and Delta have told her: First they snare you, then they treat you like klong *water. Then they send you off to the death camp. Or Bangkwang.*

• • • • •

She can't let go of him. Won't. Even though the surf is washing over them as she hugs him to her chest. The sea up to their waists, boiling around them. Crashing. And her howling. "They are my mothers!"

"Yes ... but ..."

She tries to swallow her sobs. Tries to speak. "They ... They are ... because of me. I have to ... Bangkok."

He's wiping the salt spray from her eyes. His fingers like soft little wings.

"Will you help?"

"Of course. But ..."

"What?"

"We have to be smart about this. We can't just go rushing up there. Your father thinks it would be insane to go back ..."

She chokes. "He ... he doesn't understand. He just thinks ... is a terrible place because ... what happened there the last time."

"He's got a point."

Something's rising in her chest. She's feeling empty, alone. Drowning here. And her blood's starting to howl again. "I have to go alone?"

"Never," he says.

Suddenly his arms feel so warm around her back. Both their chests pounding together.

"You really are my prince."

He opens his mouth to say something, but she puts her fingers to his lips.

"Don't say anything, Michael. This is my dream."

27

HE'S KILLING HER with this razor. She's disappearing right before his eyes. Right beneath his hands. Barely a ghost of the girl he loves is left on that face.

"Now, shave the rest of me, Michael."

He feels the safety razor shaking in his hand, his stomach turning to ash as she sits here in front of him on the chair.

"Hurry, la! My eyebrows. The bus to Bangkok leaves in less than an hour."

He squirts a ball of shaving cream onto his fingers. Dabs it across her forehead. Starts slowly, with short strokes to scrape away that distinctive, womanly arch above her left eye. Her head already shaved to the smooth softness of—what? A cancer victim? A dead person. Here. In front of God and her father.

Aparecio sits on the bed in the bare hotel room in this Thai outpost north of the Malaysian border. His head freshly shaven, beard gone. Lou Gossett turned Thai monk. Saffron robe, sandals and all. The man has his back against the wall, eyes closed. Perhaps he is praying, but those pouting lips seem swollen with anger. This was not his idea after all. He wanted to stay on the beach ... like Michael.

It was not the men's plan to sell the car yesterday, nor use the money to bribe a boatman to bring them over to Thailand from Kota Bharu. To start yet another one of Tuki's masquerades here in Tak Bai. Launch on one more mission of mercy, maybe a suicide run. *Cristo.*

"Are you done yet?"

"Not quite." He scrapes away at her remaining brow, following the grain of the fine black hair from above the bridge of the nose to her temple. "I hate this."

"Please, la!"

He tries to blank out everything but that vanishing, lovely arc of hair, focus on the task at hand. But his mind drifts. Wonders if the same thoughts clawing at the back of his brain are tearing at her father too. Wonders how many tests of his love will be enough. Does he worry that at some point all of this drama, this mutilation, will be too much?

Will he one day wake up to find himself wishing he had never met this soul of Buddha? Wishing that her mysteries, her overdeveloped sense of right and wrong, her craving for the theatrical would just disappear in a puff of smoke? Or ... does he love her without conditions? *When do you know that the straw heaped on your back is within a few stalks of crushing you? Is it when the fear outweighs the desire? Can you ever see it coming?* With Filipa he never did. It was over with her weeks before he told himself that she had already checked out.

He takes a warm washcloth and wipes the last of the foam from the corners of her eyes, from behind her ears. Tuki is gone. The face here now could be a fifteen-year-old boy's. Painfully innocent. The girl totally erased except for the small piercing in her earlobes. She says that nobody will notice after she puts on the reading glasses with the thick black frames.

He wants to close his eyes like her father as she looks up at him.

"You can't stand me, la. Can't stand to look at me. I have destroyed us. We're d—"

"No. I ..."

She's crying. "I'm so sorry. This is all a big mistake. It's just that Brandy and Delta need us. Everybody is after us and ... I didn't know what else ... DON'T know what else we can ..."

"It's ok," he hears himself saying. "Everything is going to be ok. We're back in Thailand. Safe. And I have some ideas about how to get them out of jail." Never has he lied so much, so fast.

She stands up and throws her arms around him.

He sees her in the mirror. Her back. The monk's robe a dusty gold in the glow of the room's single bulb. It is a boy hugging him. But the warmth, the breasts restrained beneath the sports bra, the scent of jasmine ... still pure Tuki.

"Tell me something good. Please, Michael. Really good!"

"Yeah," says her father coming out of his trance. "I could use some of that, boy. Something good."

Suddenly he sees himself in the mirror. The robe takes him right back to his days as a sexless altar boy at St. John the Baptist in Nu Bej. And this face staring back at him? She left his brows when she shaved him. Only her brows had to go, she said, because of their fineness, their sharp arches, their essential girliness. But his head ...? The top of his head and his ears ... could be Porky Pig's.

"Michael, tell!"

"Hair grows back."

28

BANGKWANG prison is like nothing he has ever seen before. And he's seen his share of jails. The words *freaking maze* keep flashing in his mind. Massive. White. White everything. With just a few palm trees and a central tower you might see in a film like *The Lord of the Rings.*

Everything after passing beyond the big yellow doors has been a blur of corridors, security checks, waiting rooms. Crowds of visitors. Thin-lipped, blank-faced guards. Warning signs at each of his stops. Signs in Thai and English. "Family members, clergy, attorneys only. Show I.D."

Don't screw this up, buddyboy, he hears his father's voice in his head. *You're sailing solo here.*

Cristo is he solo. And from what he can tell, just about a passport photo away from being on the other side of these bars. Before they got to Bangkok, he, Tuki and Marcus split up. Traveling like monks to slip beneath the radar of the Thai police and the *nak-lin.* Separate busses and trains back to the city from Hat Yai. But now he's using the fake Malaysian passport Marcus got him on their first time through KL, the passport showing him as a Sikh, turban and all. His name, Rajender Singh. Resident of Georgetown, Penang. "Attorney at law" it says in the occupation box. Marcus must have guessed that bit would come in handy.

It's the one tool he has to access Brandy and Delta. But maybe it's a death sentence, too … if someone in Singapore, Varat Samset or Wen-Ling, took the time to check his fake I.D. and flag his alias on some criminal-watch, file-sharing database.

But so far the fake passport has worked perfectly. He's in, wearing the turban he just got at the night market in Banglamphu.

So now he's scanning the prisoners being herded into the visiting area beyond the bars, wire mesh, glass. Looking for Brandy. And he's thinking there may actually be a chance that he will be alive and free when it comes time to rendezvous with Tuki and her father. Tonight at the Wat Chai Chana Songkhram in Banglamphu. The place the old monk handed him the ruby a few hundred catastrophes ago.

But all of these prisoners look the same with their buzz cuts, dark blue shorts, light blue T-shirts. His search seems hopeless. There are about fifty stools where he can sit down opposite a prisoner and start talking by telephone. *Jesus, which one?*

Suddenly the heat of Bangkok nails him. Fluids start gushing from every pore. He wishes he were back in the monk's robe he traveled in for three days. His black pants, white shirt, Sikh's turban, legal briefcase drip with sweat. And, now that his hair is starting to grow back into thick stubble, his head has developed a killer itch. He just wants to rip off the turban and flee.

But then he sees the middle-aged dude with the crew cut and the swelling of breasts beneath his shirt. This has to be Brandy. She's wobbling like someone who has just walked out of a train wreck.

He taps on the glass to get her attention.

When she looks up, he's ready with the little sign he made with notebook paper and a colored marker. He turns his body until it is between the closest guard and Brandy, then he flashes the sign. It's his hand-drawn image of Madonna's face blowing a kiss. Beneath, in red letters:

SILK UNDERGROUND
Hollywood Girls, Girls, Girls!!!

He knows she cannot read English, but she will recognize the graphics from the sign that hangs over her club.

For a second she squints … then nods, drops down into a free booth on the far side of the bars, wire, glass.

He settles onto a metal stool opposite her and picks up his phone.

She holds a receiver on her side. "I know you, la?"

"I'm your lawyer."

She looks at him as if he's from another galaxy.

He doesn't want to say his real name, doesn't want to blow his cover on the phone in case someone is listening. So what he says is, "Dung sent me."

She squints at him again. Suddenly her eyes spread open, sparkle, bust a little bit of a smile. "Lone Ranger gone ride again!"

"So it seems," he says.

· · · · ·

He feels her arms wrap around him here in the shadows of the *wat*. Darkness has slipped over the city, but the traffic is growling along Chakrapong Road beyond the walls of the monastery.

"I had this terrible feeling you were never coming back to me."

"I only got to see Brandy for twenty minutes."

"She's ok? And Delta?"

"They are managing … but they have been separated." He doesn't say that Brandy looks half dead, that she has already been raped twice. That some of the *nak-lin*'s boys on the inside have beaten Delta, trying to get her to expose Tuki's whereabouts.

She releases him. Takes his hand and leads him to a bench. They sit. She turns her head away … as if that will keep him from looking at her. This strangely fine-featured boy monk from Pat-pong Road who has come to stay here at the monastery.

He closes his eyes, nuzzles her neck, hoping that the lingering scent of her coconut soap and jasmine will keep him bound to the woman hidden here.

"How do we get them out? Did they give you an alibi?"

He says Brandy told him a story about something that happened on the night of the murder.

"What?"

Suddenly he's not sure what to say.

"Sorry?"

"It seems your drag mothers were having a … date with a friend?"

"He can provide an alibi?"

"They said he was with them at a restaurant on the river, an upscale place called Khinlom Chom Sa Phan. And then they went back to their apartment."

"I know this friend?"

He swallows hard. "Yeah."

"A Patpong Johnny?"

"No … your father."

• • • • •

Brandy faces him through the glass separating prisoner and visitor. Holds the phone to her ear close, tenderly between thumb and forefinger, as if it is a holy object. He feels like he's talking to ghost. No, a mutation. The last time he saw her she was something of a babe. Creamy skin, blue eyes, shoulder-length chestnut hair. Almost white-looking, except for the small nose, the arch of the brows, the creases at the corners of her eyes, the high cheekbones.

She tells him that she has already been raped twice. That men held her while others fondled her breasts, sucked them. Some of the nak-lin's *boys are here on the inside. They have beaten Delta, trying to get her to expose Tuki's whereabouts.*

He closes his eyes. "I'm sorry."

She says a word in Thai or Vietnamese, spits on the floor.

"Can you tell me something that will help me get you out of here?"

Brandy looks away toward the floor.

He knows she's holding something back. "Brandy?"

She continues to stare at the floor.

He wonders how long before you die in a place like this. Whether death comes like a lightening bolt or slow, hot suffocation.

"Brandy?"

Finally she tells him. Tells him about the date she and Delta had with Marcus Aparecio. How they went out for dinner at a slick riverfront restaurant called Khinlom Chom Sa Phan. How they drank a lot of champagne, how they pretended it was Saigon during the war when everybody lived for the moment. How they drank and danced until they were too wasted to dance anymore. The three of them. How lots of people in the restaurant, like the bartender and the waitresses, must remember them, remember that they were there late into the night.

"If I can get the police to interview the restaurant staff, I think we can get you out of here."

Brandy catches his eye, then looks away as if she's seeing something, a memory maybe, or wants to say something more. She pushes back tresses of imaginary hair along the sides of her head with her palms.

"What?"

"Nothing."

"Please."

She waves her hand in front of her face.

"If you must tell Tuki about this. Tell her we sorry. Bad judgment. Blame us, not daddy. He came to the Silk Underground to talk how to help Tuki. We gave him drinks. Made him come with us to dinner. Made him dance. Her bpaa must have been very disgusted with us."

"I don't understand."

"We got very say bí tì, very tipsy. Went back to apartment with her bpaa. But when we wake up middle of the night he gone with wind, la. We just two drunk old trannies … watching reruns of the Daily Show."

"Where do you think he went?"

Brandy's eyes flash at him. "Not my business."

• • • • •

A gasp of air escapes her mouth.

"He must be very lonely, very needy, la. Brandy and Delta too," she says after a long pause. Stands up. Grunts.

"I think I understand." He's not sure why he says this.

"No you don't."

"You're right."

"My *bpaa* was supposed to meet me here this afternoon ... He never showed."

"Oh."

"Yes, *oh*, la. My blood is turning to sand."

29

SHE FEELS something strained, tight in the way he squeezes her hand, knows he is trying to comfort her. Tells herself that's what he's doing. But his touch is having the opposite affect. She knows she is not pretty to him. Maybe not even a woman to him anymore. She feels lost to herself. As lost as Michael has seemed during all of this flight. Lost from any clear plan to return the ruby to Ayutthaya. Lost from any strategy to escape the police and the *nak-lin*. Lost from any chance to cleanse herself and Prem's ghost from all of the bad karma.

And now her father's lost to her. Again. Maybe there is no future. Maybe everything stops for her here in Bangkok. Like any second, la. If it must, she hopes it ends with a bullet, not Bangkwang or the Bridge Over the River Kwai Death Camp.

"Let's get out of here. Maybe walking will help. We could go to my guest house."

Her thighs tighten. The grind and buzz of traffic along Chakrapong Road, the heat and wetness of his body, the choking night here in the monastery garden. They make her want to run into the temple, throw herself facedown before the golden statue of Buddha.

"It's too dangerous, la. The police, *nak-lin*, might see."

He hugs her from behind. Holds her against him, his arms across her breasts, his sex pressing the cleft at the top of her legs. She thinks of Prem. Her dead lover. The *pung chao* junkie. And the man she has never told anybody about. Not even her father or Michael. The evil for which she has no words. The man she tries never—like never, ever, la—to think about. Sunny's bastard friend on Cape Cod. Wan-Lo. Those men. They were like this sometimes, full of tight embraces. Hard … when she knew they were really scared. Needy. Fear brought out some kind of craving in them, a violent need.

Buddha, tell me all men are not this way, la. Not my father. And not this one either. Not Michael! Not like Wan-Lo.

· · · · ·

"You want to fuck me, love?" Wan-Lo's breath stinks of fish sauce and garlic. "You want to spread your ass for me one more time before we die?"

She tries to pull away. But he has her from behind. One arm around her neck. The other under the waistband of her skirt, probing with fat fingers.

"I like kathoey saloey like you. Little girls with dicks. But you know that, don't you?"

"Let me go, la ..."

"Don't be like that." He yanks, tears the little black mini off her hips, her thong too. "Now bend over, bitch!"

He doubles her over the large stainless steel stove, her cheeks inches away from a back burner, its blue flames hissing beneath a pot of pad thai.

"You're burning me!"

"Shut the fuck up!" He knots her hair in his hands, pushes her face toward the flames.

She squeezes her eyes shut, braces for his thrust.

A jackhammer of flesh.

She feels something starting to crack deep inside. A fissure rupturing right at her core. Millions of little knives slice the muscles at the tops of her legs.

"Please ... just kill me," she says in Thai.
"Fucking A, baby."

· · · · ·

"Let me go. Take your hands off me, Michael!" She's suddenly gasping for air.

"What's wrong?"

"Every ... thing," she says, as she runs off to the *wat*, to Buddha.

30

"I'M NOT INTERESTED in your stories of a couple of shit-faced *katoeys* dancing at Khinlom Chom Sa Phan restaurant, counselor. I'm not going all the way over there to see if someone remembers them. I already told you that." Varat Samset sits on his desk in Bangkok Central, sucks on a wooden toothpick. He turns, looks out the window. Blinks as if to refocus his eyes on the purple haze of pollution blanketing the office buildings, hotels, *wats*.

The desk fan's broken, the room a steam bath in the monsoonal heat. Tears of moisture slide down the concrete walls.

"But it's an air-tight alibi," Michael says. "Please. You can't just let those innocent—"

"Innocent what, counselor? Flabby-ass old Viet ladyboys? You want me to picture them slobbering and hugging all over some *farang* on the dance floor of one of my fair city's riverfront restaurant bars? Shame on them for ever going near that restaurant. It's a nice place. Your innocent buttfucks are accessories to ... let me count the crimes: murder, arson, aiding and abetting a fugitive, theft of a national treasure ... Shall I go on? There are more."

"They are going to die in there."

"That's up to you."

He feels the flames building in his head. "You know what, Detective? I used to think you were a good cop trying to do the best job you know how. But you're a dickweed!"

The short, fat Thai takes off his thick glasses, stares at Michael. "You came to my office to call me names?"

"You have no reason to hold Brandy and Delta at Bangkwang, and you know it. This is illegal. This is police harassment. This is—"

"You shut up!" Samset drops to his feet. Looks for a second like he's going to swing at Michael. Stops two feet away. Fishes in his breast pocket for his Kents. Lights one.

"Just give us a break here."

"Break? You're already getting a break. This is not your country, counselor. Not Hollywood either. We have extradition agreements with Singapore. You are a wanted man there now, after your little jail break. One call from me, you will be on the next flight to Changi Prison. Maybe fifty-year vacation, complete with daily—what you Americans say—corn holing."

"Your sidekick Wen-Ling set up the whole thing, then arranged to have us killed. She'll do anything to get the Heart of Warriors back, won't she?"

"Wen-Ling is no sidekick of mine. She's on her own."

"What do you mean?"

"Wen-Ling is not Thai police."

"Then who—"

"*Silab.*"

"What?"

"*Nuy lachikan lab.* Thai National Security Agency. Very James Bond … I had nothing to do with what happened to you after you were arrested in Singapore. Once we had you in custody, Wen-Ling and the Singapore police shut me out. Seemed like they had some kind of private agenda."

"Really?"

"Yes, really. So, now you pay close attention! I got an open murder case here and lots of pressure to solve it. Huge pressure. Thaksin Kittikachorn was a very powerful man. Many people high up want your *katoey* girlfriend's head, ok?"

"Maybe I can get her to give up the ruby if you get the queens out of jail and drop all charges against them and Tuki."

"You think I give a shit about that stone? That's Wen-Ling's problem."

"I told you more than a month ago. Tuki said the *nak-lin* killed Kittikachorn. You have the throwing star. How's a drag queen ever going to learn to toss one of those?"

Samset takes a long hit on his Kent, flicks it on the ground. Crushes it. "Here's the bottom line, counselor. Bring in your girlfriend. And the man you claim was dancing with the *katoeys* the night of the murder."

"I knew you would say that. And I can deliver. But … but I'm going to need some guarantees. No arrests. No harassment. No—"

"I just want to talk to them, ok? No arrests, nothing. I promise."

"Why should I trust you? You put Brandy and Delta in Bangkwang."

"I did what I had to do."

"For what?"

"To stop you from running. To get you back here in Bangkok. To talk to Tuki Aparecio."

"About the murder."

"About what she saw that night. About these shadows you call *nak-lin*. About the *jao pho*."

"She says they want more than just the ruby."

"Then don't you think you could use an ally?"

31

NIGHT AGAIN. She's sitting, lotus position, with a dozen monks in front of the golden Buddha in the *wat*, meditating, when she feels a hand on her shoulder. Knows it's him, those long, strong fingers.

He says nothing. Presses his hands together in the traditional Thai greeting, bows deeply to her from the waist. He's wearing his monk's robe too. She's really glad to see him, thinks he looks so cute with those big ears. And his hair a kind of dark fuzz now. But her mouth is dry as dust, dry with worry over how she left things with him last night. *Luang kho ngu hao.* Her hand is in the cobra's throat again.

He leans to her ear, whispers. "Can we start fresh?"

Her heart gives a little cry.

She stands up, bows to him. Looks around at these monks, friends. They have accepted her here. No questions asked. But it would be beyond rude to bring her personal troubles into the temple.

"Come."

Outside the entrance to the temple, they put on their sandals. She leads him into the garden.

"I'm sorry," he says. "I'm sorry for whatever I did."

She presses her forehead to his chest, feels something strong, confident beating there. "You did nothing, la. I'm just a mess."

"Do you trust me?"

"You still love me?"

"To the stars and back."

A little smile forms at the corners of her mouth. She kisses his neck. "I'm so sorry I got you into all of this."

"I talked to Varat Samset today."

"That can't be good."

"He gave me the idea that he wants to help us."

"Help us?"

"He wants to talk to you and Marcus."

"Then put us in the Big Tiger with Brandy and Delta."

"Maybe not. He said he has no patience for thugs raising hell among Bangkok's upper crust with a throwing star murder. He's feeling the heat from his bosses to solve this case. He says the thugs need to be squashed."

"That's what my father said too."

"You talked to him?"

She says that she saw him last night. He came to the *wat* after she saw Michael. Her *bpaa* came back to make sure she was safe. Said he had been on a little scouting mission. Said he was tired of playing games with the *jao pho*, the godfathers, and Sunny Jan-luchai. Said if the police couldn't stop Sunny and his boys, then he would.

"Where's your father now?"

"Gone again, la. I tried to stop him. But he said what he had to do, it couldn't wait."

"We have to find him."

She thinks she hears a new note in his voice. Not just urgency, but commitment. As if something is starting to stir deep inside him.

"*Ni sua pa chorake*, la."

"What?"

"Out of the frying pan into the fire."

• • • • •

She's pumped on adrenaline when the two of them get back to the beach house her boss at the Saigon Princess keeps on the fringe of Atlantic City. Giddy from a night of hip hop. Juiced from partying with some truly fly brothers and sisters, at the House of Blues. She's not feeling the cool October night at all when someone jumps out of a bush and bashes her boss René with the butt of a pistol. His great, James-Earl-Jones body deflates, collapses onto a dark walk by the side door.

"Don't say motherfucking word, bitch!" Someone wrenches her arms behind her back, duct tapes her wrists together in one swift move. Pulls a woolen watch cap down over her head.

The man who binds her wrists cups a hand over her mouth, says something she doesn't quite catch in Thai.

René groans from the ground.

Someone kicks open the door to the beach house.

"Now you gone see what happen when you shit on people try help you, try protect you business. Try protect you girl Tuki from Mr. Thaksin Kittikachorn. You gone see what happen when you don't pay Robsulee."

"I can pay, I swear I can. I've been winning at the tables again. I just had a dry spell there for awhile. I ..." René's voice sounds broken.

"Too late, nigger."

"Don't hurt him." She hears her voice pleading.

The man with his hand over her mouth tells her in Thai to fuck herself. "You fat, old nigger boy owe us lot of money. Now we collect debt. No more monkey business."

She hears a sound like the splattering of water on the concrete walk, on skin. Smells urine.

"Jesus Christ you fucking animal, you ..."

Someone kicks René. He gasps, moans ... is quiet. But the kicking continues, at least four or five more. A heavy hollow sound each time the shoe strikes him. She knows these are blows to the head from the way each blow interrupts the groans. Until there are no more groans.

"*All gone,*" somebody says.

"*Take him inside.*" Her captor's giving orders in Thai to the kicker, the pisser, maybe others. Tells them to turn on the gas stove, blow out the flames. Light a candle in the living room. Close all the windows and doors.

"*What are you doing … You can't …*"

Something slaps the side of her head so hard her ear seems to melt with a loud sucking sound.

"*I told you shut the fuck up, bitch! His debt, you debt now!*"

She doesn't know if she hears the house explode as they are driving her away in the van … or whether her battered brain just dreams it.

32

IT'S HOT, dark on the river. No moon. Red, green, white running lights of barges, ships, ferries appear, streak by. Vanish as he and Tuki charge down the Chao Phraya in a longtail boat, dressed once again in monks' robes. The unmuffled Toyota engine screaming into the night.

"Where are you taking us?" He's sitting next to her near the bows of the boat, fifteen feet forward of the boatman and his strange engine. The loose folds of their monks' robes riffle off behind them, small beating wings. Central Bangkok's lights start to fade into the mist as the boat follows the sweeping curve of the river.

"Klong Toey," she says. "Port district. My *bpaa* said he had to find a boat."

A field of bright lights appears ahead on the left. A petroleum tank farm, docks, cranes, stacks of maritime containers, warehouses, low neighborhoods.

"What are we looking for?"

"I told you, a boat."

He looks around. The river here is thick with the shadows of rice barges, coastal freighters, oil tankers swinging on moorings, tied to docks.

"There are hundreds of boats."

"This one is special. Not Thai boat, la. Not longtail."

"I don't understand."

"My father said he had to find a black speedboat. You know, la? Like the ones on that TV show *Miami Vice?*"

"A Cigarette boat?"

"That's what he called it."

"He thinks it belongs to this guy Sunny?"

"Maybe, or his friends. *Nak-lin.*"

"How does he know?"

She shrugs, looks off toward the jungle on the right side of the river. "Sometimes my *bpaa* is a mystery."

Like father like daughter, he thinks. This may be his craziest night yet in Southeast Asia. *Cristo. What is the probability of finding a small black speedboat among all these watercraft? And what if we do, then what?*

The longtail whines on through the night. The halogen lights of the port facilities on the left bank are closer now. Glowing, he thinks, like the violet of distress flares hanging in the sky over a wreck at sea.

Suddenly the boat cranks into a sharp left turn, enters a back channel. The boatman slows the engine, cuts his running lights, shouts something in Thai.

"What's he saying?"

"He thinks we'll find the black boat up ahead in this *klong.*"

"How's he know?"

She shrugs. "You're a boat guy, a fisherman. Don't you know all the boats in your harbor, in New Bedford?"

"I'm getting a bad feeling about this."

· · · · ·

They find the black Cigarette nestled between a raft of houseboats tied up at a wharf just short of the place where an expressway bridge spans the *klong*. Opposite the wharf, across the narrow canal, he can see a waterfront restaurant, its floating docks for water taxis, longtails. Candles flicker from the tables on the open deck built over the water on stilts.

"Oh no!" Tuki squeezes his hand.

"What?"

"The restaurant ... its name."

He sees a sign hung beneath the eaves of a golden roof: **BANGKOK DRAGONS.**

"This is not good."

"What?"

"Two of them."

"Two of what?"

"Two Bangkok Dragons."

"Two restaurants?"

"Yes, la. Very bad place."

"Where's the other one?"

"Cape Cod."

"I don't know it."

"Living Hell."

"Where?"

"Bass River. You know, West Yarmouth by the bridge?"

He can't picture it. "A take-out place?"

"We had tables, too ... A few upstairs ... and outside on the grass."

He feels something flash in his guts. What does she mean *we*? "You think this place is a front for the *nak-lin*?"

She gives him a beaten look.

For just a second he really wishes he were back home on the Cape. Home where he could get some perspective from his own father. Home where he could find an ally in Detective Sergeant Lou Votolatto from the Barnstable County State Police C-PAC Unit ... Instead of floating out here in his monk's robe, with nothing but his skinhead girlfriend.

But then he feels something else stirring inside him. Something smoky, hot. Something that began to flare earlier tonight when he knew that Tuki, that all of them, could be dead by to-morrow unless he gets to her father fast. *Like get your net in the water and start fishing for serious,* meninho. Cristo! *Maybe these are strange waters, but you sure as hell know how to fish. Let's go. You flew halfway around the world to help. So help! It's way past time to unload that damn stone … and deal with karma later.*

"Do you have the ruby?"

She doesn't answer for a second, seems to be lost in a thought or a dream. "The monks were keeping it for me, but I have it now."

"Then we've got everything we need."

"My father was a fool to come here alone."

For some reason he pictures a shadowy figure in a green satin jacket. Feels his back teeth grinding, his fingers balling into fists. The air is pungent with the scent of fish.

33

"I SHOULD have known, la."

"What?"

"This is a ladyboy place."

They've just stepped through the front door. She's taking in the scene. The restaurant looks a bit like the inside of the *wat* back in Banglanphu. Airy, high ceilings, lots of golden shrines. But not Buddha's. Dragons. Some immense.

The air is ripe with the odor of fish. And new scents. Vinegar, basil, coconut, hot peppers. Tables packed with what look like upscale diners, a combination of Thai couples and groups of men. Japanese sex tourists. The servers are just kids. Drop-dead gorgeous, in little hot pants. Nipple pasties with silver serpents on them. Never had these back on Cape Cod.

She's scanning the crowd at the bar for her father. Thinking this is definitely not the place two people dressed in monks robes—as they are—would come, when suddenly she's imagining the smooth face of Prem, her gentle river lion. The junkie. Murdered son of the murdered father. Maybe it's the sad looks on the faces of the men, or the hungry smiles of the *kathoey* waitresses, that bring Prem back to her. She doesn't know. All she knows is that when she surfaces from the tart scent of his skin, she feels the barrel of a gun poking her beneath her left arm. Sees a black fire in Michael's eyes.

"*Suwat di crap*, princess," says the gunner. The voice, the smirk, the schoolboy looks from her nightmares. Sunny Janluechai. In the flesh. "Your father waiting for you. The cat on his ninth life."

She wants to bite a hole in that smug babyface. The prick she remembers from New York, Atlantic City, the Cape. Here. Not just a figment of her father's paranoia. With a gun on her again. The same gold chains around his neck, the five-hundred-dollar shoes. Prem's age. Michael's age. But shorter. Shoulders of an ape.

"Screw you."

"Maybe you get your chance, girlfriend ... Maybe you screw me right front you American boyfriend." The little shit turns to Michael. "You like that, wise guy? See you girl fucking me?"

Michael's face is flushing with anger. He looks ready to explode. She knows that if he does, he's dead. The *kathoey* hostess moving up behind him probably has a weapon hidden beneath the menus in her hand. Time to change the energy here, bring the attention back to her.

"You suck, la!"

He jabs the barrel of his gun against her ribs so hard something in her side cracks. "Let's go see you *bpaa*. Talk about ruby." He pushes her through a swinging door into the kitchen, nods to Michael. "You too, loverboy!"

They walk through the kitchen past the cooks stirring their woks, cleaning fish, scooping *lad nar* from pots. No one looks at them. It's as if she and Michael are already dead, ghosts. Sunny opens a back door near the freight dock, herds them across a parking lot into a small warehouse. Inside, he pushes them into a dark room filled with freezers and restaurant equipment, furniture. When they reach a trap door, he forces them down concrete stairs into a cellar. The room reeks of durian fruit.

When her eyes adjust to the low light of a single bulb, she sees three *nak-lin* with automatic weapons sitting at a table playing *ma-jong* and drinking bottles of Singha beer. None of them wearing a green jacket. Across the room, amid towers of fruit crates, sits her father. He has been stripped to his undershorts, duct-taped to a folding chair wedged into a corner. The luster is gone from his coffee skin. His arms and legs look chalky. His head hangs dead.

"Hey, monkey face! Wake up. I bring someone see you." Sunny slaps her father viciously across the cheek.

Her father stirs, opens his eyes. Doesn't seem to have the strength or the will to lift his chin off his chest.

"You tell ugly daughter how you come here middle of last night, dressed like cat burglar, try strangle me with ninja *manriki* chain."

Her father glares at Sunny.

His captor slaps him again. "Stupid nigger boy. I thought I already killed you once."

A couple of the guards laugh.

"Leave him alone!"

"Shut up, sit down!" Sunny pushes her onto the damp, cool concrete floor. Steps away, pointing his gun. Motions for Michael to sit beside her.

Marcus raises his head, seems to see her for the first time. "I'm sorry, sugar."

"Are you all right, la?" She knows, can see, this is a dumb thing to say. But her heart needs to say something. She can't think straight.

"Ok, princess. Now you turn be hero. You give me ruby ... or watch daddy die."

She looks at Michael. He seems to be trying to say something to her with his eyes. They are agates of black fire, but she can't read them.

"Don't tell him anything," says her father.

"Let my father go. Let Michael go, la ... Then we talk about ruby."

Sunny cocks his little pistol, tells his boys to tie a towel around her father's forehead like a bandana.

"He won't kill you if he doesn't have the ruby," Marcus says.

Sunny presses his pistol to the towel over her father's temple. "Where ruby? Say, bitch!"

Michael kicks her foot. Shakes his head like *don't tell.*

"You tell! Or I shoot."

"I lost it," she says, just stalling for time.

"Bullshit!"

She sees the muzzle flash, her *bpaa*'s eyes squeeze shut. The echo of the gunshot hangs in the damp cellar air. A spot of blood starts to bloom on the towel around Marcus' head. Then his eyes open. Blink. The shot has just grazed his skull.

"That just warning. Little scratch. Next time you lie, he dead. Then I kill boyfriend."

Michael kicks her again, gives her a look. He must be telling her to keep stalling. He must know something.

"It's not here, ok, la?"

"Search her," Sunny tells his boys.

One of them grabs her from behind, stands her on her feet. Grabs the free end of her saffron robe, tugs. She stands there in nothing but her black sports bra and panties.

A *nak-lin* with a flashlight looks in her mouth while Sunny hands his pistol to one of the guards, pulls out a pocket knife. Cuts off her bra, panties with quick flicks of the blade.

His fat fingers probe under her tongue, the outer edges of her teeth. Then he slides his hands down her cheeks, feels the soft flesh under her jaw, behind her ears, neck, shoulders, her armpits. Lets both hands settle over her breasts.

She closes her eyes. Maybe, just maybe, this isn't really happening to her.

But it is. His mouth is on her right breast. The nipple between his lips, his teeth. Biting.

"Bastard!"

He puts the edge of his little knife alongside her nose. "See this, princess? You shut up or I'll poke a dozen holes in your silicone balloons."

She freezes, pinches her eyes closed again.

His hands move down her belly, her back. "I know you are hiding it somewhere."

Two fingers go up her ass.

She moans.

"I said shut up!" His hands, fingers moving slowly over her crotch.

She's picturing a swarm of centipedes, when something jerks deep in her groin. Rips from inside her.

"What's this?"

"Tampon." She coughs as he pulls it out by the string. "I'm having my period."

He dangles the tampon in front of his face, hers. Eyes the swollen, but unstained, gauze. Says, "You not really *kathoey*. Wait I tell Robsulee."

That name again. A ghost. A mystery. The name she never asked René about, because she did not want to disturb the cocoon of security he wove around her ... as long as he paid Sunny and Robsulee the protection money. The cocoon that kept her safe from Prem's family.

The trapdoor crashes open. Down the steps comes Varat Samset, riot gun pointing at Sunny, shouting.

"Nobody moves!"

But the *nak-lin* have other ideas ...

They let loose with their weapons. A monsoon of smoke, racket, bullets.

When the shooting stops, she's on the floor with Michael covering her body with his own, breathing in hard, loud pants. Michael's ok. So is her father. The three *nak-lin* are bleeding out on the floor. Varat Samset lies in a heap, a bullet hole where his right eye used to be. *Shit.*

Sunny Janluechai has vanished. *Double shit, la.*

34

MICHAEL'S on the floor, back against some fruit cases, eyes closed, trying to let his breathing settle. Holding her as she sobs against his chest, wrapping her in her robe again, when he hears a familiar voice.

"We meet again, American."

He looks up, sees Wen-Ling standing on the cellar stairs. She's wearing a green silk pants suit, waving a small machine gun in front of her, an Uzi maybe. Smoke rising from its barrel in the damp air.

"Jesus, give me a break!" Marcus is still taped in his chair. "Not her again."

"I should have known you would be here too." Michael's throat burns from the fire still raging in his belly.

"Lucky for you."

"What are you talking about, Michael?" Tuki opens her eyes, looks around at the carnage.

"Her," he says. "Wen-Ling."

"You called the police about this?" Tuki demands. "You had them follow us?"

"I couldn't let us walk into a trap with no way out, no back up. I called Samset before we got in the boat. I should have known she would turn up too. She smells that ruby the way a shark scents blood."

She offers a bottle of water to Tuki. "Let's just say I just have a nose for trouble. Where's the ruby, Tuki?"

"*Nam yen pla tai.*"

"Tuki. I really need that ruby."

Tuki finally reaches out and takes the bottle of water. "Who are you? A dirty cop? *Nak-lin?*"

Wen-Ling tightens her fingers on the grips of her gun.

"She's some kind of government agent. Samset told me."

"*Silab?* National Security Agency? *Nuy lachikan lab?*"

"My job is to return the Heart of Warriors to the people of Thailand."

"Don't trust her," says Tuki's *bpaa*. His voice has the conviction of a man who may know more than he's saying. "She's a viper."

"I got you out of Changi Prison, old boy."

"You tried to have us killed in Singapore and—"

"Those boatmen were supposed to carry you to Jahore. Something went wrong. They were freelancers … or working for someone else."

"Likely story." Aparecio again.

"Where's the ruby, Tuki?"

"I don't trust you, la."

"Trust? You want to talk about trust. You bought your freedom from me in Singapore with a glass ruby."

"*Len kap sak sak ti hua.* You play with the dog, it will lick your mouth."

"We don't have time for proverbs. The *nak-lin* will be coming back here. Give me the stone. I can get you out of here. Out of Thailand. You'll be free."

"And dead," says her father.

"First thing tomorrow morning. Just like I got Brandy and Delta out of Bangkwang. She slides her hand to the inside pocket of her suit jacket, pulls out an envelope with the United Airlines logo, hands the tickets to Michael.

"What?"

"Here. Talk to them." Wen-Ling punches a number into a cell phone, passes it to Tuki.

Delta answers. She talks to her. Thai, Vietnamese, pidjin English. The only clue he has about what is going on is the widening eyes, the first smile he has seen on Tuki's face in days.

"What?"

"They're at the Silk Underground. They're free."

"Now hurry. Where is the ruby?"

Words rise in his throat. The fire inside him seems to have burned through some kind of shroud that has been blinding him. He sees clearly. Sees how to help. Sees that this is the moment when they give up the stone and make their break for the good old U.S. of A. "We should end this, Tuki. I think we have to trust her."

"You want me to give her the Heart?"

"It gets the monkey off our backs."

"ONE. One of the monkeys." Her father is rubbing his face with his hands, a man trying to rise above a nightmare. "You think Sunny's done with us, after this mess … and all the rest? Jesus Christ!"

"Give me the ruby, Tuki," says Wen-Ling. I can take care of this Sunny person."

"It's not just Sunny. There are others … A guy in a green jacket …"

"I can help. Just give me the ruby!"

Tuki turns to Michael, her father, back to Michael.

Something's screaming in his head. He scrambles to his feet, lifts her with him. "Tuki. Trust me. Let me help. Please."

She looks around at the bodies, Varat Samset's torpedoed eye socket.

"Ok," she says, bites her upper lip for a second. "The ruby's in the tampon."

"What?" Wen-Ling squints her eyes, confused.

"I put it inside a tampon."

He pictures the swollen gauze dangling by a string from Sunny's hand.

"It must be on the floor somewhere." He starts to scan the ground.

"I don't think so," says her father.

"What? Why?"

"He put it in his pocket."

"Sunny?"

"When the shooting started, the tampon was on the floor by me. I saw him pick it up."

"So he's fucking got off with it?"

"I'm sorry." Tuki's voice is a whisper.

Wen-Ling just stands there amid the bodies, as if waiting for the ceiling to collapse on them all.

"I followed you on that train from Bangkok to Penang weeks ago, Michael, thinking you could lead me to Tuki and the ruby. Then I chased the three of you to Singapore and back. For what? Nothing. And now look at this mess."

No one speaks. The air's heavy with the stench of riddled guts, gunpowder, fresh blood.

"Get out of here, Michael!" Wen-Ling says, "Go back to America. Before this old man and the *kathoey* get you killed."

Michael glances around at the ruined corpses, still feels something burning deep inside him. But now it's more like a low, warm buzz. Maybe even a satisfaction that brings with it clarity. He sees that all these bodies and the blood here are not signs of his failure. They are by-products of a certain kind of triumph. Fishing. It's as if he's standing on a deck up to his knees in cod fish heads, guts, blood. The aftermath of a slammer trip offshore on the *Rosa Lee*.

He hears his father's voice and his own. Shouting to the birds, the sky. To anyone up there who will listen. *Muito obrigado, Cristo Salvador! I needed help … to help myself. And others.*

Now guide me home, Sweet Jesus.

• • • • •

Bangkok Suvarnabhumi International Airport. They are waiting in line at the United counter for their boarding passes, clutching their legit U.S. passports like gold, rechecking their carry-on bags to make sure they have no gels, sprays, liquids or sharp objects, when Tuki's father nudges him.

"Does this mean anything to you?" Her *bpaa* hands him a small Swiss army knife. The plastic face plate is broken off one side of the knife. The red face plate on the other side bears the icon of a Labrador retriever and the words The Black Dog.

"Where did you get this?"

"Sunny dropped it in the cellar."

He handed his pistol to one of the guards, pulled out a pocket knife. Cut off her bra, panties. Quick flicks of the blade.

"It's from a store ... with shops on Martha's Vineyard and Cape Cod."

"What's that have to do with anything, Michael? With Sunny?" Marcus sounds impatient.

"I don't know yet. But I think we need to find out."

"I'll put the knife in my suitcase, and—"

Tuki takes his hand. "Do you think we can get the ruby back?"

35

"STOP the car, la!" She feels like she's going to be sick.

Michael swerves to the side of the highway. His jeep coughs, stalls dead.

They've just crossed the Cape Cod Canal, the Bourne Bridge, cleared the traffic circle at Bourndale and started north toward Sandwich village along the edge of the canal. Tracing the threshold of the Cape.

She leaps out the door, bends over, heaves in the sand. Tastes the clams, shrimp, tomato sauce from the *paella* she ate last night back in New Bedford. Some restaurant Michael called a piece of Portugal.

She thought she was ready for this, ready for the Cape again. Prayed to Buddha that she could handle this place with her father and Michael at her side. But five days of R&R in Nu Bej, five nights in the attic room at Tio Tommy's house after the flight from Bangkok, has not been enough to calm the scorpions in her belly. Now they're in her chest. Head, too. Stinging.

She has to run, la. Blot out the pain. Banish thoughts of the ruby, Sunny. Wan-Lo. And the serpent she has never met,

Robsulee. Banish festering thoughts about taking revenge on those monsters for what they've done to her.

She's got to find that canal. Got to pray.

I take refuge in the Buddha, the incomparably honored one
I take refuge in the Dharma, honorable for its purity
I take refuge in the Sangha, honorable for its harmonious life ...

It's the third Saturday in June. Global-warming heat. Cape traffic rushing along in a solid cue, drivers clamped to their steering wheel, eyes glazed with visions of blue beaches, cold bottles of Sam Adams. Blind.

She doesn't care, starts across the road. Without even a glance at traffic, her lips murmuring in prayer, looking like some loony kid. Tank top, cutoffs, crew cut. Brakes screech. SUVs, minivans skid to a halt. Someone honks, gives her the finger as she weaves through the chaos ... Then she's across. Scrambling through the thirty yards of brush, crossing the railroad tracks toward the bike path, the canal.

All the evil karma I've committed
On account of greed, anger, carelessness
Born of my body, my mouth, my thought
I make full confession ...

She pictures hitting the water in the Cape Cod Canal. Vanishing. With not even a ripple marking the spot in the swirling current. *So easy, arms over your head and dive, la.* Freeing her *bpaa* and Michael—sweet, beautiful Michael—from this endless quest for a stolen stone, the search for a killer. Her nagging impulse for revenge. Freeing them to get on with their lives before it is too late. Before she gets them all killed. Dragon lady from hell. *Kathoey saloey.* A storm of evil karma. Just like Wen-Ling said.

• • • • •

She's just starting to feel the peace of the Buddha when Michael reaches her. Just starting to imagine herself turning slowly in the eddies of the canal, sinking into the silence. The water a soft hug.

"Jesus. Are you ok?" His hand catches hers from behind, snaps her around, pulls her to him.

"No."

A pair of fishermen on the edge of the canal turn, stare. The buzz-cut boy with breasts, tears streaming. Folding into the arms of the Portagee ... who's panting in his red polo shirt, jeans.

"What's the matter?"

"Nothing."

"Tuki."

"Can't you just leave me alone, la? I don't want to talk about it."

• • • • •

"Get over it, kathoey bitch." Wan-Lo rips the wool watch cap off her head. Her long Rasta braids now a tangled nest. She tries to brush them out of her eyes, but her hands are still bound at the wrists with duct tape. She doesn't need clear vision to see she's hostage to fucking Sunny Janluechai.

When he drags her to her feet in the back of the rented van, he sniffs the air, smells the urine.

"You piss self."

She almost asks him what's he expect, her tied in the back of a van all night, driving from Atlantic City to who knows where. But her ear continues ringing from that crack he gave her to the head back in Atlantic City, and she doesn't want another. She just blinks at the morning sky, a pale sun, tries to stretch the hem of her little black dress as far down on her thighs as she can with her hands bound. The late-October air makes her shiver.

"So long New York City. Sayanora Saigon Princess. Say hello to Cape Cod, dragon girl." He pushes her out of the van into a parking lot behind what must be a restaurant.

She can smell duck sauce and rice vinegar going rancid in the garbage cans. Sees a fat man smiling at her. He's wearing a dirty chef's apron. Looking like one of the Chinese Thais from the provinces south of Bangkok.

"That niggerboy, René, blown to bits. All gone," says Sunny. "You got new master now.

She pictures a shadow jumping out of a bush, bashing René with the butt of a pistol. His great, James-Earl-Jones body deflating, collapsing onto the dark walk.

The pig in the apron smiles, rubs his crotch with two plump hands.

"Now you say very please meet you to Mister Wan-Lo."

"Si so hai khwai fang."

"What, bitch?" He hits her. Palm of the hand to the heel of her jaw. Her head going up in flames.

"Nothing." She does not say again that she will not play the fiddle for the water buffalo, not cast pearls to a swine. Her voice is gone. Too bad. She has an odd feeling that she could say whatever she wants. They have gone to a lot of trouble to bring her here, don't want to kill her. Not yet anyway.

"Come to daddy," says Wan-Lo. He opens his arms, pulls her against his rolls of blubber. She smells his sweat, overflowing with the tart odor of garlic, the woody, sweet scent of opium.

What can she do but melt into his flesh, lower her forehead to his chest.

"See, Wan-Lo like you, baby. I think he take good care you while we negotiate with Mr. Thaksin Kittikachorn. He gone pay lot for you. Why he want you so bad, Tuki Aparecio?"

She says nothing, thinks of the way Prem felt when he hugged her, his tight, muscular embrace. So different from this pig's.

"You fucking with his boy, yeah?"

"He left me." She sees the River House ablaze. The walls, the windows, first. Then the roof. Finally the broad deck on stilts flaring, collapsing into the klong with a hiss.

"Maybe he want you back."

"She my girl now," says Wan-Lo. Squeezes her. "Right honey. You Wan-Lo's little kitchen dragon."

Nam ron pla pen, nam yen pla tai, she thinks. In hot water the fish lives, in cold water the fish dies.

36

HE'S STANDING at Packer's Wharf in Vineyard Haven with a stone the size of Nantucket in his chest, when the *Rosa Lee* edges alongside.

"Jesus," says Tio Tommy, tossing a bowline from the foredeck, "What the hell happened to you, Mo?"

His father backs the trawler down, stops her. Comes out of the wheelhouse, heaves the forward spring line, the stern line, to his son. "*Cristo*, you look worse than when you got off that plane a week ago."

"You think I don't know that?" He's already regretting having called his father's cell, busting up the *Rosa Lee*'s trip, for this fool's errand. Should have known that when an only son with a stone in his chest, a torn note in his voice, calls a man like Caesar Decastro, the old man's going to haul his net, come running full-steam ahead.

"Where's your skinny girlfriend?"

"I don't know now."

"Oh, Christ, here we go again." His father ducks back into the wheelhouse, shuts down the fish boat's big Caterpillar.

"We needed a break from each other."

"This is why you called me, buddy boy? This is why Tommy and me quit on a slammer set of cod and steamed in here?"

"I'm sorry, ok?"

"The way you was talking, I thought someone tried to kill you or something."

"I kind of feel like that."

"How many times have I told you, you got to stop with this lawyering? Got to stop the Clark Kent stuff? You aren't cut out for it."

"Dad."

"These Lois Lane types are poison to you, buddy! Look what happened last time. That poor Indian girl ended up with a bullet in—"

"Don't. Please."

"I begged you not to go flying off to Bangkok after this one. My god, a drag queen. A—"

"Look, we went through this about six times last week at Tio Tommy's house. She's as much a woman as Mom was. So can we just stop with the judgments?"

"Then talk to me."

He drops down onto the boat from the wharf. His beard hair almost as dark and long as the hair on his head. Face sweat-soaked, dirty. Puffy eyes. Rumpled clothes.

"Why do you look like you been sleeping in the fishhold? What did that dolly do to you?"

"Her name's Tuki, ok?"

"Give me the bloody details."

"I left her at the Daniel Webster Inn. She rented a room."

"In Sandwich village?"

"Yeah. She started acting kind of crazy yesterday. And she was sick to her stomach. Said she needed to be alone for awhile."

"Her dad's with her?"

"Far as I know. I just kind of left them there. With my jeep and everything."

"What?"

"I got on those railroad tracks and walked. I walked the whole way down to Falmouth. Then I kept going on the bike trail to Woods Hole."

"*Cristo*, kid."

"It took me all night."

"That's like twenty-five miles. More."

"I knew I was in trouble when I found myself on the ferry to the Vineyard and had no memory of ever getting on. No idea why I was going to the Vineyard."

"Maybe this isn't just about Tuki. You ever think of that?"

He settles to the deck next to the winch and puts his head in his hands.

"I'm in love with her."

"That's what you said about the other one, too. The Indian girl."

"I can't stop thinking about death. I picture it. With my eyes wide open."

"I've been afraid this was coming."

• • • • •

He remembers a year ago.

Cape Cod Hospital, Hyannis. He's lying in a bed. His dad there. Not crying now. A frozen look on his face. The look he gets when the Rosa Lee *is just about on the fishing grounds. When he's staring at his fish finder, deciding exactly where he wants to set-out for the first haul.*

"Is she dead, Dad?"

"She never regained consciousness ... I'm sorry, son."

His father was talking about Awasha Patterson. Awasha the brave. Awasha who threw herself in front of a bullet to save him. Awasha the troubled. Awasha who held his heart for that short spring. Whispered to it in the language of the ancient Wampanoags. Made love to him in a bait shack.

The wind's up, churning the waves. Lifting strands of black hair off her back. She stands in the bright sun balancing on jagged granite ... in her yellow fleece pullover and jeans. Petite, almost anorexic, except for full breasts. Eyes set on the horizon. In the land of Maushop. Indian land. Aquinnah ...

A convulsion starts to rise in his chest. He feels his mother Maria.

She's taking his hand, hugging him as they stand in the shadow of the band concert gazebo on this late-October day in Chatham. The leaves in the little park a faded yellow, red, brown.

She's pale, thin. Almost as thin as Tuki. When did she lose the weight? All his life she has been an earth mother with soft caramel skin. Wild, black curls, sparkling brown eyes, a laugh that rolls through a crowd and makes everyone smile. A woman whose royalty roots in her capacity to make everyone around her feel safe and admired with the touch of her hand.

"The doctor says I have a cancer growing in my ovaries."

"Shit!"

"Yeah, really. Shit!"

The gulls swoop. Dive. Screeching.

"Are they dead, Dad?"

"I'm sorry, son."

Jesus. He sees them all. His mother. Awasha. Tuki. The women he's lost, he's loved. Sees them in flashes, flickers. In the dust sparkling, spreading in a mosaic caught by the sun's rays. Glossy black hair. Crimson lips. Cleopatra eyes. Women beckoning to him. Opening their mouths. Holding brilliant oval rubies the size of playing marbles on their tongues ... Then the flesh melts off their cheeks. Lips shrivel, disappear. Teeth, jaws crumble. Eyes fade to sockets. The ruby goes up in smoke.

"I wish Mom were here," he says.

His father stares out at the harbor, his eyes moist for his wife. Dead just weeks after her diagnosis, sixteen months gone. "She would know what to say."

"You think you could lend me a gun?"

37

SHE FINALLY tosses out her pride, calls his cell. Catches him over breakfast at the Art Cliff Diner in Vineyard Haven.

She says she's been praying for two days. But it's not working. She still feels sick, something sour in her belly. Says she's really lost her focus. Knows she needs to try to find the ruby and get it back to the Thai people. Get all this bad karma off her back and Prem's, too. But she can't stop thinking about killing somebody. And she's a thousand times sorry. Sorry for everything. She needs him. Can't live without him. Loves him. She swears to Buddha. *Don't be mad. Please come back from the Vineyard.*

Please help me.

Her father has disappeared again. With the Jeep. Said there's something he has to do, and she thinks he's going to try getting revenge for her on Sunny and others. Because she told Aparecio about some horrible things he did to her. Especially a bastard she knows named Wan-Lo. Right here on the Cape. Her *bpaa* doesn't have a cell phone. Definitely not a good thing. She's afraid for him. Afraid for them all. *Please, Michael. Please come, la. My head is way down the serpent's throat.*

She hears the clinking of silverware on china. Pictures him glaring at his omelet, wishing he were already out fishing.

"Do you remember Lou Votolatto?" he says.

"The detective who almost got me killed?"

"The cop who cleared you of murder in Provincetown."

"He used to call me *Lollypop*."

"Maybe he can help us."

"No police, Michael. Promise."

"I'm going to have to rent a car somewhere."

She thinks of a song she used to sing onstage back in Bangkok, her diva phase. "Get Here" by Oleta Adams. The song that was running through her head when she sent the email months ago begging him to come to Bangkok. The song running now. "I don't care how you get here ..." *I need you right here. Right now. By my side …*

"Hold on."

"I'm really scared."

"I'm coming."

"Help me find my *bpaa*. He only thinks he knows what he's dealing with."

"What's that supposed to mean?"

"There are things I should have told you."

• • • • •

Sunset. Hardings Beach, South Chatham. Late May. Nobody else is here but the seagulls. She feels the bastard's immense arms, pulling her from behind against his fat belly, legs. His slick sweat oiling her bare rump, his fingers rubbing the insides of her thighs, her secret places. Just as they have three times a week for almost eight months. His breath heavy with fried pork, Sriratcha chili sauce, basil, opium.

"Smoke." He slides the hard, bitter tip of the little opium pipe between her lips. "Smoke, little kitchen dragon."

Little kitchen dragon. This is what he calls her. Since Sunny left her here last October, she's been Wan-Lo's slave. The noodle girl in the kitchen of Bangkok Dragons, the living ghost in the Asian take-out joint by the bridge in Bass River. West Yarmouth. The strange little kathoey *with the vagina.*

She's the one who sleeps chained to a cot in the basement of the restaurant. The one he sometimes takes back to his house in East Dennis, binds to his bed with purple velvet cords. The one he makes lie there beside him with a .38 cocked at her temple.

He has a cheap sleeping bag spread out on the beach. Lies here like Jabba the Hut, she thinks, with his shirt open, pants down. Prick weeping semen against the backs of her legs. She can tell he's getting bored with her. Has fucked her so many times in so many ways, nothing is novel. Nothing humiliates her now that she has begun to smoke the lavender serpent with him.

So this is the new kick he's trying, now that spring is in full bloom, the weather warm. Sex on the beach. He brings her out here to this empty beach in Chatham, gets her stoned. Strips her naked, fondles her tiny body. Makes her suck him while he watches the sun slip into Nantucket Sound. It's cold, messy. The sand blows on her. And he won't let her bathe for days afterwards.

What else can she do but inhale the serpent, close her eyes, and do the deed for the fat bastard, for Wan-Lo. Cape Cod restaurateur extraordinaire. *While she dreams of Prem. Pretends he's still her man, here with her by the water. Not the cowardly river lion, lost somewhere in* Krung Thep. *In Bangkok, with his wife and babies. Not the son of the man who has put a price on her head. Not the oldest child of the man Sunny seems to have been teasing with ever-more-expensive price tags on Tuki's soul. For months and months. Not the* pung chao *addict who will never come to save her before Sunny, Wan-Lo and Thaksin Kittikachorn tire of this hostage game. Before she leaves this Earth.*

"More smoke, la," *she says.*

He pushes her head between his sumo legs. "Smoke me, baby."

A prayer coils through her mind. The words chanting. All that we are is what we have thought ... *She squeezes her eyes tight, asks Buddha what terrible things has she done and thought to wither like this. So totally alone. Maybe it will bring more misery on her, but right now she's thinking murder. First, this fat bastard, then Sunny. After that maybe she's going to find the wench he works for. Robsulee. The name. That one. The name she tried to block out of her mind, to call a coincidence, when she heard Sunny saying Robsulee during his shakedown back in New York. The one Prem* called to in his pung chao *dream, the name he whispered once when they were making love.*

Maybe the same Robsulee who calls Wan-Lo every Thursday at Bangkok Dragons. Maybe that's who she kills, too.

It is not the Buddha's way. But the Buddha was never raped three times a week for eight-and-a-half lunar months. She wants to exterminate them all. The only questions are how and when and where.

38

IT'S MAYBE an hour before sunset when they roll up to the wind-mill-shaped restaurant by the bridge. The summer traffic crawling along Route 28. A gaggle of kayakers paddling in Bass River.

"You think your dad's here?"

"I hope we're not too late."

"This is really the place?"

"You think I could forget?" Her voice has a low, angry note.

He looks at the windmill, can hardly picture it as her prison, her torture chamber. It was a fudge shop the last time he drove this way. That must have been back in his law school days when he went on a pub crawl of the Mid-Cape with some buddies. It's not your typical replica Cape windmill, not gray cedar shingles. This one is a bright, shiny red, green trim, golden roof. He's surprised the West Yarmouth Zoning Board permits such flamboyance.

The sign at the entrance to the parking lot says **BANGKOK DRAGONS, Thai & Chinese Cooking** in carved, red letters. A mix of local pick-up trucks and vacationing SUVs fill the parking lot. There's a line of folks at the take-out window, more people eating out of Styrofoam boxes at picnic tables off to the side, over-looking the river, now a mottled maze of darkening shadows stretching off the western shore.

"Here's where they held you hostage, the windmill?"

She closes her eyes, bites her lower lip, feel fingernails scraping the inside of her stomach again. "This is really hard for me, la."

He stops the rental Honda in a parking space, looks at her for a minute while her lids are closed. Her shaved brows have grown back with angular, fetching arcs. Her hair now a thick, black teddybear. Hip, edgy. She's wearing subtle eye shadow, eye liner. Her lips a crimson gloss. Jade pendants dangling from her ears. Breasts swelling smartly beneath the charcoal tanktop. Nails long, sharp, glossy black. She's back from the land of Buddha. No more holy-man disguises. Pure woman. Hollywood. Charlie's Angel. Ready for prime time. With a flask of mace ... and his father's service pistol, a .45 automatic, stashed in her handbag.

She opens her eyes, blinks to refocus herself.

"I don't think your father's here."

"Why?"

"I don't see my jeep."

"Wan-Lo's car, either. He always parks by the kitchen door."

"What kind of car?"

"Pink Cadillac."

"I should have guessed."

"He thinks he's a rock star."

"Now what?"

"This is going to be hard for me, la."

"What?"

"We have to look at Wan-Lo's house."

"What makes you think Marcus will be there?"

"Because back at the hotel, when I was feeling crazy, I told him that Wan-Lo is the key to the puzzle."

"To get the ruby back?"

She shakes her head. It's more than just the ruby. She's already told him this. Especially for her father. Especially now that he knows how Sunny and Wan-Lo held her hostage at the Bangkok Dragons. How Wan-Lo tortured her. The Heart of Warriors is just a prop, a clue. A bonus.

Finally, he thinks he gets the big picture here. Following the trail of the ruby will lead them to the people behind the killing of Thaksin Kittikachorn, lead them to Sunny Janluechai, this pig named Wan-Lo. Possibly. And others he can't even imagine yet. A shadow in a green satin jacket. The people who shot Varat Samset. The people who marked them all for death on that fishing boat off Changi Airport. There's a gang at work here, Thai mafia. *Nak-lin. Jao pho,* godfathers who must be exposed, brought to justice.

"No, Michael. Not exposed. Not brought to justice. Killed. Slaughtered!"

Her words rattle in his head. He's never heard such bitterness from her before.

"Is this about reprisal now?"

"What is reprisal?"

"Getting even, squaring accounts, settling old scores. Revenge."

"I already told you. Since I came back to Cape Cod, I can't stop thinking about killing."

"What about returning the ruby? What about cleansing yourself and Prem's spirit of bad karma?"

"*Wan phra mai hon dieo.*"

"What?"

"Every dog will have his day."

"Maybe you should give me that gun back."

• • • • •

He sees the jeep, his green Wrangler with the mangled fender, the gashed left side-panels, up ahead. The jeep is pulled off to the side of this back road leading alongside a pond in Dennis. The sun is down now. A violet dusk is settling over Cape Cod. The pines and oaks, the pond-side houses, the docks, the water fading to shadows as he drives by the jeep. He keeps going until he spots a dirt road leading into the woods.

"This is it," she says. "I remember. Motherfucker."

Her swearing grates against something beneath the heels of his jaw, under his back teeth. He doesn't like it. The swearing's not like her. Not like his Cinderella. He feels the left pocket to make sure he has the .45, to make sure that she can't go off half-cocked with lethal force at her finger tips.

When he's a couple hundred yards past the dirt road, he pulls the Honda into a cluster of scrub pines.

"There's a trail along the pond," she says, leads him to a path.

It's really dark now. He does not have a flashlight, could not see the trail through the pines, except for the lights glowing from Wan-Lo's house. The other houses around the pond have specks of dull light glowing from a window here and there, but Wan-Lo's place seems to have every light lit, inside and outside. As if beckoning, signaling. Maybe to Tuki and him. Or maybe the *nak-lin*.

From a hundred yards away he can see that this is a modern saltbox, two-car garage attached. Upscale but a little over the top, like the pink caddie parked out front. There's an orange-and-blue-lit fountain spewing into a reflecting pool, a geyser soaking golden statues of mermaids in the midst of the driveway circle. Music is drifting softly from the open windows. Marvin Gaye singing "Let's Get It On," blending with the gentle splashing of the fountain. Oddly peaceful.

"It's time to face the crocodile, la."

He pictures Bangkok.

There's a black Cigarette boat, tucked between a raft of houseboats tied up at a wharf just short of the place where an expressway bridge spans the klong. Opposite the wharf across the narrow canal he can see a waterfront restaurant, its floating docks for water taxis, longtails. Candles flicker from the tables on the open deck built over the water on stilts.

"This could be a trap ... like the last time."

"I don't think so."

"Why?"

"That's not Wan-Lo's music. It's my *bpaa*'s, la."

She says this is her father's way of signaling her that he's here. All is well. Wan-Lo is addicted to Elvis. But for her father, it's all about Marvin Gaye. He's got every version of every song Marvin Gaye ever sang on the iPod he bought in New Bedford. And the man must be driving Wan-Lo's sound system from the iPod right now. Somehow knows that she and Michael are coming.

"So you want to walk right up to the front door and knock?"

She squeezes his hand. "Maybe you better go. Give me the gun. If Wan-Lo answers the door—if he even twitches, la—I'll blow the fat piece of shit away."

"Maybe there's a better way," he says.

But she has already grabbed the gun from his pocket.

39

SHE CAN'T HELP IT. She likes the feel of racking the .45 and shoving it in the fat bastard's mouth. Until he gags. Until someone else knows what it's like to have a sickness, a terror, an alien something inside you clawing to get out.

She's so twitchy she almost shot her father when he came to the door looking *ninja* in his black watch cap, black turtleneck, black pants, black sneakers. And it seems the dude has been making himself at home. Having a cigar and a glass of scotch. As if he always knew that Tuki and Michael would track him down through a process of elimination.

Now they're all in the large master bathroom on the second floor. Marcus, Michael, her. And Wan-Lo. Her father has hog-tied him with extension cords, hands and feet behind his back. He's lying on his side in the big green spa tub. His neck straining to keep his head above water. His clothes are still on. He's shivering—the water's that cold.

"Do you know what this bastard did to me?" She turns to her father, to Michael.

They look at her with odd, helpless looks. Like maybe they don't want to know all the dirty details. Can't know. Will never know. Even though she has already told them. Has been unpacking her heart to them for the last half hour ... She sees that now her stories have given her all the power. They are just witnesses. Freaking out almost as much as the scumbag in the tub.

"You want to die now, la?" She's five inches from his face, screaming.

His breath stinks of fish sauce and garlic. "You want to fuck me, love? You want to spread your ass for me one more time before we die?"

She pulls the gun out of his mouth.

He gives her a little smile. "*Kathoey saloey.* I thought you were dead. What happened to your hair?"

"Where's Sunny, you fat, fucking piece of *gioza.* You dumpling."

"You tell me. That little prick owes me money."

She tries to pull away. But he has her from behind. One arm around her neck. The other under the waistband of her skirt, probing with fat fingers.

Something's stretching to the breaking point behind her eyes. She rams the gun back down his throat. "Can I kill him?"

Her father has his fingers pressed to his mouth as if he's praying, thinking. Watching Michael, whose cheeks, lips, have gone pale. His eyes sad, glazed. Clueless.

"Can I?"

"Fuck it," says her father. "After what he ... You have every right."

"No." Michael comes out of his trance. "Ask him about the woman."

He yanks, tears the mini off her hips, tears her thong. "Bend over, bitch!"

She can feel her fingers tightening on the pistol.

He's doubling her over the large stainless steel stove, her cheeks inches away from a back burner, its blue flames hissing ...

"What?"

She can see Michael trying to find the words, his fist actually pounding against his forehead, jaw slacking.

He knots her hair in his hands, pushes her face toward the flames. She squeezes her eyes shut, braces for his thrust.

"Tuki."

She opens her eyes.

"Tuki." His voice. Her knight's voice. Her man's. Shrill. But from another planet. "Tuki. That woman. The name. Ask him."

The name. The name of Sunny's boss in New York. The name from Prem's pung chao *dream, the one he whispered when they were making love. The one who was calling Wan-Lo every Thursday.*

She pulls the pistol out of his mouth, jams it against the bridge of his nose. "Where's Robsulee, you dung beetle?"

"Provincetown."

She feels something starting to tear deep inside, a rift rupturing right beneath her lungs. Imagines him pushing her face toward his sumo legs as the sun sets over Nantucket Sound. Feels herself gagging. The dry heaves rising again.

"Smoke me, la," she says. Thrusts the barrel of the gun back in his mouth. Pulls the trigger.

On the empty chamber.

"Provincetown Follies," says Wan-Lo again. This time garbled, muted by the gun in the mouth ... just before she squeezes the trigger again.

• • • • •

When the fat bastard has sexed himself to sleep, when he's facedown in his drool, lost in his opium dream, she breathes deep, tries to clear the lavender serpent from her lungs, knows that it is now or never that she makes her move. Whatever ransom negotiations for her that were unfolding between Sunny Janluechai, the mysterious Robsulee and Thaksin Kittikachorn seem to have broken down. Wan-Lo has grown tired of warehousing her, fucking her. And now he and Sunny have begun to hassle her about the Heart of Warriors. They know about the stone. And they want it, la. It's just a matter of days before they beat its location out of her. Tuki's time left on Earth is short.

But she's not ready to die yet. She believes the Buddha has plans for her. She has songs to sing. She has a stolen ruby, big as a fish's eye. But first she has to get out from under this pig on the king bed. It's not easy. Not with her wrists bound by velvet cord to the slats in the headboard. Not with the barrel of the snub-nosed pistol in his hand hard against her temple. She prays to the Buddha to make her like a snake. Slick, invisible, silent. Repeats this mantra again and again. Slick, invisible, silent. Until she has nosed the gun away from her face, pushed it out of his hand with her tongue, teeth, chin.

And now she's the snake, making herself thin as a blade of grass, sliding on her belly from beneath his steaming hulk. When her legs, hips, back, shoulders are clear, she slithers toward the headboard until she can taste the cord binding her right wrist. She pulls at the knot with her teeth.

He stirs, moans, flails an arm.

She lies still, chanting the mantra in her head. Slick, invisible, silent. It seems like hours before she feels safe to move. Slowly, she starts again on the knot at her wrist with her teeth. Feels, at last, a loosening. Tugs. When her wrist is free she tears at the knot on her other wrist. Now teeth and free hand working together.

He stirs again. Says her name, feels for her.

She slides against him, forces her lips and tongue to nuzzle the folds of his neck … until his breathing eases, his heart slows, he snores.

Then she rolls out of bed. Runs. Runs like the typhoon winds. Out of the bedroom, down the stairs, into the driveway where the absurd fountain is doing its thing with the mermaids. She's still naked when she slides into the driver's seat of his Caddie. A bundle of clothes in her arms, the night receipts from the Dragons clutched in one hand. The ignition key in the other. The Heart of Warriors scratching her rectum. Snatched—at last—from where she hid it in plain view for more than eight months. Stuck with chewing gum in the belly button of the statue of Buddha on a shelf behind the cash register.

The first glow of sunrise lights the way as she eases the car down the driveway, finds the main road, heads for the Hyannis Mall.

At ten she's standing at the front door to Macy's when it opens.

By noon she's on the midday bus to Provincetown, looking for all the world like Janet Jackson. With four suitcases full of every dress, shoe, wig, costume jewel that a diva's heart could desire. Like she's starting over, la. She heard the queens back in New York say that Provincetown in the summer is Mecca for a showgirl. There's this amazing drag theatre called

Provincetown Follies that looks like a castle made of wood. So here she comes. A new town, a new look. Ready for the stage again. And maybe, for the first time in years, she'll find someone to help her feel safe, do something with this ruby ... and take her mind off revenge.

Fat chance.

40

HE has been thanking *Sao Joao o Baptista* for hours that there were no bullets in the .45, that his father forgot to tell him the clip was empty. And he forgot to check.

Que merda, what shit, as Tio Tommy says. But at least no one new is dead. Yet. Tuki's not a killer. The fat guy was still tied up in the tub blubbering and weeping—the water mercifully drained out now—when the three of them took off in two cars for an Orleans' motel. After ripping out the sparkplug wires on the Caddy.

Now it's almost midnight and her father, in his weird black threads, is unpacking a duffle bag full of weapons that they stole from Wan-Lo onto the motel bed. Michael feels dull, scraping pains rising out of his belly, burning through the muscles in his lower back, chest. Morphing into a white-hot jet of flames under his scalp.

"Sawed-off 12-gauge, two Uzis, couple of little Walthers, M-16, snub-nose police special, banana clips, a shit-load of ammo. And check out this relic." Marcus waves a long-barreled pistol in the air, sites down its barrel at a table lamp. The gun looks like a six-shooter out of *The Good, the Bad and the Ugly*.

"What's that?"

"A .44 magnum target pistol. Wan-Lo was prepared for the apocalypse."

He knows the gun laws, has defended a dozen illegal-possession-of-a-firearm cases as a public defender. There's enough contraband here to put Wan-Lo in jail for about twenty years. He says they could take the weapons back to the house in Dennis, stash them in the trunk of the Caddy, call this state cop he knows to make the bust on Wan-Lo.

"We're way past cops," says her father. "You want another chicken-shit mess like we had overseas? Tuki's still technically a fugitive in Thailand, right? You think your cop buddy won't run an Interpol check on her? And didn't she leave here with unfinished business two years ago?"

He gets up, walks to the vanity, opens one of the small bottles of water that came with the room. Downs it in one gulp, hoping to cool the blow torch searing the roots of his hair, his cortex … All it does is give him gas.

"What do you want to do, Tuki? You know Lou Votolatto. He's a good cop. He can help us. Vigilante justice never works. People get killed."

Awasha's bleeding out on the floor. Three EMTs pressing enormous gauze pads to her right cheek, chest.

She sits on the beige carpet, lotus position, back against the wall. Has said almost nothing since she pulled the trigger twice on Wan-Lo. And spit in his face.

"Tuki?"

She opens her eyes. They look black, glazed. Tearing. But on fire.

He wonders what terror she's reliving, whether her silent prayers to the Buddha are helping at all. Can't even imagine. He's too sick with Awasha's blood on his hands, too scared Tuki's sailing beyond his reach, his heart.

"Let me call Lou … please."

She closes her eyes again, resumes chanting in Thai.

Her father takes her hand. "We have to go to Provincetown and end this thing ourselves. This is our chance. It won't come again. As soon as Wan-Lo can get to a phone, we're dead. You know that? You want to watch Michael die?"

"That's not fair. *Cristo*, Marcus," he says. "Are you crazy? *Violencia gera violencia*."

"What?"

It's a lesson his mind has suddenly dredged up from his altar boy days. "Violence begets violence."

Her father jumps to his feet, does some sort of weird move like Bruce Lee in a ninja film. Then he grabs the sawed-off 12-gauge, pumps a shell into the chamber, points the weapon at Michael.

"Maybe you better go. This is family business. It has nothing to do with you."

The roots of his hair flare. "Are you actually pointing a gun at me?"

"Tuki and I have to handle this our own way, Michael."

"Jesus Christ, put the damn gun down. This has everything to do with me. You think I flew halfway around the world and back, nearly got myself killed a half-dozen times, for what? A lark?"

"This is personal. You heard what that fat pig did to Tuki."

"Weren't you listening a minute ago? We can send him to jail forever."

"That won't stop anything."

"Let Wan-Lo rat on his friends. Let the law put the bite on our pal Sunny and whoever it is he works for—this Robsulee person."

Marcus holds the shotgun, but settles onto one of the twin beds. His large, thin frame sagging, a sad look in his eyes.

Michael's in the middle of the room, pacing. "Trust me. Lou Votolatto's a magician. If anyone can shut down this *nak-lin* operation, he's the man. Get off this revenge kick, will you? Tuki, tell him."

She remains in the lotus position on the floor, has not opened her eyes, her lips moving silently. Maybe she hasn't even been listening.

"Tuki."

She opens her eyes. "You still don't understand, Michael."

"What?"

"Sunny tried to blow my *bpaa* up ... And Robsulee was the one who sent him."

"Are you talking about Atlantic City?"

"It was a terrible night."

"I thought that was some guy named René."

"I was René," says Marcus, "for about thirty-five years.

"What?"

He says René Parish is the alias he took when he went back to Nam to start his bar the Black Cat. The entertainment business in Saigon, 1968, was dicy, full of hustlers, gangsters, CIA-types. Everybody working an angle. Nobody using his real name because he knew that someday, when he got way, WAY clear of Vietnam and the rackets, he might want a clean slate. Only Tuki's mother knew René's real name, used it on Tuki's birth certificate to assure her daughter legal U.S. citizenship. Sometime right before Saigon fell, Misty must have told her secret to Brandy and Delta.

"Everybody called me René or Boo back then … and I just hung on to the name. Saw no reason to go back to Marcus. That is until Sunnyboy tried to kill me."

Michael is experiencing something like a sudden loss of cabin pressure. "You were the restaurant guy in New York where Tuki …?"

"The Saigon Princess was my baby … My little piece of paradise when Tuki dropped in out of the blue."

"You knew all along she was your daughter?"

"She came with a letter from Brandy and Delta."

"But you didn't tell her, didn't show her the letter?"

"It was safer that she didn't know."

"I don't understand."

"I had a bit of a gambling problem."

Marcus says he was into the *nak-lin* for quite a bit of money. Into Robsulee. She controlled the streets north of Hester in Chinatown. Somehow Robsulee found out that a rich Thai in Bangkok named Thaksin Kittikachorn was offering a lot of money to anyone who could find Tuki. With the help of her enforcer Sunny, she traced Tuki to the Saigon Princess. The squat, little bastard started shaking him down for ten grand a month. After he missed several payments, Sunny put the hammer down. Tried to blow him up at his beach house in Atlantic City. Kidnapped Tuki.

"So you played dead for awhile to shake the heat, to make Sunny think you were dead. Resurfaced as Marcus Aparecio."

Tuki stirs. "After that terrible summer in Provincetown … I finally found him, found my father. He called me in the hospital."

"You've been on the run from Sunny and Robsulee ever since? They chased you all over the planet. For blood money."

"And the ruby," she says.

"But they have the stone now. So?"

"Like I've been saying, Michael. This is personal."

"Why?"

She gives him a dark, wet look. "I just know it is, ok, la?"

"How?"

She fishes in the pocket of her shorts and pulls out a tiny leather change purse. Inside is a small, laminated color photograph. Looks to have been an image downloaded from a computer. Tuki is standing beside a black Benz limo, looking like a glamorous teenager dressed in a golden shantung silk sheath with a Nehru collar. Pumps to match. Hair up off her neck in a French roll. And next to her a tall, thin Thai male, hair slicked back. Tan suit and denim button-down shirt open at the neck.

Written on the back in red ink, gouged into the laminate, are the words, "I'll see you both in Hell."

"What's this?"

"It's a picture of Prem and me. Our first date. Bangkok, early nineties. Seems like another life."

"Where did you get it?"

"Sunny came to the Dragons the night before I escaped, started asking me about the ruby. I told him I didn't know anything. That's when he gave me this picture. He said, "From Robsulee. Read it and weep." Then he pointed his finger at me and pulled the trigger."

"Where did Robsulee get this picture?"

"It was Prem's. His driver took it."

"Robsulee knew your ex?"

"I don't know … maybe. I think."

"When were you going to tell me about this?"

She says she didn't think it was important. It was all a long time ago in Bangkok, Prem called out "Robsulee." Tuki didn't know what he was talking about. Didn't even know Robsulee was a name. Prem was really high on *pung chao*.

He sits down on the floor next to her, leans his back against the wall, head sizzling, starting to fill with smoke.

"So was it her who wrote the inscription? She's threatening you?"

"That's what I've been asking the Buddha."

"And?"

"I think she must have known about me and Prem for a long time. I think she was in no hurry to destroy me. Maybe she liked knowing that Wan-Lo was making me suffer."

"Now what?"

"I have to find her, la. Before she finds me."

"Why?"

Her eyes drift to the twin bed covered with the arsenal confiscated from Wan-Lo's. "I think I'm going to need all of those guns."

"This is not what I meant back in Thailand when I said we needed to go on the offensive."

"*Mai dai duai monk o ao duai khatha.* If you can't get it by prayer, Michael, you must use a spell."

He feels the top of his head sputter, crackle. Then burst into flame. He squeezes his eyes shut, pushes back the waves in his head, watches the fire racing through his lids, red-and-gold rockets.

It's happening again. His friend, his love, saying goodbye with her eyes. Sinking into a trance. Walking right into the bullets. And him feeling the need to bark until his voice is gone.

He gets up off the floor, reeling from the bonfire that used to be his brain. Wants to touch her cheek. But holds back. It's only a sad and lovely mask after all. She's already chosen, opted for the fight. Not him, not them. Not life. Not now. Like that night she just plain disappeared from Provincetown. He's sure there's much more darkness he doesn't know about her life, especially from two years ago here on the Cape. Even though he was her lawyer. *Cristo!*

"Count me out of this."

He opens the door to the motel room, walks out. Sparks flying off his eyes, his ears, into the night. His throat already raw as the howling starts. To hell with Sunny. To hell with the *nak-lin*. To hell with a phantom in a green jacket. He really needs to go fishing … or talk to the cops.

41

ON THE WAY to P-town in the rental car, she feels the sudden urge to heave again. Makes her father pull off to the side of Route 6 in Truro, vomits her yogurt and peach breakfast into the bushes outside a dry cleaners.

When she gets back into the car, she wipes her lips on her forearm, sticks a piece of Dentyne in her mouth, says she wants to see the National Seashore. Wants to see the lighthouse called Highland Light.

He drives, following the signs to the lighthouse that point off onto a side road. Weird old dude in the black turtleneck, black pants. Clothes she has never seen before last night. But something about the look seems vaguely familiar. Like some hep jazzman in one of the clubs they used to go to in Atlantic City or New York. Or something more sinister. After he stops the car in the lighthouse parking lot, he tugs unconsciously at the collar of his turtleneck. Trying to let some heat escape from his shoulders and chest. He stares out into the fog from the lighthouse parking lot. Visibility is down to about a hundred feet. The lighthouse tower just a dark gray shadow in the milky air, fog horn bleating out into the murk.

"What's this all about?"

"I don't know, la." She opens the door to the car. "I want to walk."

"We could do that in Provincetown."

"I need to be alone, *Bpaa*. I need to ask the Buddha what is happening to me, ok?"

"Are you getting cold feet?"

"Sometimes I just need to listen to the ocean … and think about things."

"We have to do this. End this. There's no turning back."

"What if Michael's right, what if this is all a huge mistake?"

"Have you forgotten what these people can do?"

"I've been thinking about the last time I was at the Follies," she says as she gets out of the car and starts down the foggy trail toward the sound of the surf. Claws in her heart. "Thinking about singing … and you … and Vietnam … and my mother … and Michael. What if I've lost him?"

· · · · ·

It feels like the summer of 1966. A hot time in the Mekong Delta. Smokey Robinson and the Supremes ooze from the bars around Dong Koi Street in Saigon. Her mother is still a schoolgirl in Cholon when Radio Vietnam introduces the Isley Brothers, the new soldiers' anthem—a special favorite for all the brothers out there like Marcus Aparecio. The song is "This Old Heart of Mine." What a tune! It is all about getting kicked in the teeth by love … and getting up … to love again. Violins backing up the Holland, Dozier, and Holland piano-of-soul. The song winds up like a merry-go-round ride.

It is the perfect song for a Saturday night of Labor Day weekend. For her last show at Provincetown Follies. Like the rest of the audience, she wants to believe that summer is not over. That summer and love will rise again. No stopping them. Just like the song.

And there is no stopping her. The girl in black makes her entrance through the curtained door, weaves among the café tables. Singing about crazy love, blind love. She holds the mic like a torch to her lips, as she struts and sings her way right to the back of the room for a duet of bump-and-

grind action with the light-and-sound kid, then back down among the tables to fall in love with a truck driver and his wife for a verse or two. Before the song wheels into its last cycle. As the crowd claps and sings along, she mounts the runway. She is free.

This is her time, her moment to strut the boards, singing, bending to kiss the customers, plucking their tips like flower petals. Head high, chest out, hips swinging ... a sexy little kid from Cholon. A Marine's fantasy, a pair of Patpong queens named Delta and Brandy, a boat baby, a fugitive. A case cracker. A caretaker of the stolen ruby. A child of Buddha. A ball of fire. A girl who wears her heart for everyone to see ... for a man she will never have.

For lots of reasons.

But first and foremost, la, because of the Thai bastard watching her from the shadows by the main door. Sunthorn Janluechai's wearing that slick brown bomber again, gold chains. The unconscious smirk on his lips as he watches her. Probably imagining how he's going to dispose of her body.

She wishes the scene would end here, the music stop, the lights go off, because she is feeling right with the night ... And ready to run from her life, ready to draw Sunny's heat away from Michael. But she cannot stop. The crowd is pumped and shouting for more. She knew this would happen.

Maybe the diva in her hoped it would. She gave the light-and-sound kid a fourth CD to play for her encore, for a closer. But when he looks at it, she is sure he is wondering what she was thinking when she picked this piece. "The Crying Game." It is so dark, so blue.

She is violating just about every rule of cabaret by bringing the audience down from their high with this encore ... but too late. She picked her poison. And now, for the first time, she finally sees Michael sitting out there in the audience at his table in the shadows. Smiling. All she can do is lock onto his big soft eyes, listen for the music. And make her exit with style. Do what she has to do.

So she begins. The red spotlight catches her sitting on a stool at the end of the bar. She is in with the downbeat, afraid of where this song will take her. The words flow. She sings that she knows all about the crying game, has had her share of the crying game ...

The backup is just a lounge piano, rhythm guitar, drumstick keeping time on a block of wood. Brushes on a snare drum. Like a lullaby. She is not even twelve bars into the number when her body starts thinking about sleep, beautiful sleep. She is really forcing now to get the notes out of her wrecked throat, a throat nearly torn to pieces by the same person who killed Al Caste-lano. Everyone and everything is getting hazy. The song is unraveling. And she is sitting on a stool with her back against the bar … paralyzed or something.

A video is doing a slow-mo waltz through her mind. She's dancing with her handsome young attorney, kissing his cheek in the moonlight.

Her voice tells the story. "First there were kisses … Then there were sighs …"

She doesn't want any more of the crying game. Her voice is shredding into a thousand pieces. Her eyes find Michael one more time. Her knees are going weak. But she's smiling like crazy. Thinking of Brandy and Delta just as the song fades. His sweet face fades.

Then the house goes black.

A minute later she is gone. Out the kitchen door. Heading for Nantucket and the heroin-ruined wreck of her lover from Bangkok. Blasting south on Route 6 in a car shanghaied from her boss. She knows now that she has to give Prem back the ruby, have him make his father return it to Ayutthaya for the sake of all of their souls. Hopes she can get to him before Sunny can pick up her trail.

42

"ARE YOU fucking crazy, Rambo? Help you? Again? Do you think I've got a death wish?"

State Police Detective Sergeant Lou Votolatto leans his elbows on the mahogany bar, glares at the half-empty glass of Sam Adams in front of him. Cups his nose between the fingers of both hands, blows into them. Shoots a side glance at the woman sitting on his left. She tilts her head back, uses a hand to flick her long, dark hair out of her eyes, stirs something into her coffee—a shot of rum maybe—and stares away. She could be midthirties but looks ten years younger. A babe in a charcoal suit.

"I'm on my knees, Lou." He spins on his barstool, cranes his neck to look out the window, catch a glimpse of Wellfleet Harbor.

Gulls diving, swirling, plucking the baitfish on the ebb tide. The water a flat sea, indigo in the setting sun. And him in here, getting a barroom tan, at yet another of the old cop's hideouts. It's under the dining room at a place named simply Bookstore & Restaurant. A cave called the Bombshelter.

"I thought you went back fishing after ..."

He gives the cop a look like *don't go there*. He doesn't want to think about the last time he came to Lou for help, doesn't want to see Awasha Patterson's blood all over the floor, all over his hands.

"I've been in Thailand for awhile. Singapore … and Malaysia."

"I heard it's nice there. Why the fuck didn't you stay?"

"Tuki's in trouble."

"Aw, Jesus. Here we go again."

"It's not like you think."

The cop cocks an eyebrow at him.

"She didn't kill anybody," says Michael.

"That dolly's really got you by the balls, doesn't she? Oh Christ. I can't even imagine what you got yourself into this time. Please don't tell me Miss Gay Bangkok 2000 is back on the Cape … and we are going to be dancing a tango around her immigration status again."

"She found her father. She's got her U.S. passport."

"Well there's some good news. What the hell's it say in the box for gender? M or F? Or BOTH."

"Come on, don't be like that."

The cop turns to the woman next to him. "You ever meet a palooka got a thing for a drag queen before?"

She tosses her long hair again, leans back on her stool so she can get a better look at Michael, scans him head-to-toe, back up again. "*Sí coño?*"

"That's Spanish, Rambo. Case you don't get it. It means something like *are you shitting me*. Right, my dear?"

The woman scrunches up her nose and shakes her head. "Not exactly."

"I know what it means," he says, nods to Votolatto. "Is this guy bothering you?"

"All the time." Her mouth spreads into a smile. "You want to kick his *culo* for me?"

"Yeah, you want to add assault-and-battery-on-a-police-officer to your rap sheet, Rambo?" Votolatto's smiling too, raises his hand to the bartender. Two fingers, points to the woman's cup and his glass. "You drinking, counselor?"

"You two know each other?"

She nods. "Unfortunately."

Votolatto slaps him on the back. "Take that sad look off your face and have a beer with us. Chill, boy. As of half-an-hour ago we've been off the state clock. Michael Decastro meet Corporal Yemanjá Colón, recently of San Juan, Puerto Rico. I'm teaching her the ropes of criminal investigation, right sweatheart?"

She rolls her eyes, then stretches out her hand to him. "So ... you're the guy from the Provincetown Follies case? *Encantada.*"

Her hand feels hard as iron in his fingers. Warm. "Don't believe everything Lou tells you," he says.

"He told me you have *cojones* ... and a heart the size of Portugal."

He lets go of her hand. "Right now it's breaking into a hundred pieces."

"The last time this happened that little half-breed petunia had you so tied in knots, most of the time you didn't know your ear from your asshole."

He says it's different now. Really different. Tuki had an operation. She's a woman. One hundred percent. And he's head-over-heels for her. The best thing he's ever felt. But this Thai gang has been trying to kill her, and now she's freaking out. She wants to run the table on the bad guys. And he's afraid he's going to lose her the way he lost ...

The detective cups his nose between the fingers of both hands again, blows into them. "I'm sorry, Rambo. You know, I really am. But leave me out of this."

"I can't."

"Why not?"

"There's a hurricane heading for Provincetown."

"Named Tuki Aparecio?" Yemanjá Colón's speaking.

"And her *bpaa*—her father. The guy's dressed all in black. And they've got a whole lot of guns."

Votolatto tosses back half his new beer. "First, pal, you're going to treat me and the *guapa* here to dinner upstairs. They've got some Portuguese stew to die for. Then you're going to tell us what the hell's really going on. Like are we dealing with a crime here … or some kind of little violence fantasy you're having, huh?"

"I feel like my head's on fire."

"When you get like this, the fucking sky starts falling in … in case you don't remember."

· · · · ·

It's not until they have followed the Porsche down a winding road near Wichmere Harbor in Harwichport, not until they see it stop in front of a shingled summer mansion, that he realizes he's in a driveway. And there's a car rolling up behind them, its quartz headlights glaring. Awasha can't turn her car around, or back up. Cristo!

The headlights sear them from behind.

"Jesus!"

Suddenly she starts to babble. She says she thinks she sees what is happening here. What has been happening ever since Christopher Columbus used the Caribs to supply his men with Arawak concubines. Since the Pilgrims enlisted the friendship and good will of her ancestor Massasoit, sachem of the Wamponaogs, her namesake Awashonks, squaw sachem of the Sakonnets … Only to hoist the head of Massasoit's son Metacomet on a pike to rot for years as a warning to bad Indians. Only to drive Awashonk's people from their homelands.

"Goddamn it!" she says.

"What?"

"If you know your friend Lou's number, now would be the time to call him."

"Why?"

"You ever heard of Wounded Knee?"

43

P-TOWN'S jamming this Tuesday evening. The summer crowd here in full force for the start of another season of Carnival in the Magic Queendom.

Caught in the traffic, the silver rental Honda crawls east down Commercial Sreet behind a horse-drawn carriage, following the parade on this foggy night. The neon buzzing, the dance tunes pumping from the open doors of boutiques, restaurants, erotic toy shops. The boys go hand-in-hand. The girls go hand-in-hand. The straights hold each other closer. Past the galleries, past the goths hanging out on the steps of Shop Therapy. Past the bikers drinking at the Old Colony, the day trippers buying fudge and T-shirts. The lesbian African drummers in front of the Portuguese Bakery.

Ahead, she sees the rambling Victorian hotel, the Painted Lady, dressed in greens and gold and lavender. The haunted-house turrets, the widow's walks that look out on Cape Cod Bay. The drag shows in the huge ballroom on the first floor. Just as she remembers it.

Almost.

When she left town almost two years ago, the sign in big letters at the top of the Provincetown Follies marquis read

TUKI APARECIO, DIVA EXTRAORDINAIRE! Now the sign says:

ROBSULEE, QUEEN OF SPADES
&
The Sensation Dolls—Feel The Love!

"Guess we found her, darlin'," says her *bpaa*.

"She's a queen?"

"Among other things."

She closes her eyes, tilts her head back against the seat. "Oh la. Why's this ho trying to ruin my life? Why?"

"Are you sure your gun is loaded?"

"I don't even know what she looks like."

"Picture Whitney Houston in *The Bodyguard*."

She chokes. Claws in the heart again.

"What's the matter?"

"That's how I used to look."

· · · · ·

"I'm scared," she says.

It's totally dark now. Thick fog is swirling in off the bay, turning the lights of Provincetown to a halo of gold, rose, violet in the sky. They sit in their parked car in the lot by the wharf. She's staring into the mirror on the sun visor, trying not to squint to see her face as she draws on eyeliner, thickening her brows with a pencil, fingers green color contacts onto her pupils. Her father's toking on a joint, sipping from a half-pint of Jim Beam. Still dressed like a cat burglar, black watch cap down low on his forehead.

"I wish Michael were here."

Marcus glares at her, looks like he's going to say something mean. Changes his mind. "Everything's going to be all right, baby. Trust me. Tonight's just recon."

"What is *recon*?"

"We go out there to get the lay of the land, see how the queen bee runs her hive."

"Then why do I have a gun in my pocket, la? Why are we dressed like this?"

He doesn't answer, looks at his watch. "You almost ready?"

She looks in the mirror, blends in the white foundation a little more around the corners of her eyes, her ears. Then she adjusts the Michael Jackson wig she bought an hour ago in a costume boutique ... along with a pair of black leather pants, cowboy boots, the motorcycle jacket she's wearing. Thank Buddha, her father's U.S. Visa card works.

"You think Sunny could recognize me, *Bpaa?*"

"What's your name again?"

• • • • •

The scariest part for her is waiting in the queue before they open the doors for the late show at the Follies. Scary knowing that the other people in the line, the straights, the day trippers, maybe some of Sunny's boys, are checking her out. Sniffing around to see if she's just another drag king or something more lethal. She hopes she doesn't throw up.

It's beyond weird, being back in the Follies after all this time. Strangers working the bar. No Ritchie, no Duke, no Nikki with her cute little Russian accent and her Janis Joplin soul. Different light-and-sound kids up there in the balcony. No one she's ever heard of in the line-up of Sensation Dolls, not even that slut Silver. And in all her nights here, she never actually watched a show, never sat at one of these little tables and had a club kid in drag flirting, hounding her to buy a drink.

The inside of the Painted Lady. Michael says it reminds him of a speakeasy in a movie about Mafia kings. The ballroom two stories high, eighty feet long, complete with glass chandeliers, a rotating disco ball. Ten golden columns hold up the ceiling, which has actual frescoes of nude Greeks. And a balcony around the second floor of the ballroom. The light and sound kids hanging out up there in their shorts and T-shirts, working the spots and the soundboard.

Downstairs the wallpaper is red brocade. To top off the whole scene, that wide, semi-circular staircase sweeping down from the dressing room on the second floor. A landing branching off to the little stage and runway. This is how the girls make their entrances, down these stairs. Queens of the night. How she used to love it.

Celine Dion weeps from the sound system, her signature anthem from *Titanic*, "My Heart Will Go On." Tuki tries to hum along. Can't. A terrible tightening in her belly. So she orders an eight-dollar beer to get the dragon waitress out of her face, prays for the lights to go down soon. *Like bring on Robsulee, la. Let me see the ho behind more than two years of misery and death, a whole lot of rotten* plaa.

Her right hand's sweating as it fondles Caesar Decastro's pistol in her jacket, the gun now loaded with bullets from Wan-Lo's stash. It's almost like going out onstage for a show, being up there in the spotlights. She has to walk this walk alone. Whatever goes down in the next hour is totally up to her. No Michael. And no Marcus, no *Bpaa*. He's off on his own mission impossible, he says. He can't come in here. Robsulee might recognize him. Even though he's a slender, fitter, balder, bearded, dressed-in-black version of the René she used to shake down back in New York. Back before Robsulee's strange morph from queen bee of the extortion rackets north of Hester into a total P-town showgirl. And Sunny, la. Sunny could be back in town, already rallying the local *nak-lin*. Sunny would make Marcus in a second. *Kill us both in the blink of an eye, la. Before I get within spitting distance of the Queen of Spades. Before I rip her eyes out.*

"*Wan phra mai mi hon dieo,*" she says quietly. "Show time."

· · · · ·

The ho's ripping me off. That's what she's thinking after the house lights dim, the blue spot picks up Robsulee at the top of the circular staircase. The slut's wearing a black evening dress, a diamond choker glittering at her throat. Slowly, her head starts to rise. She does indeed look like Whitney Houston. Skin just a bit darker, iced-coffee-and-cream. Her fingers begin a rhythmic snap, her hips picking up the beat, the mic rising to her lips.

The ho! The ho is stealing her old routine. Her mind staggers, stutters. And for a second she's the one up there unpacking her heart, singing "Exhale." The way Tuki used to every night for the crowd.

The background guitars and strings cut in. Her voice is a woman lost in a memory of love on a hot slow night in the delta. The Mississippi ... the Mekong ... the Chao Prya, Bangkok. And, oh yes, la. Love in a beach house in Malaysia where the tigers roam the coconut grove. All night long.

Down the stairs she comes, three steps on the beat. She pauses. Her body does a slow burn to the pain of the lyrics. Then she takes three more steps in a kind of lazy shimmy, her voice gaining strength with each step like an approaching freight train.

She strolls the runway. Voguing—chin high, three strides, turn, smile, pose. When she hits the chorus, she starts with the "Shoop, shoop, shoop, shoo be doop, shoop, shoop." Then holds the mike out low at arm's length, a signal for the audience to pick up the refrain. As they do, she scans the crowd. People wave creased bills her way.

Robsulee's folding the dollars into her cleavage when the music stops, the applause rings. And Tuki's eyes fall on Sunny Janluechai sitting at a table on the right side of the runway with three of his thugs. Protection for the Queen of Spades. Bodyguards, scoping out the crowd. Not yet seeing through her Michael Jackson drag.

If ever there were a moment to kill the ho, it's now. She fingers the trigger.

44

HE'S READY to give up for the night. It's close to midnight, and he has been in P-town for hours, lingering in the shadows outside the Painted Lady. Waiting for the Follies to let out. Hoping to pick up Tuki's trail, or spot a Thai in a green jacket before, well, the fucking sky falls in, as Lou says.

But he's coming up empty. He's heading back to the parking lot by the wharves for his Jeep when *aí está*, there it is. The silver Honda, three rows up ahead. Marcus in his black ninja gear, bent over, blowing a joint in the front seat. It's just dumb Portagee luck finding the car like this … and Marcus. He never would have recognized Tuki in the Michael Jackson drag. Especially not with her running the way she is, streaking for the Honda with a gun in her hand.

Suddenly he's a big fan of central community parking for bringing them together like this. But he's feeling pretty freaking clueless about what to do next. Part of him wants to get on his phone to Lou Votolatto and his new sidekick that Latina, Colón. But what would they do but tell him again to get out of here and stop bugging them unless a crime has gone down? *A capital crime,*

Rambo. Like murder. Not assault or indecent exposure. Well, shit, something just happened. Tuki's flashing a piece. Why? Did she shoot someone? He can't tell. All he can tell is that she's sick to her stomach now, puking out her guts on the pavement before she slips into the car. The fear must be just eating her up.

He feels the blood swelling in his arms, his hands. Wants to rush to her, hold her, comfort her. But something tells him to hold back. He's stumbled into the middle of a nightmare he doesn't understand. When he did this before, Awasha Patterson ended up dead. *Never again.* Tuki probably has some Thai proverb to cover this, something about haste and waste.

The Honda's engine fires, the headlights come on. It starts toward the pay booth. *Cristo.* What to do now is no longer the question. The question is will Tuki and her *bpaa* get away before he can follow. *Merde.*

· · · · ·

He finally catches up to them at a traffic light on Route 6. They're headed south. He's just three cars back. The fog has lifted a little, but not too much. Perfect.

The Honda veers off the highway and starts west on the back roads of Truro, heading toward Cape Cod Bay. The twists and turns are too familiar. Sometimes he sees them in his dreams. This is the way you get to Shangri-La. The dead man's house. Big Al Costelano's. The victim in the Provincetown Follies murder case. A rich boy's party compound complete with a Thai-style teak pavilion, a futuristic master crib called the Glass House. A half-dozen tiny bungalows, for his drag queen concubines like Tuki, on the fringes of a lagoon. The place where Tuki lived. The place where she got to him one summer night.

· · · · ·

She's crying so hard that she cannot pay the cabbie when they reach Shangri-La. There's a party raging in the pavilion. She is clearly in no shape to meet people. But he can't just leave his client standing in the parking lot, can't just hand her over to one of the bouncers. She's crying so hard she can't even walk on her own. So he wraps an arm around her, guides her down a side path to her bungalow.

As soon as they get to her place, she collapses on the bed and buries her head in a pillow. Sobs are still coming. The room is in shadows. Just the porch light on. And he doesn't see any reason to change this. He just wants to let her fall asleep. Part of him wants to stay with her, just to watch over her, make sure she does not try to hurt herself. The other part screams for him to get the hell out of here. Blow her off.

He cannot decide.

But first he has to calm her down. Maybe a stiff drink will do the trick. A survey of the fridge and cabinets turns up a dusty bottle of B&B. He pours them both about three ounces, takes the drinks over to the bed, sits beside her. She rises up on one elbow, wipes the tears from her cheeks. Her big black eyes stare at him as she reaches out for the glass. The light from outside makes the sun streaks in her hair look silver.

"What is this?"

"Some monks in Italy or Spain or somewhere make this. It is a five-hundred-year-old recipe to soothe the heart."

She sips, squints like someone who has never felt the fire of brandy in her throat before. Takes another sip, a big one, just to make sure she did not imagine that sweet heat.

"Careful. It's pretty strong."

She sets the glass on the bed, rubs her eyes.

"Tonight, I need strong, la!"

45

"I WANTED TO, but I couldn't do it, I couldn't pull the trigger, la … And I had to *uak*."

"What?"

"Vomit."

"It's ok," Marcus says. "I got this under control. I found out where she lives, this Shangri-La place. We're going to end this tonight."

"Tonight?"

"This all started with me. It will end with me."

"*Bpaa*."

"You can wait in the car."

"Why was she wearing my drag? Doing Whitney the same way I …?"

He shrugs, hasn't the faintest. "Just point me toward Shangri-La."

She says the road to the compound dead-ends in a driveway up ahead in the woods. There's an Asian-looking entrance gate, always two guys in suits on security detail when she lived here. But who knows now? It's a different game, isn't it?

Right, he says. While she was inside the Follies checking out Robsulee in the flesh, he was tossing back drinks at a backstreet gay bar called the Atlantic House, chatting up the barflies about the Queen of Spades. What he learned is that Robsulee sashayed into P-town from New York City the winter after the tranny pimp Al Costelano was killed. After all his property, including the Painted Lady and Shangri-La, went up for auction. She bought the whole package. Rumor has it, paid cash.

She tells him heads-up. Shangri-La is close. They round the corner as the road crests a hill in the woods. There's the gate on the right, the parking lot beyond, blurry in the fog. She remembers how it used to be full of Jags, Benzes, Porsches. Now it's empty, except for a black Escalade. Four Asian dudes smoking in the violet glow of the light at the top of the steps leading down to the pavilion, lagoon, bungalows, the Glass House. One of the men is short, broad shoulders, thick neck.

"Fucking Sunny," says her father.

"Turn around and keep driving, la." She feels like *uak*ing again.

. . . . .

"I don't think he saw us," says her *bpaa*, wheeling the Honda into a U-turn and accelerating.

"Please, let's just get out of here."

"Eventually Wan-Lo's probably going to get his fat ass out of that bathtub. When he tells his homeboys what happened, the sky will rain shit."

"I think we should call Michael." She reaches in her jacket pocket and pulls out her new cell phone.

"He can't know about tonight." Her father is looking at her, not the road. "Don't you see? Not ever."

They crest a hill in the center of the narrow road. Oncoming headlights flare through the fog right in front of them.

"Look out!"

Her father swerves the Honda. A Jeep rushes by on their left, disappears over the hill.

"Shit."

"Stop the car, *Bpaa*."

• • • • •

She's still dry-heaving out the door when the black Escalade rolls up behind them. Still wiping off her lips on her jacket sleeve, still blinking the tears out of her eyes, when she feels the gun barrel press against her temple.

"We meet again, Patpong girl." Sunny says. "Hands on head. You, out of car."

She feels his fingernails in her neck, lifting her free of the Honda. Lying on the ground behind the car is her father, one of the *nak-lin* pressing his face into the soft mud, the gravel, with a foot. Another one of Sunny's thugs is binding Marcus' wrists with plastic wire ties.

Sunny rips the wig off her head, the black nylon wig cap. Her hair a million little black spikes.

"Wait 'til Robsulee see you now," he says.

He clips her hands behind her back with wire ties, frisks her. Scores her phone, the pistol, the Black Dog pocket knife her father found the night Varat Samset died in Klong Toey. He opens the knife, scrapes the edge against her upper lip. Smiles. "I missed this knife."

• • • • •

They hurtle through the fog, the darkness, in the Escalade for about fifteen minutes. Sunny, three *nak-lin*, Tuki, her father. Sunny is making and receiving calls in the front seat, but she can't hear what he's saying. They head south on a mix of back roads, Route 6, back roads again. At some point she sees a road sign announcing that they are in Eastham. Then they turn off on a dirt lane, stop in front of a small barn, a primo, maroon sixties Jaguar XKE parked in the shadows.

Sunny pushes her and her *bpaa* inside through a small door cut in the side of the building. She sees that the space is all but filled with the hull of a large wooden sailboat under-construction. The Beatles are singing "Dear Prudence" loudly from a stereo in some far-off corner. A few florescent light tubes high above cast milky shadows over what is obviously someone's boat shop.

She's squeezing her eyes to adjust to the light, when she feels hot breath on her left cheek, smells champagne.

"What a disappointment, la." The voice sounds like her own, but deeper. Black, homegirl. Like from the South. A bit masculine-but-not-masculine. Smoother ... with the notes rising at the end of the sentence.

She turns toward the hot breath, the scent of fermented grapes, sees Whitney Houston's clone, six inches from her face. Sees the ho in the black evening dress, diamond choker. This close the eyeliner looks gothic, the fake lashes too long, the cheek rouge and lipstick too loud. The foundation clotted slightly on the tiny hairs of her lips and chin.

"You really look like shit, Tuki Aparecio."

"So do you, bitch." The words just fly from her mouth.

"Sassy, though."

She continues staring at the ho, not blinking, sizing her up. Like size ten at least. Black pumps big enough for Michael. Rob-sulee's a freaking Amazon.

"Sunny, tell her how much money it has cost me to get her here."

The twerp bites his upper lip as if he is thinking. "Five hundred thousand dollars, maybe little more. Not counting what you pay for Painted Lady and Shangri-La."

"Look at you. The diva extraordinaire of Provincetown, the Queen of Patpong Road, Prem Kittikachorn's dream lover. The perfect girl. Look. You've destroyed yourself. You look like some kind of poor little rickshaw boy."

She feels the heat rising in her, pushing back her prayers to the Buddha for patience, calm. Thinks of her father, Michael. "People care about me."

As soon as she says this, she sees the ho's lips twist into a smile. "Not for long, honey." She turns to Sunny. "Show her, my love."

He puts the pistol Tuki was carrying right between her father's eyes. Michael's father's .45. Fires. The night thunders, a typhoon of blood and bone.

46

HE'S LEFT his Jeep farther up the road, is creeping through the brush toward the barn, the Escalade, the Jag, when he hears the gunshot, Tuki's howl.

Something stabs at his guts, short, hard strokes.

Three guys pop out of the Escalade with weapons in hand. Two rush into the barn. The third stands guard at the door with a shotgun. The fog is thick, but he can see that none of them is wearing a green jacket.

Part of him wishes he had his father's gun, the .45 that Tuki snatched. But another part of him knows that he's incompetent with handguns, that he's much better off—at least for now—with this baseball bat he's carrying. His Louisville Slugger from Little League. The one he always keeps in the jeep. His fish club.

He's almost at the barn when he hears shouting inside, Tuki howling again. The Beatles, "Eleanor Rigby," on a stereo.

"You killed him!" Her. The voice torn.

"I think you next, bitch." Sunny says.

No. Not again.

Something flares in his mind. A lightning strike. Sizzling. As he leaps from the fog, the shadows. Swinging the bat. Clipping the guard on the side of the jaw with a line drive. A second later the guard is down, out, dragged off into the scrub pine and poison ivy. And Michael is outside the little door to the barn with the guard's shotgun in one hand, his bat in the other.

The urge to burst in shooting is almost impossible to resist. He grinds his teeth, tells himself to count to ten. Think.

Tuki's keening, high, piercing notes of pain in counterpoint to "Eleanor Rigby."

"What good she to us, now?" asks Sunny. "We have ruby. Her nigger dead."

"I want her to suffer … like I have suffered. I want her to know what it's like to lose someone …" A strange draggy voice.

"Let me end this now."

"After all the stories about her from Thailand, after all the money Thaksin Kittikachorn offered for her, after her glamorous summer in P-town when that Costelano was protecting her from us, I expected an absolute siren. I dreamed about bringing a goddess to her knees."

"She pathetic."

"Worse than that. Am I right, girlfriend? You feel like nothing at all. Your soul's ripped out by the throat. Your heart's a stone. Because Robsulee took him away from you. Fucked your welching, thieving father once and for all. Just like I fucked your boyfriend Michael Decastro and fed him to the fish."

Again the stabbing in the guts, the urge to burst through the door, shotgun blazing. Shouting. *No. I'm here.* But what would that do except seal their deaths?

Tuki's sobbing has changed to a low moan. "Just shoot me. Kill me, la."

"Not 'til you hurt, slut. The way I hurt after Prem left me in New York. After he went back to Bangkok and went all gooey over your skinny ass."

He hears the rustle of clothing, a thud like a blow to the body. Tuki grunts.

"Feel my pain!"

Another blow, another groan. Like his mother's moaning in her last days of cancer. *Cristo.*

"Goodbye, sweet Tuki … Finish her. Torch the place. Bring my Jaguar home."

Jingle of keys being passed.

The door flies open.

The drag queen bursts out into the dark and the fog, makes a beeline for the Escalade. The two bodyguards scurrying behind her. They get in the SUV, start the engine, turn up the stereo, a Patti Labelle disco tune. Split the scene. They don't even seem to notice that one guy's missing. Or that Michael is pressed against the wall of the barn.

He pumps a round into the chamber of the shotgun, charges into the boat shop.

• • • • •

She's lying on the ground, pulled into the fetal position. Sunny's kicking at her knees, her belly, her groin. Pointing a Luger at her. Michael raises the shotgun, aims at the bastard's head, shoots. The little fuck doesn't even see it coming. Just buckles at the knees. He's falling when Michael pumps and fires again. Sunny hits the floor, a man with fishmeal for a face.

• • • • •

He doesn't know how long he's on the ground holding her to her chest. He just knows that when he opens his eyes his pants are wet from the pools of blood that have flowed from Marcus Aparecio, Sunny Janluchai. And her. She has not turned to engage him, just sat there in the blood, hugging her belly, whimpering as he embraces her from behind.

"It's all over," he says.

She just moans. Wipes her bloody hands on her face to quell the tears. Rocks her body.

"I have to call the police. We're going to need Lou."

"It's too late."

47

THE LAST THING she remembers is Michael talking on the cell phone. There's been a shooting. Two dead.

"Three," she says. Slips into a dream.

• • • • •

Saigon. Summer 1968.

An American in a red tank top and jeans sits at a table in the back of a girly bar called the Black Cat, nursing a Budweiser. His face is lost in shadows and the smoke from the joint he's smoking. He looks like Lou Gossett Jr. in An Officer and a Gentleman, *a refugee like her from somebody else's war.*

Spilling from the sound system, the Supremes. "Baby Love."

The spotlight picks her up. Picks up her mother, Misty, Huong-Mei, making her entrance with a sexy shuffle from behind a curtain at the end of the T-shaped runway bar. She's wearing a gold kimono stitched with little red dragons. Her lips glisten bright crimson. Liner accents the shape of her eyes. Her hair is pinned up in loose geisha folds. A golden-skinned goddess. And a private dancer. Pure body heat. She can feel the sweat beading in the small of her back, behind her ears, between her breasts. As she sashays down the runway in that kimono, kisses up to the mic, showing some leg. Bringing the night down. Rocking the poles. Working the edge.

The crowd already howling, jamming.

They clap, sing along. She struts the bar. Hears the click of her pumps on the wood. She's free. This is her time, her moment, singing, bending to kiss the customers, plucking their tips like flower petals. Head high, chest out, hips swinging …. a sexy kid from Cholon, a Marine's fantasy. A stroke of lightning. A girl who wears her heart for everyone to see … for the black man in the red tank top at the back of the room. The man who with the nod of his head rescued her from sin, from whoring. She's all of these things, riding the wave.

The humid air shimmers. Smoke in the spotlights.

She has barely started. The kimono covering all of her surprises. She throws her head back, launches into the second verse. Shakes her hair out in an explosion of curls. The shoes come off. The kimono is history. She works a pole dance in her black bra and G-string. Now she slips out of the bra and slinks off the edge of the bar. Weaves among the tables toward the back of the room, toward the man in her life. The only man. This fresh, dark man. The man whose baby she carries. This man she loves. This Marcus Aparecio, this René Parrish. This Michael Decastro.

As she dances, sings along with Diana Ross, the air grows thick in the room. The golden spotlight flickers across her skin. She feels a moist heat. Smells the incense, the weed, the opium … the ginger and the charcoal fires … the water buffalo and the rice paddies … the river and the plaa …. the sweat of men … the milk of mothers.

Outside on the Saigon River, on the Mekong, the white mist is rising over the water. The current sweeping rafts of flowering white water hyacinths downstream along with the muddy flood of the monsoon; egrets hitch rides on bits of broken houses, abandoned rice barges, bodies. Children. Everything flowing to the South China Sea.

And in the shadows, almost beyond her field of vision, a man in a green satin jacket.

The crowd is howling. She bends over, kisses her man on the mouth. The father of her child. Fears that this would be a good time for the nak-lin *to take a shot, or toss a throwing star, at the two of them. The three.*

· · · · ·

She bolts up from her sleep, shrieking. The bed a strange iron monster surrounding her with milky blankets, beeping monitors, a web of electronic sensors glued to her chest. An I.V. needle pinching her forearm.

And Michael, sweet Michael, standing over her. Covering her right hand with his. Looking ashen, sleepless.

"Hey … hey," he says softly. "It's all over."

"Michael."

She's remembering. The foggy night. The boat shed. The Beatles. "Baby Love." Saigon. The Black Cat. A man in a green satin jacket.

"You're in the hospital. Hyannis."

"I dreamed I was my mother. You were my father. There was a man in a green jacket. The *nak-lin.* They were going to kill us."

"You were having a nightmare."

"My father's dead."

"You lost a lot of blood."

"Sunny killed my *bpaa.*"

"I'm so sorry."

"In my dream I had a little baby in me."

He closes his eyes, turns his face away, wipes away tears from his cheeks, squeezes her hand tightly.

"We lost the baby," he says.

"Sunny killed my baby?"

"We'll have another. We'll have five."

"I want to kill Sunny."

"You don't remember?"

"What?"

"I shot him. He's gone."

She holds her breath for several seconds, feels the bruised, empty cradle of her belly, her hips. The long jagged tear in her heart. "And Robsulee too?"

He drops to one knee next to the bed, buries his face against her neck. "I'm sorry. I'm so damn sorry."

She feels his hot tears. "Maybe we're already dead."

48

HE KICKS the sand with his foot, scatters it into the ocean. A small shower of wet earth. Turns to Lou Votolatto and Yemanjá Colón who are casting for stripers in the surf off Nauset Beach, Eastham. All three of them have their pants rolled to their knees, bare toes pawing at the beach.

"Tell me the truth. The crap is just starting, isn't it?"

"Jesus, can't you see we're off-duty here, Rambo? Work is work. Fishing is fishing."

"I'm just arriving at the gates of hell."

"Are we talking about the dance you may soon be doing with the district attorney … or what this alleged Thai mob is going to do to you next?"

"The mob."

Votolatto jams the grip of his rod in the sand, turns to face Michael, hands on hips. "You really fucking amaze me sometimes. You know that?"

"Come on, Lou."

"No. I mean it. You really astound me. Like how many ways do you think you can screw the pooch?"

"It's that bad?"

"You have no idea."

He kicks up another cloud of sand.

"You said this dead guy Sunny may have been romantically involved with the drag queen."

"Robsulee."

"Where the hell do they get these names? Tell me, Colón?"

She shrugs, casts. Makes eye-contact with Michael for a second. Looks as if she wants to say something, but thinks better of it.

"You killed some mob queen's main squeeze, Mikeyboy. How
do you think that's going to play in Fruitcake Land?"

He wants to say that maybe Robsulee has the ruby. Maybe
she'll cut her losses and split. But what he says is that his girlfriend's
lost in a fog of depression. Somebody has to bury her father. His
baby is dead, goddamn it. So his head is hurting way too freaking
much right now to think, ok?

The detective presses his fingers up under his aviator sun-
glasses, rubs his eyes. "Are you listening to me? Michael?"

He blinks his eyes, nods.

"You need to get yourself a really good lawyer. Right now all the
cops and the D.A. know is that some Thai muscleman got his head
blown off with a shotgun with your prints on it."

"I already told you guys everything when you took me in for
questioning, Lou. I'm going to get arrested because I stopped that
asshole from executing Tuki?"

"And the fact that the dead black dude got his third eye from
a service pistol you borrowed from your father ... and he borrowed
from the U.S. government sometime around the Me Lai Massacre
in Nam."

"But, *Cristo*, I didn't—"

"Listen to me, you dipshit. I like you, you know that? I don't
know why, but I do."

He doesn't know how to take this compliment. So he just
holds the cop in a long, steady gaze.

"Fuck off, will you? The best thing you can do right now, kid, is go home and try to get some sleep. You look like dead donkey shit. Tell him, Colón."

She casts her line out to sea, starts to reel it in. Catches his eye again, brushes a skein of hair out of her face.

"You really love her, don't you?" Something in her voice sounds low, Latin. A little bit like his mother's. Or maybe one of his cousins. One of Tio Tommy's *meninhas*.

"It's killing me."

"Then forget this old fart." Colón nods toward Votolatto. "She needs you right now."

"I have to get her out of that hospital *pronto*."

"Before someone kills her too."

He pictures Nantucket. Two years ago. Her ex, Prem. A junkie on a suicide mission.

• • • • •

He's here as her guardian. Her first time on Nantucket. He's stationed outside the house in case something goes wrong. She's come to the island to find her ex, looking for the truth about who's framing her for the murder of Big Al Costelano.

He can hear the two of them talking as he tiptoes toward the immense plate-glass windows and sliding-glass doors that look out on the deck, the ocean, from the center of the Kittikachorn's beach house in Madaket. Hiding against the wall at the edge of the window, he sees the back of Prem's head as he sits on a couch. But most of the room is blocked from his view. Prem is smoking. The scent of burning tobacco drifts out through a screen door. He can hear her voice perfectly, but he cannot see her or understand a word. She's speaking Thai.

He cannot tell how things are going. Cannot tell whether this man from Bangkok who has stalked her on the internet and now on foot is really the one who put a knife in the belly of Costelano. The one who has framed her. Or whether he's just a lonely, desperate Joe looking for a way to curl up and die in her arms.

For a while she speaks in soft tones. Her voice sounds tender, earnest. Maybe pleading.

Prem grunts, says something abrupt, disdainful, sarcastic.

She fires back at him with hot words.

He throws his lit cigarette over his shoulder with the whip of his arm. It strikes the screen door, leaves a smudge, falls to the wooden floor, continues to burn. It is not ten feet from where Michael is hiding.

He draws his phone, wonders if he should call in the cops.

Suddenly Prem shouts something, just two or three words, then jumps to his feet. He comes around the couch. Starts jabbering again in fast short bursts. His voice rising with each new salvo. He looks pale as a drowning man scrambling for fresh air as he heads toward the screen door, the deck. A snub-nose revolver in his hand.

Michael presses himself back against the outside wall of the house, raises the phone in front of him, punches in 911. His right index finger ready to press the send button.

Prem snaps the barrel of the pistol to his temple, closes his eyes.

Tuki shrieks. Just two words. "Mai! Chi!" Suddenly, she's at his side. Tears are running down her cheeks as she tears at the gun in his hand, hugs him. Soaks his face in kisses.

Something bites into Michael's stomach. She's still in love with the man. Cristo!

In the blink of an eye, the prick collars her around the neck with his free arm, presses the gun to her head. He's crying wildly as he pulls back the hammer of his pistol with his thumb. His face contorts like that famous photograph of a prisoner being executed by a Vietnamese officer.

Michael leaps—right through the screen door. His arms flailing. His body hitting Prem and Tuki with a loud slap. The gun discharges.

They are in a heap on the floor. He can feel a burning sensation shooting all the way up his left arm. But his right hand still holds the phone, and now he's shoving it up under the unshaven chin of Prem Kittikachorn like it's a weapon, screaming.

"Don't move, fucker!"

"You think you can save her?"

49

THE *ROSA LEE* plows into the short, steep swells southwest of Hyannis. The hum of the engine, the calls of the gulls the only sounds.

In the wheelhouse Michael's father steers, shifts his weight for balance as the boat rolls. She thinks he has the body of a footballer, the hair of a wanderer. Shaggy, black threads tending toward gray.

"How far out you want to go, princess?"

She shrugs, afraid to open her mouth. Afraid she will start spouting the Heart Sutra, saying, *All the way. I want to go all the way to the inn of the eighth happiness. Beyond. To the emptiness, la.*

Her eyes close, lips purse. She sits in one of the captain's seats of the eighty-foot steel trawler, cradling what looks like a tin of biscuits. Michael stands behind her with his arms around her shoulders, staring ahead into the sparkling seas of Nantucket Sound. The breakwater of Hyannisport, the Kennedy compound already a mile astern. It's mid-morning. Tio Tommy is down below in the galley making a fish stew. She can smell the garlic, the peppers, onion. Pungent fish. The *plaa*.

They've come out here to scatter the ashes of Marcus Aparecio.

"He loved the ocean," she says.

Gone, gone, gone beyond.

She pictures the walks they had on the beach outside his place in Atlantic City before Sunny blew it up. The walks on the beaches of Penang, of Vietnam too. Those long walks, with the hot salt winds when they were just getting to know each other. When she was falling in love with this passionate dark man, letting herself be a little girl again.

"I love you." Michael squeezes her from behind, kisses her ear.

She shivers. *Form is emptiness and emptiness is form.*

"We can go as far as you want."

In emptiness there is no eye, ear, nose, tongue, body, mind.

"I know this is hard."

No forms, sounds, smells, tastes, touches or objects of mind.

His kiss, the whispering in her ear again. "How can I make this easier?"

No decay, no death, no extinction of decay, of death either.

She opens her eyes, sees the sparkling seas of the sound. "Maybe it's time."

The sea that surges, falls, resurges, is the life that is born, dies, is reborn again.

"You want to stop the boat?"

"No." Her voice empty as the wind. The Heart Sutra speaking. "There is no stopping, no path."

"But ..." He looks confused.

"I will let him go now." She rises from the chair, goes out the door to the catwalk, can of ashes clutched to her chest.

Form does not differ from emptiness; whatever is form, that is emptiness, whatever is emptiness, that is form.

He grabs for her free hand.

Her fingers slip away.

There is no suffering, no origination, no cognition.

"Tuki, wait."

She takes the can, takes Marcus, takes ashes, takes nothing. In both her hands. Raises it over her head. The wind whirring in her ears now. In her chest.

No attainment and non-attainment.

"Can I say something?"

She closes her eyes again. *The Bodhisattva dwells in the absence of thoughts.*

"I really want to say something."

She feels him behind her, beside her. His heat. His big Potuguese heart. Something surging in him. "Everything is ok, la."

"Then this," he says. "*O senhor é meu pastor.* The Lord is my shepherd. *Eu não quererei.* I shall not want …"

When he has finished she looks at him, looks at this sweet, sad man. This man who wears his worry on his forehead. His love in his eyes.

"I must let him go." She kisses his tears.

"Tuki …" he says, as if there is more he wants to add.

But it is already too late.

She is heaving the can in the air. It is spinning, rising, arcing across the horizon. A clutch of gulls diving for it as it falls, hits, tumbles in a wave, bursts open. Whitish, gray dust spilling out. Floating. Is gone.

"He has not been made to tremble," she says. "He has overcome … and in the end he attains Nirvana."

In her mind the great spell, the unequalled spell, allayer of all suffering, echoes. The Prajnaparamita. *Gone, gone, gone beyond, gone altogether beyond, O what an awakening, all-hail!*

But from her mouth. A dark moan with no form, no emptiness. Only wave upon wave of pain.

• • • • •

"What's happening?" she asks when she finally wakes up.

"We're fishing," he says. "*Bacalhau.* Cod fish. My father thought we needed to get away from everything on the Cape for awhile."

She's somewhere deep in the belly of the boat. It's dark, damp, smelling of diesel. The rumble of the engine, the grinding of steel cables, the shuddering of the boat as it tugs on the net. They seem to be coming from all around her. From the man spooning up behind her in the berth. From beneath her lungs too. All these sounds.

"How long have I been asleep?"

"I'm going to say ten hours."

"I never sleep that long."

"When my mother died I went to bed for three days."

"Oh, la. Where are we?"

"East of Nantucket."

"That island again."

"What do you mean?"

"Prem."

• • • • •

Her second time on the island … and her last. She promised Prem that she would come to him here. Alone this time—no crazy Portuguese lawyer jumping through screens—if Prem told her what he knew about the killing of Al Costelano. She would come to him at the beach house in Madaket. Come to him before the pung chao, *the heroin, swallows him up forever.*

He has delivered. Her sad river lion. He has led her, led the police, to the real killer. Now she's free. Banged up, her vocal chords wrecked from a choking at the hands of the killer in Oak Bluffs before the police took him down. But free. Clear. All charges dropped. Her lawyer—her impossible new love—turned loose to find a life.

So … it's her time to pay up, to give back the magnificent ruby before it causes her any more misery. Time to stand by her river lion until he dreams himself into oblivion. Two of a kind, she thinks, her and Prem. Misfits, damaged goods, strangers.

They are in bed. In the dark of midnight. The king bed in the master bedroom at the end of the hall. The one that looks out over the Jacuzzi on its own end of the deck, out on the Atlantic surf rolling in all the way from Africa. He has Lionel Ritchie playing on the sound system like old times at the River House back in Bangkok. The song is "Stuck on You."

He's cold. Shivering even though it is a hot late-summer night, trembling as he surfaces from his heroin dream. She takes off her dress, her bra, her thong. All but the lambskin gaff that pulls back her little penis. Undresses him too. Throws the clothes on the white rug, follows them like a trail to the spa. Leads him into the steaming water of the Jacuzzi, leaving the champagne-colored comforter, the sheets, the pillows heaped together behind her on the frozen bed. She's trying to pretend for a moment it's years and years ago when he was her young river lion, she was the teenage queen of the Patpong. When they used to bathe each other at the River House, make love, hold each other for hours in the bath and watch the coming of the morning sun turn the prangs of Bangkok's temples into golden pillars.

She's pressing her chin to the top of his head, singing along softly with Lionel. Feeling the heat of the water washing away her sadness. Trying not to miss Michael, when four men burst into the room. One of them Sunny. With a pistol in his hand. Prem's pistol, the .357, that was on the nightstand.

"You game is up, Patpong bitch."

Prem opens his eyes. Seems to recognize Sunny. Moans.

"Give me stone now."

Prem stirs against her breasts, speaks in a voice that seems to come out of the water. Wet, low. "It has evil karma."

Something freezes in her belly. Just tonight she gave Prem back the gem. Tucked it in the pocket of his shorts. "I threw it in the sea, la."

"Don't lie to me, ho."

"If I tell you where it is, you will let her go?" asks Prem.

Sunny steps closer. Almost to the edge of the Jacuzzi. Looks down at her nakedness. Seems to be going over something in his mind. "I don't think I can do that."

"Then shoot us now … And tell Robsulee …" He throws his arm up in the air, flips Sunny the bird, closes his eyes.

Sunny points the gun at him, curses.

"I can take you to the ruby," says Prem.

"Do it."

"Not until she's gone."

Sunny points the pistol at her. Between her eyes. "Get out tub."

She feels the warm water rushing off her in a sheet as she stands up. Prem's fingers tightening in her right hand.

"I'm sorry." Prem is speaking in Thai.

She doesn't know what's happening. At this point doesn't care. What's her life worth anyway? Prem dying. Her cute lawyer gone. She's just waiting for the bullet.

"Please. Go," Prem says.

"What?"

"He's giving you a chance."

"I count to ten," says Sunny.

"Go."

She looks at Prem.

"Neung." One.

He's lying in the tub smiling the way he used to smile back in Bangkok after a night of love.

"Sawng." Two.

"Remember me," he says.

"Saam." Three.

How could I not, she thinks.

"Sii." Four.

I will dream you just as I will dream a bar girl named Misty … and the marine who loved her. Forever, la.

"Haa." Five.

"Tuki."

"Hok." Six.

Prem points to the railing around the deck. "Jump!"

"Jet." Seven.

"Now!"

She feels him press the ruby into her hand … just before she throws herself over the railing, drops twelve feet to the ground. Her legs, it seems, already running. Beach sand is flying from beneath her feet when she hears the gunshot.

50

"YOU WANT to level with me, Mo?" His father comes up the steps from the galley, offers him a mug of coffee, a piece of eggy Portuguese bread topped with tomato, onion, sardines.

He hits the autopilot button, takes his hands off the *Rosa Lee's* steering wheel, accepts the gift. Looks out at the horizon where the sun is just creeping over the rim of the Earth, a flaring, bleeding wound. The net's in the water, trawling for cod. The boat making about three knots.

"What do you want me to say?"

"How about giving me your best lawyerly advice about whether the police are going to try to lock you up for the death of that muscle guy and Tuki's father … and whether I'm going to the pokey for giving you a stolen pistol."

He takes a bite of bread, a sip of the coffee. "It could happen."

"Then how come they haven't done it yet? It's been something like four days."

"Five."

"There you go. How come?"

"I have this cop friend."

"Votolatto. The guinea."

"Yeah. Maybe he's stalled things a bit, at least until we could bury her dad, you know?"

"But the cops are probably looking for us right now."

"Your guess is as good as mine."

"How we going to face the music, kid?"

"Part of me wants to run."

"I didn't raise you like that."

"Tuki's caving in with grief. I'm not sure she can take much—"

"The girl's in a world of hurt. I'll give you that. Kind of changes things, doesn't it?"

He looks out to the east. Wonders if it is Tuki's pain that has made his father finally see her as a girl. The sun bleeding out all over the ocean now.

"I just wish we could stay out here fishing for about a hundred years."

"We could be in the old country, at least the Azores, in nine, ten days."

"What about Tommy? What's he going to say? A trip like that?"

"He don't give a shit. He's my brother."

"But …"

"He can feel the *tempestade* in her. In you too."

"Listen to us, talking like we're already fugitives."

"I'm not saying run. Never run. Just take a sabbatical, go see all the cousins on Sao Miguel."

"Isn't it nice to think so?"

"Give Tuki a little time to get back on her feet. Give the law a chance to see you shot that guy in self-defense."

"The law," he says. "That's the problem."

"You lost me there."

He closes his eyes, inhales. Pictures scales. "You taught me to believe in justice, in the rule of law. I took an oath when I became a lawyer."

"Sometimes you have to answer to a higher authority."

"That's the part I really seem to screw up. When I lead with my heart, my soul, good people—people I love, end up dead."

His father takes a pack of Winston's out of his shirt pocket, shakes out a cigarette. Lights it.

"This mean you want to haul in the net and turn around?"

"I don't want to get anybody else hurt."

"What about Tuki? She's sinking."

"I think she needs more than Sao Miguel and the cousins."

"How about we drop you two on Nantucket?"

"Nantucket?"

"You take a couple of days in some romantic inn. Drink a little wine, eat some fresh scallops. Sing to her, rub her feet ... Whatever you do together ..."

"And then?"

"We go to your cop friend and turn ourselves in. Tommy will bail us out. *Claro.*"

"Let me talk with Tuki."

• • • • •

She's standing in the bows of the *Rosa Lee*, black sweatpants and his white fisherman's sweater. Her arms spread, wings. Him holding her from behind. Kate Winslet and Leo DiCaprio in *Titanic*. The boat heading back west with the afternoon sun in their faces. Great Point Lighthouse on Nantucket showing itself, a black spike on the horizon.

"I always wanted to do this," she says, "since I saw the movie. Nothing can touch us right now."

He can feel her smiling, maybe the first smile since they set foot on Cape Cod weeks ago.

"Don't let me go."

He tightens his arms around her waist. "Not a chance."

She raises her left arm, lowers her right. Tilts them in the opposite directions. Soaring.

He leans his face alongside her neck, her cheek. Kisses the hollow beneath her jaw.

"We're going to get through this," he says.

"Hold me tighter."

He squeezes, tries not to think of their dead child.

"Tighter, la."

He nuzzles her.

Minutes pass with the salt air swirling around them, lifting. Stinging their eyes, ears. Their lips.

"I have to tell you … things … I never thought I would …" Her voice falters.

He feels her coming back down from the sky, settling onto the deck. She's heavy in his arms. Maybe with the secrets she's carrying. It's always secrets with her. The weight.

"I never told you what really happened the night Prem died."

"Ok," he says, as if these words will give her permission to unburden herself.

"It's not what you think. He didn't shoot himself …" She drops onto the deck, huddling out of the wind beneath the steel bulwarks.

When he's sitting there beside her, she tells him about that last night at Prem's parents' beach house in Nantucket. Tells him about how the *nak-lin* surprised them in the Jacuzzi, how Prem promised to give up the ruby if they let her run for it, but how he slipped her the stone at the last second. How she heard them execute him.

"So Prem's death was another one of Sunny's dirty deeds that began back in New York. Back when Sunny started his shakedown's of your father's restaurant?"

"I'm scared, la."

"Let's get off this boat in Nantucket." He tries to make his voice sound husky, seductive.

51

SHE HATES that she told him about Prem's murder.

She feels how the news is sucking the warmth from his body. More of her dirty little secrets surfacing to make him wish he had never met her, probably. Now, because she loves him, because she lost his baby and her father ... because she knows she'll lose Michael too unless she rises from the swamp ... she must take him beyond all of this drama. The deaths. The throwing star. The stolen ruby. The police who must already be looking for them. She must take him over the rainbow. Back to the Hotel California again where they can find each other. Even though sex is just about the last thing on her mind right now.

"Close your eyes, la."

He's stretched out beside her. Nude, except for his shorts, on the antique bed in this Nantucket inn. The Jared Coffin House where she first spent a night with him when they were looking for Prem. Almost two years ago.

The streetlight filters through the trees, the thin curtain. A soft glow, casting the shadows of leaves and a tall bedpost across his silvery thighs, the sheets heaped at the foot of the bed, the oak floor, the wall beyond. And tonight he is not drunk like the last time. Not passed out. Just twitchy. Scared. Trying to pretend he's Prince Charming.

Her fingers glide up his thigh, feel the curls of leg hair.

He shivers a little.

She kisses the vee at the base of his neck.

He makes a humming sound.

Her teeth bite the flesh of his shoulder softly.

"I love you."

"I love you too." She feels the urge to sing something, knows that's crazy. Kisses his lips. Tries to taste their fullness. The sweet, wet hardness of mangos.

He wraps his right arm around her shoulders.

His hand slides up the back of her neck, cups the back of her head. Fingers probing the tight, little curls she has grown back since he shaved her head in Malaysia.

Her tongue meets his, is starting to explore his mouth when she feels something stirring in her hips. The old urge to die in a tangle of limbs. To explode into a thousand bright bits like that thing white-hot stars do. Nova. Suddenly the worry is gone. The fear. Even the grieving for Marcus, for her child.

She just wants this, la. Wants to give herself to him. Wants him. Michael. The father of her child. Once more. Merciful Buddha.

And now she can feel his body wanting this too. The perfection of it all. His muscles tightening into cables, one-by-one. They wrap her, tug her. Pull her beneath him. Fill her with something there is no word for. The melting away of pain, the sweet surging, the slow dancing of paired hips. The making of a new life. The no flight that is flight.

Like that first night …

She curls an arm around his waist, closes her eyes. Smells the scent of coconut soap on his shoulders again, feels the warm wind blowing in off the ocean. The night birds fussing in the trees, the waves combing the beach. From far off in the jungle come sounds

she can't identify. Tigers, maybe. Or her own voice. Pleading. Bay-
ing for her lost child. Her father. This man in her arms.

• • • • •

"I love you." Her words silk. She brushes her fingers across his
forehead.

He thinks everything is happening to him as it did before. He
is back in Marang. In a small bedroom with a mattress on a platform suspended from the ceiling by ropes. Their bodies weaving
around each other on the swinging bed, swaying in the wind. The
moon rising over the South China Sea, washing over them in their
tender fury … Monkeys chattering.

He smells the fruit of her hair, slides his lips along the rim of
her jaw, reaches her mouth.

His lips brush hers.

Her tongue traces the edges of his mouth, the palm of her
hand settling behind his left ear, pulling him right through the surface of her hot skin. The fur rising on his chest, his legs.

He slides his lips to her collar bone, inhales her skin, her
breasts. He drinks the wetness from her mouth, her belly.

Her body is small, delicate. Immensely strong when she puts
her hands beneath his shoulders. Tears at his back with soft claws.

"I love you."

Her fingers are on the back of his neck. His ears prick to her
fast breathing. The bed sways. His body melts into hers. His
mouth, his heart, *meu cristo*, his soul. Her finest, smoothest, secret
skin against his own. A film of sweat rising on their bellies, flanks.
Eyes closed, not seeing the *tsunami* rushing toward them.

Even as they dive into the planet's blood, their own. Their
child's. And—strangest of all—their fathers' blood. Their war. The
scene he always pictures in Saigon.

• • • • •

*The boatman sits in the stern of his canoe in black pajamas, a paddle
across his lap, staring at the soldier with unmasked resentment.*

"Come, la. I take you home now," she says.

The soldier, his father—and maybe himself, too, if that makes any sense—cannot remember how long he sat in the bar watching her dance to the ballads of Smokey Robinson, the Temptations, "talkin' 'bout my girl." But he feels drunk now. His service shirt is unbuttoned to the waist, the MP chevron on his sleeve is stained with lipstick, rice whiskey, Budweiser. There is a green beret stuffed in his hip pocket, a .45 snapped into the black holster on his hip.

He knows going into the boat is a mistake. There is a reason the army has guards posted along the roads to Cholon. On the bridges over the klongs, too. Navy swift boats patrol the waterways. Cholon is teaming with people, rats, vice, crime—off-limits to GIs. But he knows. He has heard. This is how they go. His brothers … with their women. By boat, in the dark, up the Ben Nghe Channel to another world, away from the killing, the savagery, the generals. To Chinatown. To drown in the wet, golden loins of Asia for a while.

She stretches out her arm, beckons him to the boat. He sees every inch of her body calling to him from beneath that red dress. It is nothing more than the thinnest veil. A film, really.

"This is bad," he says. "Are you sure …"

"Quiet," she says. The boatman is nervous. The army shoots the ferrymen sometimes.

· · · · ·

When the bed is still, she kisses him alongside the ear.

"Please … never let me go, la."

"Where are we?"

52

HE'S ASLEEP in her arms when the police burst into the room and snap on the light. Local island cops ... along with Lou Votolatto and Yemanjá Colón.

"It didn't have to come to this, Romeo."

"Jesus Christ, Lou!"

He sits up, tries to pull the sheet over his bare legs, but Tuki has it clutched to her chest.

Colón picks up a bathrobe, hands it to Tuki. Then she snatches his boxers and jeans from a chair, tosses them to him. "You want to put these on?"

"I was going to turn myself in, Lou."

"I don't want to hear it, I swear. I could have run you in days ago. The D.A. wanted me to. But we cut you some slack. Colón went way out on a limb for you. Begged the D.A. to let you bury Tuki's father, first."

He scrambles into his shorts, a little surprised to hear about Colón's advocacy. "Honest to *Cristo*, I was coming in to see you tomorrow."

"Then how come you jumped ship …? I should never have let you …"

"We just needed a little time, Lou."

"We already picked up your old man, you know?"

"Jesus."

Colón hands Tuki her sweatpants, white fisherman's sweater. "We're all in a heap of *merde*. This new district attorney really has us in a fucking …"

Votolatto looks at Tuki. She seems shell-shocked. Pale, frozen. "Some worse than others."

"Give her a break, Lou. Those musclemen were going to kill her. She's the victim here …"

"Says you."

"And what does Robsulee say?"

"Would that be the tranny girlfriend of the guy whose face you turned to spaghetti sauce?"

"Come on, man. You know who I mean."

"Yeah. Ok. Well here's the story on that petunia, bub … We can't find her. Flat fucking vanished … So your girlfriend is the next best thing."

"Lou!"

Votolatto's cheeks sag, eyes droop. "The minute she jumped off that fish boat with you, loverboy, she gave me no choice. She's a material witness. And the D.A. says the both of you are at risk of flight."

"Aw, Christ."

"I don't think Jesus has anything to do with this cluster fuck. We got orders to lock the both of you up."

"What about my dad? Did he make bail?"

Votolatto rolls his eyes. "Didn't I tell you to get yourself a good lawyer?"

"What do you mean?"

"Patriot Act, pal. Your old man stole a weapon from the feds and now that weapon has been involved in a killing with foreign nationals."

"My dad's a vet."

"Yeah, and they could fuck him good. You ever seen where the feds send vets gone sour?"

He closes his eyes, bites the edges of his tongue with his molars. Pictures Bangkwang prison. Recalls his interview with Brandy.

When he opens his eyes again, he has the feeling that he just remembered something important. Something more than the story of Brandy and Delta's alibi for where they were the night of Thaksin Kittikachorn's murder, the night of the first fake ruby exchange. Something else sketchy, something besides the way Marcus Aparecio and his Saigon tranny pals made a spectacle of themselves at a popular nightspot. Maybe something even darker.

… *when we wake up middle of the night he gone with wind, la. We just two drunk old trannies … watching reruns of the Daily Show."*

"Where do you think he went?"

Brandy's eyes flash at him. *"Not my business."*

He wants to talk about this with Tuki. But she's no longer here, not in the hotel room. Lou and Yemanjá Colón have left too. And a Nantucket cop is fitting him with nickel handcuffs.

53

"DOESN'T IT seem sad to you, Michael? Almost every time I see you, you're in some jam with the police."

"Who the hell's she, Mo?" His father is sitting next to him. Their backs to the wall, butts on the concrete floor of their cell in the Barnstable county lockup.

There's a woman outside the cell with one of the guards. Late thirties, early forties. Asian. She's wearing that fancy white summer suit again. Reeking of cigarettes, jasmine perfume. Straw hat, pink ribbon for a band, trailing off down her back with her ponytail.

"Dad, I'd like you to meet Wen-Ling."

His father squints at him, confused.

"We met in Thailand ... and Singapore. She helped Tuki and me out of some scrapes."

"Your son seems to have a nose for trouble."

Caesar Decastro rises to his feet, nods. His mind settling, focusing. "You going to be our angel, honey?"

She shrugs. "I have no jurisdiction here."

"You some kind of super cop?"

She smiles. "What do you think, Michael? Am I a super cop?"

He tries to remember what Varat Samset called her. *Silab*. Thai National Security. "She's a secret agent, Dad."

"Like Domino, Kissy Suzuki, Pussy Galore."

She lets go a burst of laughter. "Your father knows his James Bond girls, Michael."

"I was in Vietnam, sweetheart. They came with the territory."

She raises an eyebrow. "So does that mean you expect me to sleep with you?"

His father pops his eyebrows up—the man's alert, free of his depression, his *saudade*, for the first time in days. "Don't you think that would be kind of awkward given the circumstances?"

She laughs again. "Your father is something else, Michael."

"Get us out of here and I'll show you something else, cute stuff."

"Dad!"

She winks at the two men. "Can you help me recover something I've lost?"

"What's she talking about, Mo?"

"It's a long story," he says. "Maybe better for another time."

"Hey if I can find jumbo cod on the bottom of the ocean, I can find anything."

She puts her hands together under her chin as if she's praying, looks deep into Michael's eyes. "Where's the Heart, Michael?"

"Don't say anything, Michael …" His father elbows his ribs. "Listen, Mata Hari. We could be out of here. On bail, free men. Except this district attorney has set our bail at a million dollars and my brother Tommy can't come up with that kind of dough. I'm telling you, whatever you lost, we can find, you help us out with the bail money here."

She shakes her head. "You're going to have to do better than promises, slick."

"You can have the *Rosa Lee* if we don't deliver."

"What's that?"

"My big-ass fishing boat."

"You think Bond Girls go for fishing boats?"

"How about a candlelit dinner by the sea and some homemade Portuguese *paella*?"

"Does that have shrimp?"

Caesar smiles. "If you want shrimp ... Of course, pretty lady."

She shakes her head, seems amused. "Like son, like father."

"What's that supposed to mean?"

"Charm boys."

．　．　．　．　．

Something's wrong, really wrong. The words—English words, not Thai words—start pounding in her head the second a guard opens the door to her cell and she sees the pretty cop Colón ... with Wen-Ling.

Every time this Chinese-Thai bombshell shows up in her life some new horror presents itself. Her father seemed to sense the wench's toxins from the start. How?

Wen-Ling walks up to the cot where she's sitting. "I'm sorry about your father, Tuki. It must be very painful."

"How would you know, la?"

"And I'm sorry about your baby."

"Fuck you."

"I know you don't like me. But I'm here to help you."

"I don't need your kind of help."

Wen-Ling sighs. "I told Michael you were going to be the end of him. I warned him back in Bangkok. But he didn't listen."

"Go away, la."

"Now look at the mess you've got him into. The man's been arrested for murder. Because he tried to save you from your shadows. Again."

She feels something breaking beneath her upper ribs, turns her back on Wen-Ling to hide the tears she feels coming.

"What if I told you there's a way you can get Michael out of this jam he's in? A way to clear him of murder?"

"You want me to help you find the ruby."

"Michael and his father think they can ... but I kind of doubt they're actually up to it."

"Please leave them out of this."

"This is a girls' thing isn't it? It always has been. It's about love, not adventure."

"I wish I never saw the Heart."

"But it's way too late for that."

"I don't know where that ruby is. Why don't you just let it go? It's cursed."

"No it's not. It's just a stone … that is really important to His Majesty."

"Bhumipol?"

"Who else?"

"Who's Bhumipol?" Colón is confused.

"The king of Thailand."

"Oh."

"He wants it back in Ayutthaya, in a museum for the people to admire. It is part of the national heritage."

"So are the *nak-lin*."

"What are you two talking about?" Colón again.

"Thai gangsters."

Wen-Ling circles Tuki's cot so she can look her in the eyes. "They don't have it anymore. You know that."

"I don't know anything."

"Yes you do … Prem Kittikachorn had a lover before you, didn't he?"

"What do you want me to do?"

"First …? Remember."

· · · · ·

One night she and Prem are lying there in the hammock together at the River House on Klong Bangkok Noi after making love. He's drinking his rice whiskey and rambling on and on about his crazy life before he met her. The charcoal fire is crackling in the brazier. The longtail boats whine up and down the river. It's a clear night and she can see some stars shining above the glow of the city, the floodlights on the temple prangs. She's in her late teens, the kathoey queen of the Patpong. The diva of divas. The brightest star of the Silk Underground.

"Tell me things," she says. "Tell me a secret, la."

He tells her he learned about romance in the strangest place, a military high school where his father sent him in America. He says most of the guys in his school were a bunch of racist white boys. The few minority kids all stuck together for protection. He made a friend, a black kid on scholarship from Memphis. After their first year, they chose to be roommates. The black kid was a football star, an amazing runner, ball handler. The whole school respected him. They stayed out of his face when he came on with the eff-you-white-boys attitude.

So for three years until they graduated, no one bothered Prem or his black friend. And in their room, in their free time, they had a separate, private life apart from all the young storm troopers. A lot of Lionel Ritchie music, candle light, pot. One night they kissed.

"What was his name?" she asks.

"Everybody called him Robert then."

54

"I THOUGHT you said that Tuki was waiting for me on the *Rosa Lee*." He's pacing back and forth on the work-deck of the fishing trawler, on his cell phone to Lou Votolatto.

"Yeah, kid, that's where Colón dropped her after she was released from the pokey. Right at your old man's boat tied up with the other draggers in Hyannis."

"Well, I'm on the *Rosa Lee* right now. She's not fucking here, man."

"Calm down … you're less than an hour out on bail and you're getting up in the face of an officer of the law with the eff-word."

He inhales, holds the air in his lungs until his vision clears. "I'm sorry. This is freaking me out, Lou."

"Are you sure she's not there?"

"*Cristo!* My dad and I have been up and down this wharf three times. And all through this boat."

"Hey, kid, take a chill pill will you? Maybe she's on one of the other boats tied alongside. Maybe she went to the little girl's room somewheres, is putting on her makeup before she sees you. Maybe she went for coffee."

"You think I haven't thought of that? Goddamn it, Lou. She's not here." He sees a small codfish head lying on the deck, sends it flying with a kick.

The cop on the other end is silent.

"Lou!"

"Ok, Michael, just hold your horses, buddy. Just give me a few hours. Colón and I are up to our ears in *caca* with the higher-ups because of you and this shit storm that seems to follow your girlfriend around. Do me a favor, will you? Don't you or your old man do anything crazy."

"What's that supposed to mean?"

"It means the last time this baby doll disappeared on you for a few minutes a couple of people turned up dead."

"I don't think she would just plain take off on me, not for long."

Another pause on the line. "Well … she did before."

"What are you talking about?"

"Two years ago ... when she left us with a body, a hot tub full of blood, and her black thong on the floor of that place on Nantucket."

"It's different this time. She's different. I'm different. Everything's different."

"Just about the only difference I can see is this time I've got all the guns. Yours. And hers. Think about it, kid."

He bites the inside of his mouth, knows that somehow Votolatto's missing the point. If he could just find the right words, maybe …

"See what I mean, Romeo?"

"Yeah." There's a dark shadow taking shape in his mind. "I already told you, the last time she ran, the *nak-lin* were on her butt."

"And now it's Madame Nu."

"You mean Wen-Ling? I thought she was your new best friend."

"The feds told me to work with her, pal."

"Because they want to help the Thais get their ruby."

"That's how it looks to this dumb cop."

"You sound bitter."

"Remember how things turned out last time?"

• • • • •

"Don't touch anything!" Votolatto jams his hands against the sides of his head. "The guy's been dead a while."

Prem Kittikachorn's family's house, Madaket Beach on Nantucket. A Lionel Ritchie album playing softly on the stereo. And Prem dead, shot in the head, bleeding out in the Jacuzzi. Michael is doubled over, on the verge of heaving. Knowing that Tuki was here, too. And now she isn't.

Months later he discovers that she isn't dead, just in another universe. When she sends him a little jade statue of the Buddha. And a photograph of herself with her new-found father in Vietnam.

55

SHE'S SITTING in the lotus position on the stage of the Methodist Tabernacle in Oak Bluffs, Martha's Vineyard. Crying.

The tabernacle is a massive open-air Victorian pavilion surrounded by the gingerbread cottages of the Martha's Vineyard Camp Meeting Association. On Sunday mornings and some evenings the building pulses with people, Christian hymns. But on this sunny Tuesday afternoon Tuki is the only one here in the cool shade amid the birdsongs. It seems everyone else in town has gone to the beach.

She has come to this island, this town, on a hunch. On instinct. Come here because she cannot do what she promised Wen-Ling, cannot face any obligations until she feels clean, at peace. She's seeking nothing short of spiritual deliverance. And maybe this is the place that can provide it. She has read brochures and a Lonely Planet travel book about Cape Cod. Has read that Oak Bluffs became a center of the Methodist spiritual movement during the 1800s, that Sabbath meetings here began drawing thousands of religious believers one hundred and fifty years ago. Until, by 1880, a thousand brightly painted wooden cottages surrounded this iron-girder Tabernacle. Hordes came here by steamship each summer to cleanse their spirits.

She thinks maybe they still do, thinks maybe this place is marked by god like the Temple of the Dawn, Wat Arun, where she first reconnected with Michael so many months ago across the river from Bangkok. Maybe Oak Bluffs is an American equivalent to a holy city like Ayutthaya, where the ruby belongs. Or like Ankor Wat in Cambodia. Mystical. Maybe she can touch the face of the Buddha here, feel the presence of the All. Because if ever there were a time to free herself from a web of legal accusations, a nest of reptile carnivores, a hell of evil thoughts, that time is now, la. Maybe here she can clear her head to pray. To truly make peace with Prem, with her dead father, with her mother in Saigon who cannot face her. With Buddha and her dead child.

Her tears fall as she chants, prays for forgiveness yet again.

She wonders if it is possible to pray for pardon from things she has not yet even done, but will soon do. Because she promised Wen-Ling. Because this is the only way to save her man. To get the *nak-lin*, the *silab*, all the ghosts off her back once and for all. And because something deep in her craves this. Craves revenge.

Her eyes close, lips move silently with the words of the final *gatha* of the Diamond Sutra:

So should one view the fleeting world: a drop of dew,
a bubble in a stream, a flash of lightning in a summer cloud,
a star at dawn, a shadow, a phantom, a dream.

Her mind stretches to picture her father, stretches to see his broad, gentle smile that night at the Delta baggage claim. Ft. Lauderdale/Hollywood International Airport.

And then, suddenly, there he is. Right in front of her, la. Looking like Lou Gossett, Jr. in An Officer and a Gentleman. *Wearing his Marine Corps dress blues, as he promised—so you can't miss me, sugar. Almost like the young man her mother Misty, Huong-Mei, saw the night he walked into the bar where she was dancing off Dong Khoi in central Saigon.*

Almost that young warrior still, the black cat … except for the full beard.

Her hand, reaches out. Reaches up. Is almost touching that beard, the cheek … when she hears footsteps coming toward her in the tabernacle.

"You can't hide from me, Tuki."

She doesn't have to open her eyes to know that Chinese voice. Wen-Ling.

"I can always find you."

She opens her eyes. Sees the *silab* ho, standing before her in shorts, polo shirt, camera around her neck. The total tourist disguise.

"If you want to save Michael from the *nak-lin*, we have to find Robsulee. It's time."

"I'm not ready."

"She's hiding in some hole somewhere, crying for her lost love, petting that ruby. And planning how she's going to get even with you and Michael. Once and for all."

"Not yet. I'm …"

Wen-Ling looks at her like *no excuses, honey.* "So you want to watch her kill Michael? You know that's what she wants. For you to feel her loneliness."

She pictures Michael, his neck nearly severed by a *tonki*. His body awash in a sea of blood. Something flares in her chest, spreads into her stomach. Lower. "Where do we start?"

"You have to look beautiful. You have to be a major tease. Irresistible bait. We need to find you something to wear."

"Look at me, la. I'm nearly bald. I'm skinny as a roach. I'm a mess."

"Try to think of this as your very first date. Think of the Patpong back in the nineties. Think of Prem."

"He must be suffering from the weight of bad karma."

"Look. You can help him, too, Tuki."

"You really believe we can get the ruby?"

56

"I SWEAR I told you not to do anything crazy." Lou Votolatto takes another bite of his batter-fried codfish cheek, cocks an eyebrow at Michael.

Votolatto is on one side of him, the female detective Colón on the other. And if anybody is noticing, he or she might guess from the conversation that Michael's not exactly here by choice.

It's the dead hour between three and four in the afternoon when most of the lunch crowd has left and the happy-hour crew has not yet started to trickle in. The Rolling Stones "Beast of Burden" plays softly from the sound system. Except for a couple fishermen and a trio of college girls on holiday—all sitting on the far side of the horseshoe bar, the cops and Michael are the only folks in the tavern side of the Chatham Squire.

"I didn't do anything!"

The older cop stops chewing his cod, rolls his eyes at the ceiling, swallows. "How did you get your car out of the police lot?"

"I have a spare key. *Cristo*, man. I just drove it away."

"You ever think, maybe, we were holding that jeep for your own safety?"

"It's my car. I'm out on bail remember? I get to drive."

"Oh yeah, pal, you get to drive. Like right to the nearest gun shop."

"I don't have a gun, Lou."

"Don't give me that shit. Tell him, Colón." ·

"The guy from the Powderhorn called Hyannis PD."

"I don't know what you're talking about."

"You tried to buy a fucking gas pellet pistol." Votolatto.

"But I didn't."

"Because you guessed that the shop owner dropped a dime on you … so you took off before we could get there."

"Jesus, Lou. Maybe I just thought better of the idea."

"We sort of doubt it, Michael." Colón lets her fork fall into her *hummus bi tahini*.

Her pretty Latin face sags just *um pouco*, he thinks. Like his mother's did when he disappointed her.

"We followed you to the paintball store." Colón hasn't taken her black eyes off him. Not blinked. "We know you have a Tippmann A-5 high performance paintball marker and several belts of paint stashed in your jeep."

Something's burning right behind his eyes. The bottles behind the bar look blurry. "What do you want me to say? That I'm worried as hell about Tuki? That I'm feeling just a little vulnerable right now because some Thai gang wants my head and my girlfriend's … and all the police are doing is harassing me?"

"Oh Jesus, here we go again."

"You want me to tell you how stupid I feel? How I thought I was going to Bangkok to help my client. How I've done absolutely nothing right from the start for Tuki, even though I've spent weeks-upon-weeks, thousands-upon-thousands of dollars. I'm a failure as a lawyer. I didn't listen to my father or you. I broke the first rule of legal representation. I got emotionally involved with my client. *Cristo!*"

"Hey, listen, kid. Everybody messes up sometimes. That doesn't mean you make amends by going off on some kind of freelance rampage."

"I couldn't just sit around on a fish boat all day drinking coffee while my girlfriend's missing. While my old man tells me how screwed we are—how he should have never let me leave for Bangkok this spring."

Votolatto heaves a deep breath, growls to himself, rises slowly from his barstool. Unlocks the handcuff from Michael's wrist and his own. "Fuck it. You know what, kid? Just fuck it. I don't know why I bothered following you all over the Cape this afternoon. Why I thought if Colón and I bought you a decent meal here maybe you would stop with the goddamn Lone Ranger shit and be a good doobie just for once."

"Jesus Christ, Lou—"

"Don't Jesus Christ me. To hell with you, kid. Life's too short to put up with your kind of crap. You want to go get yourself and Miss Bangkok killed, have at it."

"Lou … I don't even know where she …"

The cop throws his napkin on the bar, turns away, starts for the door. "Tell your troubles to Colón, pal. If she'll listen. I'm going up the street, buy myself a book about bass fishing."

· · · · ·

"He'll get over it, you know?" she says, stirring the hummus on her plate with a fork.

He shakes his head, doesn't know. "My old man's just as pissed."

"They really care about you."

"It doesn't feel that way."

"You've never had a kid." *This is a mother talking.*

"Sore subject."

She puts a hand on his, looks into his eyes. "My bad."

"Yeah."

"We're going to find Tuki. You know that. She's going to be ok."

He leans back on the barstool, stares at the assorted collection of beer signs and license plates tacked to the rafters.

"You just have to let Lou and me do this our way. You can't go off like some kind of *loco* trying to save the world with a paintball gun, you know?"

"I think I'm going out of my mind."

"When I'm feeling like I want to shoot somebody or myself, I go for a long walk."

"You get like that?"

"Was my mother murdered?"

"Jesus."

"Yeah. So … you want to go for a walk?"

"I know a place."

"Are you going to try to ditch me, *hombre?*"

"You want to cuff me, don't you?"

"Maybe it would be the smart thing."

· · · · ·

He's pushing through a thicket of trees, reeds. Brambles higher than his head. She suddenly stops dead behind him. Jerks his arm with the chain between their nickel handcuffs.

"I don't think I can do this. I've got a bad feeling."

"You are about to see something you'll never forget."

"*Sí coño.* I'm in the middle of No-Freaking-Where Marsh cuffed to an indicted felon."

"You know that I shot that guy in self-defense?"

"That's your story."

"Come on, Detective. I need this." Something seems to uncoil in his mind. "Maybe you do too."

She looks around. "What's this place called?"

"The Whispers. It's some kind of secret set of trails through the marsh. Maybe deer paths, but I've also heard that rich summer folks in the mansions near here cut these trails to walk their dogs generations ago."

"It's sketchy."

"You want to hold a gun on me, too?"

"I want to go back and find Lou. At that bookstore."

"The Yellow Umbrella."

"How do you know?"

"I read. And I used to live in Chatham."

"Can I ask you something?"

"Will you keep walking down this trail? Really just another minute or so."

"If you answer my question."

"You're difficult."

"Watch yourself, Michael. You need a friend right about now."

He sighs. "Ok. What?"

"Why were you heading for Chatham when we pulled you over this afternoon?"

"That's what I want to show you."

He feels the chain between them go slack as she steps closer, sees her drop her guard, turn her head to watch a pair of quail flush from the brush to her left. He could take her right now, he could be free again.

"Keep moving," she says. "I know what you're thinking. My pistol's aimed at your head."

• • • • •

"*Chinga!*" Her voice seems a gust of wind.

"What do you think?"

They're standing in a clearing about the size of a tennis court. In the center of the sandy clearing is a hillock of black, greasy sand mixed with shells. Scallops, quahogs, sea clams, soft shell clams, razor clams, mussels. Stone chips. The mound is perhaps twenty-five feet across, three feet high near its center. The perimeter marked by the stubs of thick stakes, charred and nearly petrified by the salty winds and sea. The place has a Stonehenge feel. Across the marsh the deep blue waters of Stage Harbor churn in the strong southwest wind.

"This is a holy place," she says. There's absolute surety in her voice.

"I've been told that if you look closely you can find tiny shards of pottery. Fish, bird and animal bones."

"*Los indios.*"

"Wampanaogs."

Her cuffed hand unconsciously takes his as she inhales the scents, the sounds. He feels her muscles stiffen … before she realizes what she's doing and lets go.

"Who showed you this place?"

"I had an Indian friend. She called this a shell midden. Said it was where her ancestors came to feast a long time ago."

"You came here looking for your friend?"

"She died."

She tenses again. "My people come from Cuba and Puerto Rico and Jamaica … where we listen to the dead. The dead gather here, Michael."

"That's what my friend Awasha said. She said she used to come here as a girl and let the spirits help her sort things out."

"So you thought you'd try it today?"

"My mother died a little more than a year ago."

"After my mother was killed, I didn't talk for a year."

"I'm sorry … Maybe it was a mistake to bring you here."

The detective doesn't speak, doesn't move for more than a minute. The only noises are the melodies of songbirds in the high brush at their backs. The whir of the wind across the marsh.

"Listen …" She cocks her head into the breeze. "Sometimes I feel things. Ok? Deep things."

Her words draw his eyes away from the lines of small waves melting against the salt hay shore, draw him back to her. There's something penetrating and steady, scary in the way she's looking at him now. The way the wind whips her black hair. The way the setting sun catches on her high cheekbones, her thin nose. She could almost be Awasha's sister. His sister.

"I feel the spirits here. The ones I carry. The ones you carry. Maybe I can help you."

"I can't stop thinking about Tuki."

"I know."

"If you were her … If you were all torn up inside … where would you go … besides for a long walk?"

"You were coming here today to ask the spirits that?"

He shrugs. "Yeah … essentially … something like that."

"You could have asked me this back in the Squire."

"I thought you wanted to walk. I thought maybe this place would …"

"*Sí coño.*"

"Well, where would you go?"

She smiles. "One word."

"What?"

"Shopping."

A brick of pain melts in his brain, runs down the back of his neck. Warm, sticky, wet.

"You're not kidding?"

"I swear before the spirits."

"Tuki's at the Cape Cod Mall?"

"Probably not alone."

"Wen-Ling?"

"*Esta puta* has something up her sleeve."

"What are we waiting for?"

"Just some guy named Lou."

57

"THINK I could start a fight in this, la?"

The mall. She has just stepped from the dressing room at a shop called Caché. Wearing five-inch red pumps, peep toes, rhinestones on the heels … and a killer crimson jersey gown. It has one shoulder strap, trimmed in rhinestones, and a rhinestone wave trim down the side of the dress. The top grabs her tight around her breasts, waist, hips. It flows into a skirt with a high slit and peek-a-boo mesh overlay, falling to her ankles. A three-inch chain of rhinestones dangles from each ear, making her neck look impossibly long.

"You look stunning." Wen-Ling claps her hands. "Absolutely smashing."

"Really?"

"Totally Halle Berry at the Academy Awards … when she was working her butch hair thing."

She feels a smile growing inside her, pushes both hands through the short, black curls on her head. Leaves behind a thatch of tiny spikes and curls. This is the first time, since months ago back in Thailand, she has felt even a little pretty. A little voguey. A little ready for the runway again. Ready maybe even to sing. Ready for revenge … If she can just find the right lipstick and gloss. Some eye shadow.

Wen-Ling, still in khaki shorts and polo shirt, smiles back. A big, toothy grin. "If that dress doesn't lure Robsulee out of whatever hole she's gone down, nothing will."

"You think she's really that jealous of me?"

"Has she been trying to copy your game for years … right down to having a Thai boyfriend? Right down to giving herself that phony Asian name about ten years ago."

She shrugs. It seems so bizarre that someone would want to be her. But then she remembers all those years of drag, first in the Patpong, then in New York and P-town, when she wanted to be Janet or Whitney or Beyoncé. All those years when the loneliness was eating her from the inside out.

"She thinks you stole the love of her life from her."

"How …?"

Wen-Ling says she has found copies of emails. Prem Kittika-chorn bragged online to Robsulee about meeting Tuki in Bangkok, about loving her. After he came back to Thailand from his college in New York. After his family threatened to disinherit him unless he stayed home, got clean, went straight. After years of his being Robsulee's lover, her friend, in Greenwich Village.

"Do you have any idea how jealous she is of you?"

"How do you know so much, la?"

"I'll do whatever is necessary to get the ruby back. I'm very good at investigation. And now I see the whole story."

"Then tell me why this Robsulee cares. Prem left me too."

"In his emails to Robsulee, even after he left you, after you left Bangkok, he talked about you. He even sent her pictures of you. He couldn't let you go."

"Funny. I never heard that. The man was silent for almost five years."

"But not to Robsulee. Prem tracked you on the internet, found you in New York. I don't think it was his intention, but his emails led her right to you. He talked about this price his father had put on your head. And while you and Prem were doing your thing in Bangkok, Robsulee was building up her extortion business in New York's Chinatown. Suddenly there you were. At the Saigon Princess. Ripe for picking. Living under the wing of a guy who already owed her money for his gambling debts and protection."

"Then why didn't she just come and get the ruby as soon as she found me? Why all the drama with Sunny and the shakedowns, la. Why try to kill my father and kidnap me?"

According to Wen-Ling, Robsulee didn't seem to know about the existence of the ruby at first, didn't know Tuki still had it. But Robsulee had her held captive for so long because she suspected that something really valuable was motivating Thaksin Kittikachorn's extreme interest in finding Tuki. Besides, Rosulee seemed to enjoy knowing that Wan-Lo was making Tuki suffer. Eventually, during Tuki's captivity, Robsulee squeezed the story about the ruby out of Prem.

"That was probably right before I escaped from Wan-Lo, when he and Sunny started to hound me about the Heart."

"And not long after that, Prem appeared in Provincetown. I think he wanted to warn you, save you, before Robsulee, Sunny and their crew could crush you once and for all and grab the Heart of Warriors."

"That wench had Sunny kill Prem?"

"I'd say she wanted payback for his betrayal. The ruby and his life. She wants to strip you of everything that she thinks should be hers. And Michael's next on her list. She'll kill him just to torture you … unless we stop her. She can't stand the thought of your happiness. You stole Prem from her. Before Tuki Aparecio she had him all to herself. You know?"

• • • • •

Prem tells her. He says it was after one of his prep school vacations. His roommate, the black guy Robert, came back from Memphis with wigs and dresses. He said that he had stolen them from his sister. At first he dressed up for fun, danced around the dormitory in drag singing along with Roberta

Flack tunes and flirting with the other boys. But after a while, Robert started to change. After lights out in the dormitory, Robert began to wear bras, stockings, garter belts. His voice changed. He said to call him Bobbi. Prem liked it.

They flirted in the dark for months. Then they did more. They did everything. They liked the idea that at any minute one of the boys or the hall master might catch them. Sometimes Bobbi came out of the closet, and they sneaked around the dark school. Had sex in places like the library and the chapel. Once they even stole into their hall master's apartment and did it on his bed, leaving skid marks to prove it. Then one vacation Prem's mother let him and Robert use the family apartment in New York by themselves. Prem and Bobbi discovered Christopher Street—Silicone Alley—and all the tranny clubs in the Village. They split up, picked new partners. But they always came back together, fighting, crying, screaming. Loving each other.

"She used to get so jealous when she saw me with someone else. What we had was so intense. First love. A love unto death," Prem says one night, when she makes him talk after their loving. When he's riding his pung chao landslide right through the middle of the hot Krung Thep night ... and she's so smitten she can't even see he's high.

"I think my parents knew it. It was sooo intense, sooo crazy." His voice sounds wistful.

He says that his parents tried to keep him and Bobbi apart.

"All through college they kept throwing these rich Chinese-American chicks at me. I played along. I cannot handle my father's anger. I was actually engaged once. But in my heart, I never came back to the straight ... And Bobbi and I always found a way to get lost together ... until my mother dragged me back here, back home ... And then I found you."

· · · · ·

"We strike while that bitch is deep in her pain." Wen-Ling's clipping a rhinestone choker around Tuki's neck.

"Chua chet thi, di chet." Her voice sounds ironic, skeptical.

"You're the reason she's lost another man."

"Sunny was a bastard."

"So tonight we get even."

Tuki feels something jagged in her belly. Something ripped and dead. She knows what it's like to lose the people she loves. First Prem, then her father. The baby. She remembers her father calling Wen-Ling a viper, her father insinuating he knew things he was not telling about Wen-Ling. What if Wen-Ling is just getting her all pumped up on fear, on dread, for dark purposes? What if Wen-Ling is sacrificing her to get the ruby?

"Maybe you should go to Provincetown alone, la."

"Are you prepared to see Michael dead?"

Her heart seizes. "What if Robsulee has a weapon?"

"You're going to have one too."

58

"THEY WERE HERE. This afternoon. Two attractive women. One Asian. The other, as you say, *exotic*. Short hair." The shopkeeper in Caché smiles a bit at the memory. As if maybe Tuki and Wen-Ling made her sales day.

"Can I call it, or can I call it, boys?" Colón is feeling pleased with herself. Of all the stores in the Cape Cod Mall, she started their search for Tuki here. Said a woman just knows these kinds of things about another woman. Knows her style. Knows the kind of shop that will call to her.

"They buy anything?" Votolatto, all business. His squinting eyes, sagging cheeks clear enough signs that his shift was over two hours ago. He's beat. Probably can't believe he's still on the job, and will be for hours more if the Portagee and the Latina get their way.

"The one with the short hair. Yeah. She didn't look like much when the two of them came in here. But when they put her in that hot, red dress with the slit up the side. Added some jewelry … She was smokin'."

It's that picture again. The one he clicked in his mind the first time he saw her onstage. The house lights going dim. A blue spotlight picking up a figure in a red evening dress standing at the top of the steps. A diamond choker glittering at her throat.

"Come on." His voice has jumped an octave.

"Now what, Rambo?"

"She's headed for Provincetown."

"With Madame Nu?"

"She bought that dress for the Follies."

"You think they're looking for that Robsu-whoever?"

His chest tightens, bursts. "I think all hell's about to break loose."

"I knew it," says Colón. "I told you guys. I heard it from the saints."

Votolatto squeezes his eyes shut in pain. "Don't start with that voodoo shit."

• • • • •

The Lower Cape traffic has become a special form of Purgatory as cars flood the Cape for the Fouth-of-July weekend. So … it's not until after nine thirty when one of the waitresses, in the drag of a Hooters Girl, leads the two cops and Michael to an empty table at the back of the Follies. The intermission between the featured drag acts, a sort of half-hour open mic session for fresh talent and wannabee queens, is in full bloom. A popular interlude with audiences. Comedy lurks in the possibilities for slipping falsies, forgotten lyrics, clumsy dancing, hideous clothing, makeup from the halls of vampire crypts.

But right now nobody's laughing. She's onstage. Her. His love. Three bars into Gladys Knight's "Midnight Train to Georgia." Right here, right now, right before his eyes. P-town is burning.

Snares are tightening around his spine, his belly. He has this feeling that at any second the whole place is going to blow itself apart in a hurricane of hot winds, flaring sparks. She has waltzed right in here. Straight-up claimed center stage in what is effectively Robsulee's living room … and used to be hers. She's daring Robsulee to come out and fight. Daring her to bring it on.

Votolatto drops into his chair wide-eyed. "What's going on here?"

"*De puta madre*," says Colón. "There's that spook."

She nods her head toward the bar across the room. In the dark, dusty light Michael sees her. As if for the first time all over again. That woman on the overnight express out of Bangkok. That woman in the expensive white suit. Reeking of cigarettes, pungent perfume, Mae Kong whiskey. Jasmine. The witch in a French-style straw hat. Broad brim, pink ribbon for a band, trailing off down her back with her ponytail.

Right now one hand holds what looks like a burbon and soda. The other is tucked under the suit jacket folded on her lap.

"She's packing, Lou." Colón feels for her shoulder holster.

"We have to get Tuki out of here. Get her off that stage."

"Wait," says Votolatto. "We don't know who else is armed."

The horns swell. The piano cuts in. The spotlights flare silver, gold. Tuki's voice seeps from the sound system. Low, raspy. Sultry. Straining. Singing about leaving a life. About going back to a simpler place and time. About a one-way ticket.

The light-and-sound kids in the balcony have a mic too. They're singing the background vocals, swaying. Dancing a little kick-and-shuffle up there in the shadows.

She struts, a slow pause-and-go. She holds the mic like a torch to her lips.

He starts to stand. Starts to go to her.

Votolatto grabs him by the belt, jerks him back in his seat. "You want to get her killed?"

The room seems incredibly dark now. The lights fading purple, blue. Her voice that midnight train, those broken dreams in the lyrics. Exposing a terrible longing in her soul. In his.

He feels it. That *saudade*. Sees it. Sees it just as he has seen it before. That half-dream that has haunted him for years. That scene from *The Dear Hunter*. He sees Saigon.

And her. Tuki. She's the one laying claim to the dark soldiers' bar now. Her, this wonder in the red dress with that long leg breaking through the slit. The rhinestones. Dancing on the bar. Hips pumping to the rhythm. The Americans and the B-girls staring up at her from their seats, nursing their Budweisers, their fake champagne. The GI's faces lost in shadows. His dad's, her dad's. The black-haired, smoky sirens of Asia … Her voice healing their wounds. Comforting their losses. Swelling in their hearts. In his heart.

While her eyes keep searching. The faces in the crowd. The darkness. Singing about his love, her love. His world, her world …

Then she sees him, rising from his seat. Trying to shake off Votolatto's hold.

Her eyes hold him. Pleading. Telling him … as clearly as the lyrics … that she loves him … But this world—this here, this now—is too much. Too dangerous. Her lips are trembling, her left arm stretching out, trying to push him back. Her voice coaxing. He's got to go … got to go …

But he can't help himself. He can't sit down, won't sit. Can't just go. Not now. Not without her. Not the way his father left his hooch girl Meng in Saigon, the way her father left her mother. Stray cats slinking off into the shadows.

Doesn't she see? He can't lose her again. Can't let her stay up there on that stage. No matter what kind of bargain she made with Wen-Ling. No matter how much she loves singing this song … or how much she thinks this is destiny, this showdown with Robsulee. He can smell the heat, the ozone. The electricity in the air. The storm coming.

He's throwing off the cop's hands. He doesn't care anymore about how all this violence started. Doesn't care who really killed Thaksin Kittikachorn. Or who's got a stolen ruby. He's just feeling, just knowing deep in his bones, that he must take her away from this place, this battle. Take her with him.

So … the lover is pushing his way toward her through the GI's, the Saigon bar girls, the dragon waitresses, the P-town Fourth-of-July crowd …

… when someone kills the lights.

59

ONE SECOND her heart is stretching for him. For those full lips.
The olive cheeks with the stubble of a beard coming on. Her voice
warning him to back off, to go. To let her finish this, end this fight.

The next second she's in total darkness, and all she can hear is
the sound of someone slipping a CD into the disk changer. Then
a piano. The lead-in to Bonnie Tyler's "Total Eclipse of the Heart."

A voice cuts in. Singing on cue, deeper than her own. Richer.
Harsher.

Telling her to turn around. A command. Singing from somewhere above and behind her. Somewhere up there in the balcony.
The blackness.

A silvery spot snaps on.

She looks up, over her shoulder. Sees the spot swing to the
singer at the top of the circular staircase that the showgirls use for
their entrance. Robsulee is magnificent. All curves … in a low-cut,
blue-sequin sheath. Slit to the hip. Four-inch heels. A frisky little
wig that nearly copies Tuki's own hair. And there on her bare chest
is the Heart of Warriors. Dangling from a thick, gold chain above
her cleavage. Just as Wen-Ling predicted.

"Tonight we'll call her, tell her you're on your way. I'll bet you a thousand dollars she'll come out of hiding to see you sing."

"Then what, la?"

"I grab her ass ... I grab the ruby. The nightmare's over."

The crowd's cheering the return of Rubsulee, the Queen of Spades, as the piano plays through the next bars of the song.

That command to turn around again. The challenge. The call. She's a singer. She knows what Robsulee wants. A response to the call. A duet. If she can. Right here. Right now. Onstage. Like Bonnie Tyler and Kareen Antonn on YouTube. A duel of the divas. Like *you up to this, bitch?*

"Turn around."

She stares into the dark. Looking for Wen-Ling. Wondering when the *silap* will make her move on Robsulee. Grab the ho, grab the stolen ruby, end the nightmare ... Hoping Michael has heard her warning. Hoping he'll let Wen-Ling finish this ... any second.

But the only person she can see is Robsulee, making her way slowly down the steps.

Tuki raises the mic to her lips. Closes her eyes, turns her back on the ho. And starts to sing, picks up the lyrics where Robsulee left off.

A golden spot swings to her, frames her in a pool of light. The crowd cheers, feels the tension of a duel.

Robsulee is almost down the stairs.

But Tuki won't look.

Where's Wen-Ling?

The voice is louder. Sharper. Still demanding that she turn around. Robsulee's on the stage, moving toward her.

Where's Wen-Ling?

Nothing she can do but hold her ground and sing. Even as the queen stalks her ... The spotlight goes red, surrounds them both. Catches the audience too. She can see the silhouettes of bodies, faces in the crowd. She looks toward the bar, looks for Wen-Ling. *Grab her. Grab the ruby, la. End the nightmare. Before it's too late. Before this powder keg blows.* She feels the words. She feels the need in the words of the song. Feels the eclipse coming, the loss. The massive ruby just sucking in all the light. A red darkness spreading.

It's sinking over the stage, covering her heart. Robulee's nearly toe-to-toe with her. Their voices harmonizing. Their eyes welding on each other's. In each other's. Their mics weapons that they shake as they sing. Arms pounding the air. Challenge. Telling each other there's nothing they can do. They're falling apart. Both of them. Maybe dying here …

Or killing.

She sees the sparks in Robsulee's eyes. And the tears. The anger. The shame. The urge to devour Michael and her … Prem, too. He's in the ho's eyes as well. Her poor, scared river lion. Eyes glazed with *pung chao*. And for a second she just channels that hatred and loss. Feels the jagged thing in her belly again, tearing, dying. Wants to reach out to this other singer, this other self.

She's reaching. Reaching out to Buddha, asking to end this. To bring help. Praying. *Bring Wen-Ling … or somebody.* Bring light. Or no light. Like *mai dai duai monko ao duai khatha.* If you can't get it by prayer … use a spell. *Do or die, la.*

Do it now.

That's what she's thinking when she feels the first cold slash across her thigh. A sting, a jolt, that runs right to her toes, detonates charges in her hips, spine, right behind her eyes.

She staggers for a second, gasps. Before her vision clears, she feels a second sting as if something's ripping her. Twice in the same spot. She loses her place in the song. Stares at her leg, sure that she'll see the blood rushing from the wound.

But there's no blood. No rent fabric, torn skin … Just a smile on the face of her clone. Like *gotcha.*

The Queen of Spades twirls away across the stage. The song moves into its instrumental bridge. An organ, guitars, drums.

She's looking out into the audience for help, for Wen-Ling, trying to figure out what the hell just stung her, when the bridge circles back to the lyrics. Robsulee taunts her from across the stage. *Turn around.*

The queen is singing again about falling apart. Starting a slow circle around Tuki. Closing in, stalking her the way one Thai boxer in a ring stalks another. And for just an instant there's a little flash of light from the wench's hand. Robsulee has something small concealed in her hand that's not holding the mic.

Something arcs in her brain. Now she knows that it is as she feared. Wen-Ling's not going to save her. That she's being sacrificed for a piece of red stone. And that Michael's hanging back because … because he thinks that's what she wants. She's on her own here.

For an instant she turns her back on Robsulee, closes her eyes, puts her hands on her breasts as if to feel the pain in the lyrics. And the real pain of her terror. When she turns back to face the queen she has a steel nail file—the one Wen-Ling told her to hide in her bra. It's in her free hand. She waves it for the Queen of Spades to see. To fear, maybe.

Tuki inhales, finds her voice. Picks up the duet. Sings along with Robsulee about need, about darkness. About a terrible hunger for love. As they circle each other. Their arms slashing at the air. Stage smoke starting to swirl around them as the piano pounds toward the climax of the song.

Robsulee's grinning now. Closing in on her. Almost to arm's length. Flicking something that looks like a pen, rhythmically at Tuki's face. Bellowing that forever's going to start tonight.

The orphan child of Saigon calls on Buddha for strength. But something far different than the Heart Sutra, something raw and wild is rising in this love child of the Black Cat Bar. Something seething from the crescendo in the music, her pelvis, her own voice. She's no longer seeing the black Amazon, coming in for the kill. Not seeing some twisted version or her own face or her mother's looming toward her.

Wan-Lo has her from behind. One arm around her neck. The other under the waistband of her skirt, probing with fat fingers. He's tearing the mini off her hips, her thong too. Doubles her over the steel stove, her cheeks inches away from a back burner, its blue flames hissing. Sunny's scraping his Black Dog pocketknife across her upper lip. Putting a pistol between her bpaa's eyes. Marcus is opening his mouth to tell her something. When the gun cracks. The night thunders, a monsoon of blood and bone blinds her … until every ounce of her feels the urge to kill.

She drops her mic, lunges toward the Queen of Spades. The hand with the nail file aiming for the ho's heart. The other grabbing for the ruby in the dim red light.

Her hand's already on the queen's neck, the file's just inches from home, when Robsulee hits her with the stun-gun pen. The first jolt catches her in the wrist of her attack hand. Ripping right up her arm, shoulder, neck. Going off with a flash in her skull. The second strikes her low in the belly. Not a whip lash, but a hundred talons tearing her to pieces, fitful, jagged strokes …

Until she's a fading plume of sparks, hot ash settling onto the dark stage. Her throat feeling like it's rupturing as she tries to swallow, blacks out.

She never sees the throwing star sail through the air, slice open Robsulee's neck. Never feels Michael draw her to his chest. Never hears Lou Votolatto and Yemanjá Colón calling in police back-up, EMTs. Never sees Wen-Ling searching through the gore for the stolen stone. Before the lights come back up.

60

WHEN he wakes up, it's 9:17. Morning. He's in Tuki's hospital room. A nurse, white woman the size of a sumo wrestler, is shaking him, asking him where his girlfriend is.

The bed where she has been resting, sedated, since the ambulance brought her to Hyannis late last night, is empty. The room smells strongly of puke. The sheets flung on the floor, stained with slick mucus, yellow bile, blood.

"What happened in here, pal?"

"*Cristo.*" He's in a fog, shaky, coming out of a dream he can't remember … except for the sound of clucking chickens.

"Who pulled out your girlfriend's IV?"

He tries to answer, but no sound comes out of his mouth.

"Someone was sick in here."

"Sleep … I was asleep." He gets to his feet, rubs his eyes.

"What's this?" The nurse is staring at the vanity mirror in the bathroom.

There's a note scribbled across the mirror in deep red lipstick.

I love you Michael

Something twists in his chest. He smells the vomit again, feels acid rising in his throat. Heaves a few ounces of stale coffee into the sink.

"Jesus. What the hell?"

Suddenly he knows, sees it all. "She's gone."

"You mean bolted? Just ripped out her own IV? She walked out of here?"

He stares at the blue hospital johnny crumpled in a corner of the bathroom, the empty paper bag where he stowed her clothes last night. "She shouldn't be hard to find."

"Oh yeah?"

"A pretty dark girl in a red prom dress."

"Did you hurt her?"

He has to think. "We need to call the state police."

· · · · ·

By the time Lou Votolatto finally calls back, Michael's on the *Rosa Lee*. The fish boat still tied to a wharf at Hyannis' inner harbor. He's sitting at the galley table, nursing his can of Coke. Trying to pick last night's blood out from beneath his fingernails. Watching his father smoke one cigarette after another, turn the air into a lung-burning soup.

"We just found her evening dress in a changing room at Marshalls in the mall." Votolatto's voice sounds strained over the phone. "It looks like our gal shoplifted herself a new wardrobe and skedaddled."

"Do you know what this is doing to me?"

"I wish I could say we'll find her, kid. But she's a slippery fish."

"*Cristo.* Why, Lou?"

"Why did she run? I haven't the faintest. Women are a mystery to me … Colón says your girl's on a mission of some sort."

"Is that supposed to make me feel less like a piece of *merde?*"

His father gives him a worried look. Crushes out a cigarette, lights another.

"I'm sorry, Michael. I really am. I should have known everything would go to hell as soon as you said she was heading for P-town. That fucking zoo."

"I don't even know where to start to look."

"One thing you can bet on. Tuki's not hanging with Madame Nu anymore … Unless your girl has some kind of death wish I don't know about."

"What?"

"You see the way she whipped that throwing star last night? See the gash it made in the Queen of Spades' neck? Almost took the fucking head right off the shoulders," says Lou.

For a second he pictures the throwing star Varat Samset showed him back in Bangkok. Shivers.

"You got Wen-Ling in jail."

"Are you shitting me? She's like your girlfriend, bubba. These Asian chicks, they just vanish into thin air."

He says, "You know, Wen-Ling's some kind of Thai spook. The Feds are backing her up, right?"

"Well, fuck that. Spook or not. She can't just go around wasting people on my beat. Even if it's just some piece-of-shit gangster queen."

He pictures Robsulee making her entrance down the circular steps in the Follies last night, the blue sheath painted on her curves, the golden chain around her neck and … Something in his head, right behind his temples begins to ache. "The killing. The running. Everything. Tuki says this is about a lot more than that ruby."

Caesar Decastro crushes out his cigarette as if he's trying to kill the butt. Gets up from his seat, heads out to the work deck, shaking his head.

"The one the queen was wearing last night?" Lou Votolatto coughs. You think it's about more than that? I don't know, pal. It was a hell of a stone. Big enough for some people to kill for."

"So you saw it?"

"Not after the killing."

• • • • •

She's brushing back tears as she looks out the window of the
Cape Air twin-engine Cessna. In the haze ahead she can see the
sky scrapers of Boston. There's bright blue water below. For some
reason it reminds her of her father, of scattering his ashes with
Michael on the *Rosa Lee*.

Her lips begin to move without sound, the Heart Sutra
swelling behind her lungs.

Form is emptiness and emptiness is form.

In emptiness there is no eye, ear, nose, tongue, body, mind.

No forms, sounds, smells, tastes, touches or objects of mind.

No decay, no death, no extinction of decay, of death either.

*The sea that surges, falls, resurges, is the life that is born, dies, is reborn
again.*

Form does not differ from emptiness.

Whatever is form, that is emptiness.

Whatever is emptiness, that is form.

There is no suffering, no origination, no cognition.

No attainment and non-attainment.

"No stopping ... no path," she says aloud.

"What'd you say, dear?" The old lady sitting across from her
seems concerned.

Tuki tries to smile. But the tears are really starting to come,
running down her cheeks.

"Are you ok, sweetie?"

What's she supposed to say?

*Oh, yes, la. No problem. Just something in my eye ... And a couple
other little things. Like I'm running away from the man I love, the man
who loves me. Again. To save his life ... I hope. Running away again from
the police and a silap Chinese Thai wench who tried to sacrifice me to a
dragon. I'm running in the baggy jeans, orange tank-top, cardigan and sandals I just kind of borrowed at Marshalls.*

*Running with $823 in cash, a Thai passport and a Visa card I lifted
from Wen-Ling's purse—just in case, la—on the drive to Provincetown*

last night. Running with an overseas airline ticket out of Boston I bought this morning.

And one last thing ... I'm running with an immense stolen ruby I swallowed right before I crashed last night at the Follies. The one that ripped my throat so bad I can hardly talk. The one I huaaed into my hands this morning in the hospital. The one wrapped in a condom, pressed deep in my birth canal. The one I'm not sure I want to give back now ... after all this misery. The one that feels just right tucked in there, la ... and I don't know why. What if the stone is my karma ... and my fortune? My only balm for a heart that is a bag of trash torn open by the typhoon winds?

61

"I WANTED to tell you this in person, kid." Lou Votolatto gives him a sad-eyed look. "You want to sit down?"

The cop's alone at a waterside-table in the Mattakeese Wharf restaurant on Barnstable Harbor. He's spooning fish broth from a bowl of *bouillabaisse*, nursing a scotch on the rocks. Outside the sun is setting over Barnstable Harbor. The water mercurial, spreading, stretching to the dark, low silhouette of Sandy Neck's marshes and barrier beach. Gulls and bats swooping, diving. Black comets against a crimson sky.

Michael stands there over the table. His eyes pits of sleeplessness. It has been three days since Tuki disappeared.

"Come on, sit. Will you? I have some very good news."

The fisherman, the failed lawyer, the lover of long shots settles into a chair, squints at the cop who shoves a glass of red wine toward him.

"*Toma.* Take it. *Beba.* Isn't that how they say it in Portagee? Drink. You and your father are free men."

"Really?"

"Cheers." Votolatto clinks his scotch to Michael's glass.

"Off the hook?"

"Yes, kid. Once again you dodged the bullet. The D.A.'s dropping the charges. Said you're free to go … wherever. Fishing if you want. The feds are going to back off of your old man for the gun charge."

"Because of what Wen-Ling did?"

"Yes and no. Your girlfriend was right. Maybe righter than she knows. Looks like this mess is about way more than a stolen ruby. It's pretty clear to everybody that you, your pop, Tuki—you all—just kind of got caught in the crossfire so to speak … The feds are pretty embarrassed about forcing Madame Nu on us after all that has happened."

"She murdered Robsulee. Freaking assassination. Like some sort of gangland thing you read about."

"Yeah, that's exactly what I told the feds. What the fuck were they thinking ever trusting that freaking dragon lady?"

Michael takes a long swallow of his wine.

"All I can figure is she had somebody big in our government or Thailand's by the balls … The feds had to make us all play along with her."

"Sometimes I feel just plain stupid," says Michael.

"What do you mean?"

"I used to think I knew who the bad guys were."

"But now you're not even a little bit sure. Like there's anarchy in the streets."

"Something like that."

"Join the club, brother."

"But I just don't get it, Lou."

He says that a few months ago he thought Tuki's problems came from being falsely accused of killing Thaksin Kittikachorn in Bangkok. That all he had to do was to lead the Thai cops to the gangsters who really committed the murder. Then he, Tuki and her dad could start fresh.

"That's kind of the other thing I want to talk to you about."

It's as if Michael doesn't hear the cop, just continues his rant. Says that when he came into this whole thing with Tuki it was like he just had a simple murder case to help the police solve. But now her father's dead, a Thai detective's dead. The two gangsters he thought of as the bad guys? Dead. His girlfriend? Vanished. His life? A wreck again. He's been hit by a hurricane. Because of a stolen gem. A scorned lover. And this disaster calling herself Wen-Ling. Who in the hell does she think she is?

"Listen to me, will you, shithead? Listen. Ok? That's what I'm trying to tell you."

"What?"

"Madame Nu. She's a ringer."

"A what?"

"A ringer. An imposter."

Michael takes a drink of his wine. "My head hurts."

"The D.A. and the U.S. attorney spoke to the Thai ambassador this morning. The Thai government has no one working in intelligence fitting Madame Nu's description, never heard of anyone called Wen-Ling."

"Yeah right."

"The King of Thailand and the Thai state department deny knowing anything about a stolen historic ruby. Or a plan to repatriate it."

"You're kidding. You saw the stone on Robsulee when—"

"Yeah. I saw something that looked like a big-ass ruby. The Thais acknowledge that a ruby called the Heart of Warriors disappeared from some ancient shrine or temple decades ago. But the stone doesn't seem to have been on any official radar screen except as a lost antiquity."

"What are you saying?"

"That ruby we saw may or may not be the Heart of Warriors. Who's to know? But one thing seems clear."

"Yeah?"

"Our Wen-Ling is a freelancer. She has her own plans for that stone. And she has killed before Provincetown for it. We have proof."

Michael can barely believe what he's hearing, knocks off the rest of his glass of red. Doesn't even taste it as it goes down.

Votolatto says that the state police lab rats in Boston just got finished looking at all the stuff on Sunny Janluchai's cell phone. Seems like there were quite a few pictures.

"But there's one I want you to help me with."

The cop fishes in his briefcase, pulls out a manila envelope. Draws out an 8 x 10 color print. Typical cell phone shot. Grainy, blurry. Dark. It's night in the photo. But there's enough light to give the picture.

The outdoor deck of a traditional Thai teak house. There's a life-size, bronze statue of the Buddha seated in the lotus position at one corner of the deck.

"We sent a copy of the photo to the Royal Thai Police. They confirm we're looking at the place Thaksin Kittikachorn was murdered. The so-called River House. On some kind of canal across the river from Bangkok."

"*Klong.*"

"What?"

"The canals are called *klongs.*"

"Whatever. How many people do you recognize in this picture?"

On the right side of the photo he sees two people. Tuki ina black skirt, red silk blouse. She's holding the ruby in her right hand, stretching out her arm to offer the gem to an athletic-looking Thai in a golden shirt. Age maybe mid- to late-fifties. His eyes aren't on the ruby, they are shifted toward the camera. As if he's worried about something. Maybe about being seen here.

"The guy in the golden shirt is Kittikachorn?"

"According to the Thais ... But look at the left side of the photo. This is where things get real interesting."

The left side of the photo is the darkest part of the picture, but there's enough light reflected from the city and the luminous river mist to reveal two figures where the house meets the porch rail at the far end of the deck.

The figure closest to the camera seems to have just popped out of the shadows. It's a woman, dressed in black pajamas. Her arm is cocked, just releasing a *tonki*, a shimmering silver throwing star, toward Tuki and Kittikachorn. Even in the low light and poor photo quality the angle of the jaw, nose, eyes look familiar.

"That's Wen-Ling. No doubt about it." Votolatto sucks an ice cube from his scotch glass, crunches it. "Tossing the lethal throwing star at the late, great Thaksin Kittikachorn."

"Yeah," says Michael.

"And the black guy in the green satin jacket, the one deepest in the shadows a few feet behind her there … he's Tuki's father, isn't he?"

Michael feels something with long fangs taking him by the neck, clamping down on his windpipe. It's not just the discovery that her father was there the night of the murder. It's the look on the face of Marcus Aparecio. His eyes are bugged out, mouth open in a silent scream. It is the look of a man totally surprised, a man bearing witness to a massacre. Maybe the look of a man betrayed.

"What the hell?"

"Yeah."

"So Sunny didn't kill Kittikachorn? Wen-Ling beat him to it. But Sunny was there."

"Yeah, probably with a *posse* of his own."

"You think Wen-Ling and Tuki's dad are somehow connected? You think he was in on the killing? Or do you think he followed Tuki to the River House to cover her back?"

"Who knows? Does it matter? The guy's toast. Kittikachorn's toast. The Queen of Spades is toast. Sunny Janluchai is toast. All fucking toast. For what? Vanity? Ego? A rock? Stuff we don't even have a clue about?"

"Wen-Ling's out there, and Tuki …"

Votolatto sighs. "The D.A. told me and Colón to close the book on this one … I'm sorry, kid."

"I don't understand, Lou." He feels the fangs squeezing into his neck, his larynx starting to shatter.

"ICE says someone named Wen-Ling Yan flew out of Boston three days ago on—get this—a freshly minted Vietnamese diplomatic passport. Headed for Hanoi. It's over."

He wants to say, *Not until I find Tuki*. But his voice, his breath … Gone.

Epilogue

EARLY OCTOBER. Chatham. The leaves on the vines, the trees, the brush, the marsh grass surrounding the trail into the Whispers have turned brown, yellow, a rusty red. The southwest wind gusts in off Nantucket Sound, churning the water of Stage Harbor to foam in the crystal light.

When Michael reaches the sandy clearing, Yemanjá Colón is sitting, her legs drawn in beneath her, on the ancient midden surrounded by a black, sandy mix of empty shells and stone chips. Everything salt crusted. Colón seems to fit with the scene. Looks almost like a Wampanoag woman with her black hair whipping in the wind, her dark complexion, leather jacket, earth-tone slacks. There's something piercing, scary, in the way she's staring at him. And she's reminding him once again of the Indian woman who showed him this place ... who gave her life for him in the shooting at Harwichport a year ago. Reminding him of Awasha Patterson. Reminding him of his mother, of the sister he never had ... Reminding him of Tuki, too.

"Let me guess," he says. "You asked me to come here because you've been talking to the dead again."

"Sometimes the spirits demand things of us."

"I've had enough of the dead and gone."

She looks at him with a sad intensity. He can feel her reading him, reaching out to him.

"*Mira*, I know this is just about the last place you want to be … I know you feel dead too … I know you've been hiding out there on your papa's boat." She nods to the sea. "But you can't just fish forever, Michael. You can't hide from your grief."

Part of him wants to say, *You don't have any idea what I carry inside me, what fishing helps me forget. Don't know what a fresh breeze and a rolling sea can help a man put behind him.* But part of him is churning with questions, wanting answers. Every time he gets back ashore after a trip on the *Rosa Lee*, the *preguntas*, the *questãos*, start again. About everything he's screwed up in his life. But especially about this hole in his chest that seems to grow by the day.

"Why did you ask me to meet you here, Detective?"

She doesn't speak, doesn't move. Just stares at him. The wind hums across the marsh.

"You told me once that a person can talk to the spirits here. That it's a healing place."

"I'm not sure I believe in any of that anymore."

"Well I do. And sometimes—well, actually, *frequentemente*—in the last few months I've felt the need to come here, to listen. To try to heal."

Something deep in his guts twists and he blurts, "Is it working?"

She gives him a sad-eyed look as if he's a fish squirming in a net. "I'm having my own troubles letting go of that night the Queen of Spades died, Michael … and all the rest."

"But what do I have to do with any of …?"

She says that she found something … Something that Lou would never tell him about. Not because he wants to be a *cabron*. But because he thinks he needs to protect Michael.

"I can take care of myself."

"That's what you think."

"Just tell me … Ok?"

She shifts her weight on her toosh, doesn't take her eyes off him. "When I can't sleep, when the spirits won't talk to me … I surf the web. My kid and my grandmother, who live with me, think I'm addicted."

"Are you?"

Her gaze feels like she's squeezing him. "I found something last week on YouTube."

"I don't understand."

"It won't heal a broken heart, but maybe it will help."

He gives her a look like *spill, talk to me*.

Then she tells him. She was searching for videos of Vietnamese singers because … because the spirits were hounding her maybe … or she was hounding herself. She could not let go of the image from that night at the Provincetown Follies. The night of the half-African-American, half-Vietnamese diva. The wonder in the red dress. The siren of Asia … The horns swelling. The piano cutting in. The spotlights flaring. The voice seeping from the sound system. Low, raspy. Sultry. Straining. Singing about leaving a life, about a one-way ticket to a simpler place and time. As if right then and there Tuki was telling them what she was already planning to do. And him, Michael, watching with his heart in his throat.

So … *oyé* … she was surfing the web. On her fourth *cafecito*, eyes on sticks. Playing her hunch, scrolling through YouTube videos of Vietnamese bars, clubs, singers, when she stumbled across a clip from a bar called MTV in Ho Chi Minh City. Saigon. There in living color, was a hip, dark female onstage, surrounded by male dancers working a gangsta look and singing backup. The diva—little orange dress, golden hair to the shoulder, light chocolate skin—belting out "Midnight Train to Georgia" in Vietnamese.

"It was her? Tuki?"

"Without a doubt."

"And Lou knows?"

"I told him. Showed him the video."

"And he wasn't going to tell me?"

"He says she's toxic for you."

"What do you think?"

She bites her lower lip for a second. "I think you're a big boy … I think you have the right to decide for yourself."

"What aren't you telling me?"

She covers her mouth with her hand, squeezes her lips. Now maybe she's sorry she ever got into this with him.

"Come on, Yemanjá. You know something."

"Lou thinks she has the ruby. He thinks that's why she bolted."

"What do you think?"

"I think that if she has that stone, she's going to have another problem with Wen-Ling."

A string of little explosions erupt in his chest, popping one after another. A chain reaction, sinking into his belly, lower into his legs. He feels any second he could lose his balance.

"You think she still loves me?" he says at last.

For the first time in minutes, she takes her eyes off him, stares out to sea. An odd look on her face. She seems to be brushing back tears with both hands. "How could she not?"

RANDALL PEFFER established himself with his first book, *Watermen*, a documentary of the lives of the Chesapeake's fishermen. It won the *Baltimore Sun's* Critic's Choice award and was Maryland Book of the Year.

In 2000 he published *Logs of the Dead Pirates Society*, a literary memoir that evokes the natural drama of life aboard a traditional research schooner sailing the coast of Cape Cod.

Randy is the author of over three hundred travel-lifestyle features for magazines like *National Geographic, National Geographic Traveler, Smithsonian, Reader's Digest, Travel Holiday, Islands* and *Sail.* His travel features appear in most of the US major metro dailies. He is also the author of a number of travel guides for National Geographic and Lonely Planet.

For fourteen years he was the captain of the research schooner Sarah Abbot. He teaches literature and writing at Phillips Academy/Andover and has spent his summers on Cape Cod and the south coast of Massachusetts since his youth.

Killing Neptune's Daughter, his first mystery novel, appeared in 2004 accompanied by strong reviews. *Provincetown Follies, Bangkok Blues,* his second literary mystery, was a finalist for the Lambda Award in 2006. It was followed by *Old School Bones,* the second in the Cape Island Mystery series.

Randy's Civil War naval thriller, *Southern Seahawk,* launched in November, 2008. It is the first of a trilogy of Civil-War-at-sea novels about the Confederate raider Raphael Semmes, the most successful naval predator in history.

Bangkok Dragons, Cape Cod Tears is the third novel in the Cape Islands Mystery series.